continued . . .

Larkspur Road

JILL GREGORY

B

BERKLEY SENSATION, NEW YORK

THE BERKLEY PUBLISHING GROUP
Published by the Penguin Group
Penguin Group (USA) Inc.
375 Hudson Street, New York, New York 10014, USA

Penguin Group (Canada), 90 Eglinton Avenue East, Suite 700, Toronto, Ontario M4P 2Y3, Canada
(a division of Pearson Penguin Canada Inc.) • Penguin Books Ltd., 80 Strand, London WC2R 0RL,
England • Penguin Group Ireland, 25 St. Stephen's Green, Dublin 2, Ireland (a division of Penguin
Books Ltd.) • Penguin Group (Australia), 250 Camberwell Road, Camberwell, Victoria 3124, Australia
(a division of Pearson Australia Group Pty. Ltd.) • Penguin Books India Pvt. Ltd., 11 Community
Centre, Panchsheel Park, New Delhi—110 017, India • Penguin Group (NZ), 67 Apollo Drive,
Rosedale, Auckland 0632, New Zealand (a division of Pearson New Zealand Ltd.) • Penguin Books
(South Africa) (Pty.) Ltd., 24 Sturdee Avenue, Rosebank, Johannesburg 2196, South Africa

Penguin Books Ltd., Registered Offices: 80 Strand, London WC2R 0RL, England

This is a work of fiction. Names, characters, places, and incidents either are the product of the author's
imagination or are used fictitiously, and any resemblance to actual persons, living or dead, business
establishments, events, or locales is entirely coincidental. The publisher does not have any control over
and does not assume any responsibility for author or third-party websites or their content.

LARKSPUR ROAD

A Berkley Sensation Book / published by arrangement with the author

PUBLISHING HISTORY
Berkley Sensation/mass-market edition / May 2012

ISBN: 978-0-425-25089-1

BERKLEY SENSATION®
Berkley Sensation Books are published by The Berkley Publishing Group,
a division of Penguin Group (USA) Inc.,
375 Hudson Street, New York, New York 10014.
BERKLEY SENSATION® is a registered trademark of Penguin Group (USA) Inc.
The "B" design is a trademark of Penguin Group (USA) Inc.

PRINTED IN THE UNITED STATES OF AMERICA

10   9   8   7   6   5   4

ALWAYS LEARNING   **PEARSON**

To my family, with love

Acknowledgments

A huge thank-you to Leslie LaFoy, friend and quilter extraordinaire, for so generously sharing her time and expertise. Leslie, you're not only a marvelous quilter, you're a lovely friend and a patient teacher. Thanks for your invaluable help! And to Marianne Willman, my dear and wonderful friend, thank you for your wisdom and insights, and most of all, for your treasured friendship all of these years.

Chapter One

❧

"When will we get there? To Sage Ranch?"

The sleepy, but still wary voice of the boy in the passenger seat broke the silence of the moonless Montana night.

Travis Tanner glanced at his scrawny ten-year-old adopted stepson. Then back at the long, empty road leading them to Lonesome Way and his family's ranch. The vast darkness of the June night nearly obliterated the peaks of the Crazy Mountains in the distance—but not quite. A few stars gleamed, despite the clouds, illuminating the faint outline of hefty granite peaks spiraling up, dwarfing the road, the trees, and certainly the black Explorer and its two passengers driving down that lonely road.

"Soon," Travis said quietly. "We'll be there soon. Another twenty minutes, half hour, tops."

It was almost midnight and Grady had been sleeping since ten o'clock. But now the brown-haired boy with his mother's green eyes looked like he was going to be awake for the duration. Awake and uneasy.

"You need a pit stop?" Travis asked as the Explorer sped past a coyote stealing furtively through some brush at the side of the road. "There's a gas station coming up just outside of Lonesome Way."

"I'm okay," Grady mumbled. His voice sounded low, defensive. And just a tad sulky. Which matched the expression on his face ever since Travis had picked him up at Sky Harbor Airport in Phoenix the previous afternoon, after Val plopped him on a plane in L.A.

The poor kid didn't know what to expect, Travis reflected, his jaw tightening. One minute he'd been in L.A., in his big fancy new house with an Olympic-sized swimming pool, cabana, guest house, game room, and thirty-seat home theater, and the next he'd been shipped off for the summer with his adoptive father, who was no longer even married to his mother—and was on his way to a remote ranch the kid had been to only once in his life and probably didn't even remember.

Travis had been stunned when his ex-wife called him, her voice high-pitched and shaking with tension as she yelled that she and her new husband were at the end of their rope and couldn't handle Grady anymore, that they needed a break. She'd said Grady had failed a class at school and would probably need to repeat fifth grade. He hadn't bothered doing homework, he'd skipped classes, he'd mouthed off to teachers. Worse, he'd been getting into fights and had even been suspended for the last two weeks of school before summer vacation started.

"Drew's really angry—and I just can't take it anymore. The two of them . . . they just don't . . . Travis, you're his father legally, and I need you to take him for the summer! I really can't deal with any of this right now. Drew and I—we're having a big party here in a few weeks—one hundred guests—and I'm at my wit's end. There's so much to do, and Grady, he's so difficult—I just can't handle—"

"I'll come get him," Travis had said instantly. Not for

Val's sake, that was for damned sure, but for Grady's. He'd first met Val's son, then four years old, when he picked her up for their second date. Val's first husband, Kevin, had died of cancer two years before, when Grady was only a toddler.

The Grady he'd met that night had been a tiny fast-motion machine, a tousle-haired, pug-nosed imp, precocious, funny as hell, and possessing a sweet smile that had burrowed its way into Travis's heart. A year after he and Val tied the knot, Travis had legally adopted his stepson and had loved being a father to him, even after things went south between him and Val.

But lately he hadn't been able to spend as much time with his son. His latest investigation with the FBI, the death of his former partner, and Val marrying some corporate bigwig and moving with Grady to L.A. last year had made visits a lot more difficult to come by.

"I was just leaving for the ranch, Val, but I'll come to L.A. first and pick Grady up," Travis had told her.

"The ranch? You're going to the ranch?"

He hadn't bothered explaining that he'd taken an extended leave of absence from the FBI two weeks before, had found someone to rent his house outside of Phoenix, and was headed home to Lonesome Way to take some time, figure things out, and make a new start.

"Yep," was all Travis had told his ex-wife. "I'll see to it Grady gets back on track over the summer. In Montana."

After that, Val hadn't asked any questions. She'd been too relieved that Travis was taking the boy off her hands for the entire summer. Before he could say another word, she told him that he didn't need to drive all the way out to L. A.—she would put Grady on a plane, get an airline escort for him. It was as clear as daylight to Travis that all she really wanted was to ship the kid the hell out as fast as she could.

Travis's heart had plummeted when he'd picked Grady up at the airport and had seen how much his son had changed in just the past three months. For one thing, he'd shot up a couple of inches—the very beginnings of a growth spurt. But there was also scant trace of the happy kid who'd read all of the Harry Potter books twice and seen all of the movies, and who had joyously biked with Travis up and down Venice Beach last summer.

The boy who stepped off that plane and was now slouched in the passenger seat of the Explorer was withdrawn, wary, on the verge of being surly.

And Travis knew he should have been there for him—FBI or no FBI.

"Things will start looking up tomorrow," he said conversationally as they swung down the main street of his hometown of Lonesome Way. The sidewalks were deserted at this time of night, though he noted with not the slightest bit of surprise that there were lights blazing and cars crammed in the parking lot of the Double Cross Bar and Grill, the town's most popular watering hole.

When Grady didn't answer, Travis continued easily as he took the turn that would lead to Squirrel Road. "You'll have a good bed tonight, not like that lumpy one at the motel last night. You had a great time at the ranch when you were there before, remember? And Uncle Rafe's new wife, Sophie—she owns that little bakery we just passed in town. A Bun in the Oven. She makes cinnamon buns that you won't believe. Melt-in-your-mouth good. Bet she'll have some on hand tomorrow for breakfast."

"Yeah?"

For the first time Travis heard a note of interest in the boy's tone.

Food. Food is the way to a growing boy's heart. He'd have to remember that. Grady had wolfed down two burgers and a greasy bag of fries at the drive-through in Crystal Springs that afternoon.

"Sophie—she's your aunt now—usually has a chocolate cake or an apple pie around the house, too. At least that's what my niece, Ivy, tells me. You won't go hungry at Sage Ranch, that's for sure."

"I don't really remember it." Grady stared out into the darkness, a frown puckering his mouth. "I remember horses, that's about it. You put me up on a horse called Gum . . . Gumball or something, and I almost slipped off. But you caught me."

"Gumption," Travis corrected with a grin. "You were only seven. You got the hang of it before too long. You actually did great for a tenderfoot. And this summer, you'll get to do some real riding. And some real work."

Grady looked interested, and just a tad scared.

"What kind of work?" he bit out.

"Taking care of the horses, mucking out stalls, pitching hay. I haven't checked out my cabin in a while and might need some help making it habitable again. Stuff like that."

"And what if I don't want to muck out stalls and clean up crap?"

Travis shot him a measuring glance and Grady glanced away, his hands clenched in his lap.

"It's going to be a good summer, Grady," Travis told his son quietly.

"Yeah, right. Aren't you going to yell at me—for getting a D in English, and flunking earth science and getting suspended? Everyone else does. That's all they do."

"We'll talk about all of that. But not tonight." Travis kept his tone steady. "You're beat and so am I. It can wait. Unless there's something you want to say."

Grady shook his head.

"You sure? I'm listening."

"How much longer 'til we're there? I just want outta this car." Grady's tone was defiant again now. But Travis heard the misery and uncertainty beneath the words as the boy hunched his shoulders and turned away, staring out the window into the black moonless night.

Travis said nothing, merely drove another mile and then

turned into the long wide drive leading to the ranch. When Grady made out the ranch house just ahead, he stiffened and peered through the darkness at the huge rambling structure looming up in the darkness.

The porch light was on. And light gleamed in the kitchen window. For a moment Travis could almost imagine it was a dozen years earlier, that his parents were still alive, sipping coffee in the kitchen, waiting up for him and his brothers, Rafe and Jake, to get home from a date or a dance or a movie.

He shook himself back to the present and wondered how much of the ranch his son remembered. Being back in Lonesome Way was stirring his own memories big-time.

All those squabbles and tussles and laughs with Rafe and Jake. Hours spent swimming in the creek with his sister, Lissie, or racing on horseback across the pasture. Midnight poker games with his high school friends in Mick Peterson's barn. The exhilaration that had rushed through him every time he threw a winning touchdown pass or charged down the field at a football game.

And Mia. Mia Quinn.

Mia had been best friends with his younger sister, Lissie, since as far back as he could recall. She and Lissie—along with Sophie McPhee, who'd married his brother Rafe last year—had been inseparable growing up, and he'd regularly encountered Mia darting around every corner of his house when he was a kid. She'd been a scrappy little tomboy in those days, two years younger than Travis—just his sister's tiny, fast-talking friend. And Travis had never looked at her twice.

Until she hit high school. Then he'd looked, all right. Because sometime over the summer between eighth grade and her freshman year, the messy-haired tomboy had transformed into a petite blond bombshell, with pin-straight hair that flowed to her slim little waist, a gorgeous face with a mouth so lush he could almost taste its pillowy sweetness before his lips ever actually touched hers, and a body as curvy and distracting as any Victoria's Secret model.

Travis had fallen for her. Fallen hard.

They'd started dating in November of her freshman year and he'd known he loved her by Christmas. They'd been a couple all through the rest of Travis's time in high school. And not just any couple. Travis and Mia had been "the" couple—the one everyone was sure would get married and have a ton of kids.

Pulling up in the dark at the house with his son beside him, Travis flashed back for a dizzying moment on all the dates and dances and picnics he and Mia had shared—afternoons sipping Cokes and eating chocolate cream pie at Roy's Diner, weekends kissing and laughing on her front porch swing on Larkspur Road. Or all those evenings in the hay-scented barn at Sage Ranch, making out in the hayloft when no one was around. Stroking her hair, touching her beautiful, trusting face, breathing in the summer-flower scent of her, whispering how much he loved her on those hikes up to Larkspur Point.

Mia was the girl he'd planned to marry.

The girl he'd promised undying love.

And the girl he'd walked away from the day after his prom without a single backward glance.

When he'd come home a little more than a year and a half ago for Rafe and Sophie's wedding, Mia had been there, looking more gorgeous and sexy than ever in a delicious red dress, but she hadn't even glanced at him.

It was as if for her, he might never have existed.

And every time he'd tried to seek her out that day at the wedding, she'd managed to elude him. She was always busy talking to someone else—her smile breezy, happy. Her attention riveted on Sophie, or on Lissie, who'd been nine months pregnant and in fact had delivered her little girl, Molly, the very next day.

It had bothered him that he and Mia never spoke that day,

but he hadn't forced the matter. They hadn't exactly been on good terms for years now, so he knew he had no right to push himself on her, even to say hello. He'd thought he would forget all about her after he returned to Phoenix following the wedding, but that hadn't happened.

Could be a part of him had never forgotten.

"C'mon, buddy," he said as the front door opened and light spilled from the living room of the ranch house, as warm and welcoming as a fire in the hearth. Rafe, at six foot three, two inches taller than Travis but not as powerfully built, ambled out onto the lit-up porch, a welcoming grin on his face.

"There's your uncle." Travis put a hand on his son's shoulder. "We're home."

"It's your home, not mine." The sadly muttered words from the boy who unsnapped his seat belt and shoved open the Explorer's door felt like a baseball bat swung hard against his chest.

He reminded himself that bringing Grady around would take some time. Loneliness, anger, sadness . . . whatever was eating the boy from the inside out couldn't be undone in an instant.

Neither can betrayal. The thought popped into his head. He'd betrayed Mia all those years ago when they were teenagers—when he was a reckless, stupid kid in a panic over the thought of a lifetime commitment.

That kind of betrayal couldn't be undone quickly. Who was he kidding? It probably couldn't be undone at all.

Besides, the girl he'd hurt was all grown up now—and not his responsibility. Hell, when he'd come back from college the following summer and gone to see her, hoping she might give him another chance, she'd frozen him out. Looked at him like he was a chunk of crud on the bottom of her shoe. She was dating Curt Hathaway by then so she hadn't exactly been languishing after he left her. She'd gotten married to some business whiz sometime after she finished college and though from what he'd heard it hadn't ended well, she'd clearly moved on.

You can never go back. Only forward. The words that his former partner at the bureau, Joe Grisham, had told him often enough echoed through his ears. After the turmoil of the last few months, including Joe's sudden, devastating death, Travis sensed Joe was right.

He had his son to focus on now. And his future. There was an idea for a new business circling through his head. It was time to get started on building a new life for himself and Grady.

There's no going back.

He swung his long legs out of the car, grabbed Grady's duffel, and followed his son up the steps of Sage Ranch.

Chapter Two

Pale glimmers of dawn stole across the peaks of the Crazy Mountains as Mia Quinn sat with her legs curled beneath her on her front porch swing, sipping coffee from her favorite pink mug and seeing stars.

Not celestial stars   those had faded with the sunrise. Mia saw imaginary stars, glowing like brilliant sparks in a dark blue sky. Exactly like the ones in the Van Gogh painting *Starry Night*. She saw them in her mind as she envisioned the design of the quilt she'd sew this summer for her quilting group's exhibition fund-raiser.

Her grandmother, Alicia Rae Clayton, had been the undisputed leader of Bits and Pieces—Lonesome Way's quilting society—for six years before her death three years ago. It still felt a bit strange to go to meetings in the paneled basement of the community center and not have Gram there, front and center. But it was what it was, Mia always told herself as she mingled with her grandmother's closest friends and the younger quilters like herself.

She'd initially only joined the group for her grandmother's sake. It had seemed a simple enough way to make Gram happy and to spend more time with her, but she'd soon found herself fascinated with the lore and history of quilts and with the women who created them—as well as with the pleasure of comparing notes with a circle of women all devoted to creating something both useful and lovely.

Then something unexpected happened. She came to treasure it. All of it.

The hunt for just the right fabric. The excitement of mastering appliqué. The joy of seeing her design spring to life as she sat at her sewing machine for hours, feeling as if she were spinning straw into gold.

And then there was the tea and lemon scones, or coffee and pie, from A Bun in the Oven served at every Bits and Pieces meeting. Not to mention the encouragement, advice, and conversation that swirled around her like a cozy shawl.

Her heart would sing as she sketched, cut templates, and measured seams, striving to make every quilt as unique as her grandmother's while transforming simple cotton fabric into a work of lasting beauty.

Mia knew her love of quilting came directly from Gram. Her grandmother had been quilting since she was a young girl and each of her quilts was gorgeous. They graced every bed and some of the walls in the little house on Larkspur Road where Mia had grown up.

She'd moved back there from Butte in order to live with Gram during the last fragile years of Gram's life, after her own parents were gone, after her divorce from Peter Clancy.

Her favorite room was the small den that had become her grandmother's sewing studio. Gram had spent nearly all of her time there, measuring and cutting and sewing or doing meticulous embroidery and appliqué.

These days Mia often found herself glancing over at the faded butterfly quilt that hung on the sewing studio's wall as she worked on quilts of her own. That well-used quilt with its graceful checkerboard blocks and carefully stitched appliqué had won her grandmother an award at her very first quilt show at the age of nineteen.

Merely gazing at the beautifully precise squares, each one artistically connected to the whole, made her feel almost as if Gram were there beside her, peering over her shoulder with her reading glasses pushed up on her nose, smiling. Pleased.

Pleased that Mia had returned to quilting. And to Bits and Pieces.

For a while after her grandmother's death, Mia had given up quilting. She'd told everyone that during the school year she was too busy with her teaching, but eventually she'd admitted the truth to herself.

It hurt too much to attend the monthly meetings without Gram, to see all of the women who'd been Gram's friends and *not* see her grandmother's delicate, heart-shaped face, her spry figure, her silver-gray hair when she glanced around the room.

She'd rejoined only last year—seeking out the connection again and spurred on by the approach of the annual Bits and Pieces quilt show.

Always held in mid-July, the exhibition was combined with an ice cream social and quilt raffles, all of which served as a fund-raiser for local charities. This summer all of the proceeds would be distributed to the Loving Arms shelter for abused women and children.

The school year at Lonesome Way Middle School had ended just the day before, and now Mia had the luxury of several months ahead without the need to think about fifth-grade lesson plans or essays that needed grading. Without having to devote hours of time to marking up English quizzes with a red pen.

That meant an entire summer to devote to quilting— completing her own Starry Night quilt and a special square for the Bits and Pieces community quilt to be raffled off at the exhibition. She'd have plenty of time to do all that and tend her garden, plus hunt up the perfect birthday card for Tommy, her best friend's husband—Lissie was throwing him a birthday bash at the Double Cross Bar and Grill.

With the early morning air cool against her skin, the heat from the mug felt good, warming her palms as she shivered slightly in her pale gray hoodie and sweatpants. Beside her, Samson stirred and nestled closer, plopping his furry chin on her thigh.

"Sleepyhead," she murmured and stroked his ears absently.

She'd rescued the tiny gray and white mutt a few months back, after seeing a ramshackle Ford truck stop twenty feet in front of her on Old Cedar Road in the midst of a snow-storm. The driver had tossed a small dog out into the icy road and then roared off.

Mia had braked immediately, shaking with rage, and had scooped up the scrawny little guy and set him on the pas-senger seat of her Jeep.

The dog had slowly crawled onto her lap and looked up into her eyes with absolute trust. And won her heart.

A quick examination by Doc Weatherby revealed the mutt had no tags, no chip.

Which probably meant no friends and no home.

"What do you want to do with him?" the vet asked after giving the tiny bundle of fur a thorough checkup. "Want to drop him over at the shelter or should I do it later today?"

Mia had picked him up and held him close. The dog weighed no more than ten pounds, tops.

"I'd better keep him. We're in desperate need of a guard dog on Larkspur Road."

Doc Weatherby laughed.

As if understanding her words, Samson had tentatively overcome his shaking nervousness to lick her cheek.

"You sure?" the vet asked. "You haven't had a dog since Reckless died." He'd helped her put Reckless to sleep eight years before, and Mia had thought she'd never get over the grief.

"Then I guess it's time, isn't it?" she'd countered softly.

The truth was, she'd taken one look into the abandoned mutt's beautiful lonely eyes and guessed fate had put her on Old Cedar Road for a reason that day.

"Relax, big guy," she'd whispered. "You're not going anywhere except home with me."

Now Samson's head flew up as Mia's across-the-street neighbor Ellis Stone pulled up into her driveway, parked her old Dodge van, and got out, waving at Mia in the swing.

"Morning, Mia!"

"Morning, Ellis."

Ellis's husband had passed away last year. She was fifty-five and a nurse who worked the night shift at the hospital. Ellis had more energy than anyone Mia knew. She came home at seven every morning, slept until two, then babysat her eleven-year-old twin grandsons, walked vigorously for an hour around the neighborhood, did her shopping and baking, and managed most days to write an online blog for her book club, which met every other week.

To Mia's surprise, instead of letting herself into her trim little house as usual, no doubt to fall into bed, Ellis strode toward her. Samson's tail began to thump against the wood of the swing.

"Something I thought you should know." Ellis padded up the neat, flower-bedecked walkway toward the porch, weariness creasing her high forehead beneath her short-cropped rust-colored hair. A songbird chirped in Mia's dogwood tree, and from the next block came the faint sound of a dog barking.

Mia recognized that deep bark. It was Zeke's dog, Bounty. Her heart twisted a little at the familiar low, hoarse sound of her ex-fiancé's German shepherd–boxer mix. Sheriff's deputy Zeke Mueller lived only one block away. He'd rebounded with surprising speed after she broke off their engagement less than a year ago—and now he and his new wife of four months were expecting triplets.

So much for "You're the only woman I'll ever love." Zeke's exact words when he proposed.

Peter Clancy, her ex-husband, had said nearly the same thing a week before he cleaned out their joint bank account and disappeared without so much as a "Nice knowing you." Now he only called when he was two steps ahead of the bill collectors and desperate for a loan.

As if.

In high school, Travis had told her more times than she could ever count that she was the only girl for him. Ever.

The promises of a man are as meaningless as the ramblings of a fortune cookie. So Mia's mother had frequently reminded her.

According to her mother, ever since Gram's good luck wedding quilt had been destroyed in a fire weeks before her nuptials to Henry Clayton, the women in Mia's family had been cursed with bad luck when it came to love.

The quilt had been sewn by Mia's grandmother's great-grandmother in 1902 and passed down from contented mothers to joyfully-in-love daughters ever since. But after it went up in flames, the tradition of long-lasting marital bliss had seemed to go up in smoke as well.

Not only had Henry run off with a barmaid when Mia's mother was a little girl, never to be seen again, but Mia's father had frequently cheated, and her mother had time and again taken him back. Each time, she'd vowed never to let the man set foot inside the house again, and each time, she'd allowed him to return on the "condition" of a fresh start.

"I'm sorry for this news," Ellis continued, her words yanking Mia back to the present with a start. "But your aunt was brought in to the hospital last night."

"Winona?" Mia swung her legs to the ground, her amber eyes locking on Ellis's face.

Sensing something was up, Samson lifted his furry head.

"She's not . . . She's all right, isn't she?"

"Oh, she's not dead, that's for sure. Everyone in town knows Winny Pruitt's too mean to die." The instant the words came out of her mouth, Ellis looked abashed. "Sorry. Didn't mean to make a joke of it. She *is* your aunt, after all."

Not that anyone can tell, Mia thought. Everyone knew Mia's great-aunt—her grandmother's sister—wanted nothing to do with any member of her family.

Nor, for that matter, with anyone in Lonesome Way. The woman was the town loner, a self-imposed hermit. She kept to herself, rarely speaking to another soul, except for her neighbor, Abner Floyd, whose dilapidated farm bordered her cabin.

Winny was an enigma. On the few occasions when Mia had spotted her aunt in town over the past years and greeted her, Gram's younger sister had nodded brusquely, her eyes as cold as mountain snow. Then she'd turned away without uttering a word.

She did the same with everyone in Lonesome Way and most people had stopped bothering to try to speak to her on the rare occasion when she ventured into town for groceries or supplies.

Mia had no idea what had caused Gram and Winny to stop speaking to each other years ago, since even up until the day she died, Gram had refused to discuss it.

All Mia knew was that Winny had never come to a single Sunday dinner or Fourth of July barbecue, had never exchanged a birthday card or even a phone call with Gram as far back as Mia and her own older sister, Samantha, could remember.

Aunt Winny hadn't even come to Gram's funeral. Which shouldn't have been a surprise because she hadn't come to the graveyard service for Mia's parents several years before that either, after their car spun out in the worst blizzard of the decade.

"What's wrong with Winny? Is she sick?"

Mia knew she wasn't under any obligation to feel concern for her great-aunt—after all, it was Winny who'd made the decision to part ways with her family and she'd rigidly stuck to it. But it had always disappointed her that even when she'd made overtures—inviting her aunt to dinner or driving out to her cabin on Sweetwater Road to bring her a Christmas gift the year after Gram died—her aunt had stonily refused to open her door, much less even a fraction of her heart, to her only remaining family.

Whatever had happened between Gram and her sister when they were younger had caused a permanent rift, and all of Mia's overtures had been summarily rejected.

"Seems she tripped over a loose board on her front porch. Had a pretty nasty fall—sprained her foot real bad. She'll be using a cane for a while. Wasn't none too happy about it either," Ellis added with an arch of her eyebrows. "She nearly snapped Doc Grantham's head off when he told her she'd need that cane for at least three or four weeks. She's lucky it wasn't any more serious—she could have broken a hip or an arm—or worse."

"Thanks for telling me, Ellis." Mia jumped to her feet, her coffee mug gripped in one hand as she set Samson down on the porch with the other.

"I know that look." Ellis studied her. "You're thinking about going out to Sweetwater Road, trying to tend to her, aren't you?" She shook her head. "You have a big heart, Mia, but that old woman is a lost cause if I ever saw one. She's never shown a flicker of interest in you or Samantha—or your dear mother either, rest her soul. You're wasting your sympathy on her."

"Don't I know it."

"Uh-huh. So why do I still think you're planning to check up on her?"

"Call me crazy." Mia grinned. Ellis knew her too well. "She's family, Ellis, whether she likes it or not. And she's out there miles from town in the middle of nowhere. All alone."

"Honey, by now, Winona Pruitt's plenty used to being alone." Ellis's sharp hazel eyes bored into Mia's face. Then a wry smile touched the corners of her lips.

"You've already made up your mind, haven't you? You're going to Sweetwater Road to check on her."

"I'll take her some supper—just for tonight. Then I'm done. Believe me, I know she wants nothing to do with me or Samantha."

Her sister, Sam, lived in Butte with her daughter, Brittany, and a brand-new husband, and Winny had no interest in any of them either.

"In your own way, you're as stubborn as your grandmother was, you know that?" The nurse spoke fondly. "And as Winny, too, I suppose."

"Ellis, you don't have any clue what started it all, do you?"

"You mean the feud?" Ellis waved a dismissive hand. "It was all before my time. Far back as I can remember, I'd heard Winny was on the outs with your grandmother and your parents, just about everyone. I don't recall anyone ever saying what brought it all on. Which is strange, considering folks here pretty much know everybody's business and don't mind talking about it."

"Even my mom didn't know. Gram never would tell her, not during all the years Winny was gone or after she came back."

Ellis patted Samson's head. "Well, now, remember, some old things are like graves—best left undisturbed." She nodded meaningfully. "You want to bring your aunt some supper, go right ahead. But don't be surprised if she refuses to poke her head out the screen door. She didn't say a decent word to Doc Grantham the whole time she was in the ER— didn't do more than grunt and curse when he examined her foot. She's a tough bird, that one."

But even a bird needs to eat, Mia thought.

So half an hour later, after showering, pulling on her

Wranglers, a pale blue tank top, and sandals, then twisting her blond hair into a loose knot atop her head, she headed for the kitchen. First she poured Samson's kibble into a bowl and freshened his water, then she washed her hands and turned her attention to her fridge.

It wasn't as if she was going to any trouble. She had half of a roast chicken left from the previous night's supper, so she merely wrapped it in tinfoil, then nuked a potato in the microwave while tossing together a quick salad of greens, carrots, peppers, and tomatoes.

There. Done.

So don't start yelling at me from your grave, Gram, she thought as she stuffed everything into a wicker basket, grabbed a hoodie, and carried Winny's supper out to her car. *You may not have liked your sister, but you wouldn't want her to starve to death out there on Sweetwater Road, would you?*

She had just slid into the Jeep when her cell phone rang. *Samantha.*

"What's up?" Mia asked, fastening her seat belt one-handed.

"Mia, I'm scared. Really scared." Mia went stock-still as she heard the quiver in her sister's voice. "It's Brittany. God, I don't know what to do."

"Sam, take a breath. Tell me what's going on."

"Britt's *missing*. I can't find her anywhere!"

Mia felt her heart slam hard inside her chest. "What do you mean *missing*?"

"I've called every single one of her friends. *No one* knows where she is. Or else they're just not telling me!" Sam's voice rose in a crescendo of panic. "I could *kill* her right now. Alec and I are supposed to leave *tomorrow* for our honeymoon and she's . . . gone. Or hiding. Or something. Laura claims she doesn't know where Britt is, but . . ."

Her sister's voice broke, and Mia heard hard, gut-wrenching sobs.

"Give it a minute, honey, take a deep breath." Her mind was racing as she tried to think. Laura Walker. Britt's best friend. If anyone knew where she was, it would be Laura.

"Start from the beginning, Sam. Tell me the last time you saw her."

"Last night. We had a fight. She was being rude to Alec and I told her to knock it off. She flew out the door, yelling that she was spending the night at Laura's. But she didn't come home this morning—and she's not answering her cell. So I called Laura and she claimed she didn't know where Britt was. She swore that Britt did sleep over, but she was upset and woke up around five this morning and just left."

Sam sucked in a deep, shuddery breath. "No one's seen her, Mia. I've called all her friends—*and* her father. He hasn't heard from her either. I even called Wade, the boyfriend du jour, even though he and Britt broke up a month ago, but he had no clue. *No one's* seen her!"

Not good, Mia thought, fighting back her own rising panic. *Think,* she ordered herself, struggling to come up with a logical explanation.

"She might be cooling off somewhere, still pissed about the fight you two had. Try to stay calm, Sam."

But her heart clenched with the beginnings of real fear. She needed to stay cool, think clearly. Samantha had been a drama queen all her life—every issue was life-and-death, joy or despair. Mia, the little sister, had always been the cool, practical one, the one with her head screwed on tight, her feet on the ground. But at this moment, she felt on the verge of sheer terror.

Britt was a good kid, an A student, responsible. Sure, she was high-spirited and boy-crazy, but she wasn't the type to run away or give Sam cause for worry.

Fighting down the fear twisting through her, Mia spoke quickly. "She's probably grabbing breakfast somewhere—or just sitting with a coffee, pulling herself together. You said she wasn't happy about staying at her dad's while you're in Corfu."

"No, but she's not happy about much of anything these days. She's been so moody lately, snapping at Alec when he's been wonderful to her. Fighting with me over every little thing—"

"All mothers and daughters fight, Sam—," Mia began, but her sister cut her off.

"How would you know? You think it's easy living with a sixteen-year-old? Mia, you know *nothing* about what it's like—you don't even have any children of your own and at the rate you're going you—oh!" Samantha's voice cracked. "Crap, crap, crap. I'm sorry, I didn't mean that—I'm taking this out on you and it's not your fault!"

For a moment Mia couldn't speak. Her throat was too tight. Her sister's words hurt. Probably because they were true. She seemed to have a knack for getting involved in dead-end relationships. And the way things were going, that didn't seem likely to change anytime soon.

She was thirty-one, living in a small town with a limited population of men, and chances weren't great that she was going to meet her prince at the Toss and Tumble Laundromat or the Lucky Punch Saloon. True, her life was full, between her friends, her teaching, and her quilting, but it wasn't as full as she'd once thought—and hoped—it would be.

It wasn't full of love. And a man she could count on.

It wasn't full of children and laughter and a family gathered around a table—like a Norman Rockwell painting, she thought with a stab of pain that sliced deep into her heart. She drew a long breath, swallowing past the lump in her throat.

"It's okay, Sam. I know you're upset."

But the truth was, her sister was right.

She had to face the fact that after one disastrous marriage and one broken engagement, her prospects of actually finding a man in Lonesome Way she wanted to marry and stay married to—and to have a houseful of kids with—seemed to be dwindling like winter kindling.

Her two best friends, Lissie and Sophie, both had great marriages and adorable children—Lissie an exquisite moppet named Molly and Sophie a little son, Aiden, who was a miniature spitting image of Sophie's gorgeous husband, Rafe Tanner.

And in another life, if Mia and Rafe's brother Travis *had* gotten married as they'd dreamed way back in high school, they might have their own little boy now, too—one who was every bit as handsome as Travis. The thought gave her a sudden deep pang, which she quickly shook off, annoyed with herself.

After all this time, Travis Tanner should have no power to upset her. *None.*

Her infatuation with Rafe's strapping younger brother had ended too many freaking years ago. High school. She'd been an idiot back then, a stupid, naïve teenager who'd believed Travis when he whispered that he loved her, that he would always love her.

Maybe he'd believed it himself. Right up until the moment when he dumped her like a sack of mealy potatoes.

She'd obviously been the only one to give her heart away. And Travis hadn't hesitated to toss it back to her in bloody little pieces.

She'd been sixteen then. The same age Brittany was now. And she'd been full of silly, romantic dreams, believing she and Travis would be together forever—one of those blissfully happy married couples who adore each other through the decades and are surrounded by scads of children and grandchildren.

Well, she reminded herself as she listened to Sam apologize yet again, it wasn't as if her track record with men was any worse than that of the other women in her family.

"Listen, Sam, you need to hang tight right now." She kept her tone upbeat, despite the worry gripping her. "I'm sure Britt will come home soon. And if she doesn't—"

She broke off suddenly as a red convertible streaked

around the corner two blocks ahead and roared down Larkspur Road.

"Sam, wait a minute." She interrupted her sister's breathless worried chatter. "Hold on. I think . . ."

The convertible barreled closer, straight toward her.

Britt drove a red convertible. A Mustang. Steve Duncan, her father, had bought it for her on her sixteenth birthday.

Mia's gaze was glued to the flashy little car and her breath caught in her throat. "Sam, wait. Listen to me—"

The car squealed to a halt at the curb not ten feet from Mia's Jeep. The skinny sixteen-year-old driver with dirty blond hair, wearing sleep pants and a T-shirt beneath a purple hoodie, tumbled out from behind the wheel.

"Samantha, she's all right," Mia gasped. "Brittany's all right. She's *here.*"

Her sister erupted into relieved weeping so loud Mia had to hold the phone away from her ear.

"She looks fine. Don't worry. Give me a few minutes with her, honey, and I'll call you right back."

Tossing her cell onto the seat before Sam could answer, Mia sprang out of the Jeep.

"Aunt M-Mia." Leaning wearily against the convertible, her niece stared at her through tear-filled, sea blue eyes. "Please don't try to make me go back. Because I w-won't."

Britt might have her father's eyes, but the mutinous expression on her face reminded Mia strongly of the way Sam had looked countless times after their mother had grounded her.

"I *won't* stay with my dad while Mom goes on her honeymoon. And she can't make me. I'm not going back to Butte for the rest of the summer. You have to let me stay with you!"

Chapter Three

Twenty minutes later, Mia watched Brittany swallow the last buttery bite of one of Sophie's famous cinnamon buns.

"I can't make any promises," she said as the girl stared at her with pleading eyes. "Your mom gets to decide where you stay."

They were sitting at the table in Mia's small, comfortable kitchen. Wide windows framed by delicate white lace curtains opened onto the quiet, tree-lined street. Brittany's sandals were on the floor, upside down under the table, her bare feet curled beneath her. Samson lay snuggled on her lap on the pretty peach-cushioned chair.

Sitting at the opposite end of the table, Mia thought back to the little girl who'd dragged a lavender blanket everywhere she went, until the blanket had faded to a dull shade of gray by the time she entered first grade. That little girl had endlessly drawn pictures of rainbows and castles and had loved the Sleeping Beauty storybook Mia had given her for her birthday more than any other book—until she discovered *The Black Stallion* and *Little Women*, and then Harry Potter and Twilight had come along.

What had happened to that child? The young woman at her table had grown into a subdued young beauty—her long tawny blond curls tumbling down her back, shadows under her eyes the same color as the blanket she'd once carried everywhere.

"I *hate* going to my dad's house," she said miserably.

"Since when? I thought you were crazy about your new little stepbrother."

"Tate's . . . a brat." Brittany looked away as she said the words, and somehow Mia didn't believe them. "You should see how Gwen and my dad cater to him. He gets everything he wants. It's . . . lame there. I don't want to stay in that house for three days, much less three weeks."

"But all of your friends are in Butte," Mia pointed out. "Don't you—"

"I'm sick of Butte. I'm sick of everyone. I just want a break."

Tears filled the girl's eyes. And that was the most alarming thing of all. Britt didn't cry easily. She was an athlete—a soccer player and track star—and she had tons of friends, both boys and girls.

Why does she want to get away from everyone?

"Did you argue with one of your friends? With Laura?" Mia chose her words carefully. "Are you upset about breaking up with that guy you were dating—what was his name . . . Wade?"

Britt's mouth opened, closed. She swallowed. And shook her head.

"I just want to be here. With you." Her voice was so low Mia could barely catch the words. Rubbing her eyes, she looked exactly as she had when she was a little girl, exhausted and ready for a nap. "Why does everyone need to make a federal case out of it?" she burst out suddenly. "I'll get a job for the summer. Pay my own way. So what's the big deal?"

This is going nowhere, Mia thought. Whatever was up

with Britt, it might be better to discuss it after she'd had a few hours of sleep.

"You look wiped, honey."

"I woke up really early today."

Five o'clock in the morning, according to Laura.

Mia pushed to her feet, held out a hand. "Come on then. You can take a nap in the guest room. You'll feel better when you wake up."

Leading the way down the hall, she glanced back over her shoulder to see Samson trotting after them. "But you'll need to talk to your mom when you wake up," she warned.

"Can't you talk to her for me?" Brittany stumbled toward the double bed with its white wrought-iron headboard and wasted no time in pitching herself facedown on the rose and blue quilt. "If you tell Mom it's okay with you, she'll let me stay. She always listens to you."

Mia refrained from pointing out that nothing could be further from the truth. She and Samantha definitely had their differences, though they were nowhere near as drastic as whatever sisterly drama had forever separated Gram and Aunt Winny all those years ago. She and Sam loved each other and despite their widely differing temperaments—and Sam being eight years older—they'd always been close.

"I should scold you, I suppose." When Britt eyed her warily, she grinned and carefully smoothed the girl's tangled hair back from her face. "But I won't. Not right now."

Something in her niece's eyes pierced her heart. Brittany wasn't just being moody. She was truly upset.

What if there's more to this? she thought uneasily. *And what could it be?*

"Don't worry, I'll tell your mom that you're welcome to stay. But you need to talk to her, too. And accept whatever she decides."

"Sure. As long as she doesn't make me go back." Britt's eyes were already closing as she burrowed her face into the pillow.

She looked so exhausted. And so unhappy. Not at all like her usual buoyant self.

Drawing the curtains against the sunlight, Mia tiptoed out of the room, leaving her niece in semidarkness, with Samson's small furry body pressed against her side.

This has to be more than mere stress because her mother's just gotten married for the third time and going on an extended honeymoon. And because her dad has a new wife and son.

But . . . what?

Slipping out the front door, she headed back to the Jeep. The day was warming now, the sun glowing in the sapphire Montana sky. She stripped off her hoodie and tossed it in the backseat. With just her tank top and jeans, the sun felt good on her bare shoulders. She climbed behind the wheel and began automatically organizing her priorities.

First things first. Winny. Then home to play peacemaker with Samantha and Britt.

Lucky me, she thought ruefully, starting the engine. A fun-filled day of Quinn women family drama. *Not.*

Chapter Four

Though the smells of fresh coffee, fried eggs, sausage, and warm banana bread wafted through the Sage Ranch kitchen, Travis scarcely noticed. He barely even noticed the frantic activity outside as his brother's two rescued dogs, the gangly black mutt Starbucks and the little brown and black Tidbit, with his stubby tail, chased each other around the perimeter of the house—until they sounded a frantic joint alarm after spotting a squirrel impinging on their territory.

"Hey, quiet, guys," he ordered through the open window, halting the racket as the squirrel made its escape into the woods, and one of the horses whickered from the corral. Both dogs turned to gape at him, tails wagging.

Ah, home on the range. Where the dogs and the horses play.

Travis resumed rinsing his plate in the sink, then set it inside the dishwasher, hoping the two mutts hadn't wakened Grady, still asleep upstairs as of fifteen minutes ago when he'd last checked.

The boy was as worn out as a stub from that two-day drive. And who knew, maybe from all the tension in his life—and, if Travis knew Val—from all the yelling. The kid had been through a lot in the past forty-eight hours—uprooted from his home, transported hundreds of miles to a place he scarcely remembered, plopped down amid family he barely knew.

My fault, Travis thought as his older brother ambled into the kitchen. *I should have been there for him, kept him attached, connected to the ranch, to the family. But I was too busy with the FBI, chasing bad guys and trying to keep our undercover alive—while letting my kid's life go all to hell.*

He had a brief image of Nichols, the grungy undercover agent he and Joe had been monitoring for months. Nichols had infiltrated one of the largest human smuggling rings in the country, working hand in glove with soulless thugs who traded in human misery. They'd been trying to keep Nichols safe and alive as he stockpiled a landslide of evidence. Ironic that at the end of it all, it was Joe, tough, gritty Joe, Travis's grizzled veteran partner, who'd ended up dead in the blink of an eye.

"I wouldn't give a plug nickel for your thoughts right now," Rafe commented drily, pouring himself a cup of coffee and automatically refilling Travis's cup. "Looks like you woke up on the dark side of the planet."

"Guess you could say that. The planet of hard truths."

Rafe's brows rose. "Such as?"

"I let Grady down. Big-time. I should have been paying more attention, visiting the kid a hell of a lot more and making sure he spent some time with me in Arizona. And here on the ranch." Travis grimaced. "I'm legally his dad—and maybe if I hadn't been so wrapped up in trying to bust that damned smuggling ring these past months, I'd have noticed that my own boy was in trouble."

"He was with his mom—you thought he was covered.

Give yourself a break. You *did* bust that smuggling ring. Your country thanks you. So how long until the bureau needs you back?"

Travis frowned out the window at mountain peaks rearing up like giants to punch the June sky. It was a much better sight than a lot of what went on inside his head these days, like the dark trails he'd followed recently, the hellish sounds of human screams and gunfire that came back to him unbidden—and far too often—in the middle of the night. Not to mention the endless reports and paperwork, the interrogations and directives from rigid, out-of-touch supervisors who hadn't set foot in the field for decades.

He was burned out. Trying to come to grips with Joe's death. He needed this change. Needed at this point in his life to shift gears.

He'd almost forgotten how beautiful it was here. How peaceful. Arizona had its own wild spare beauty, but Montana . . . Montana was both lush and hard, a land of contrasts with its soft meadows and sharp peaks, its creeks and cattle, white-tailed deer on distant bluffs, mountain goats and elk.

It was at times an unforgiving and possibly dangerous land that welcomed visitors, challenged them, and nurtured them with deep beauty and adventure—even as it tempted them across high ridges and isolated hills where the unwary could topple off a cliff into a bottomless ravine or stumble across a puma or grizzly.

This land was good to those who called it home. It cradled its cities and towns in rough-hewn grandeur and it nourished cattle and horses and everyone who loved wide-open spaces. And it seemed to Travis it had always cupped the gentle community of Lonesome Way with particular care, tucked as it was in the shadow of the Crazy Mountains.

"Travis? Where'd you go?" His brother's voice pulled him back to Sage Ranch. "How long until you have to report back to the bureau?"

"Good question."

"You got a good answer?"

"Yeah." Travis spoke quietly. "Maybe never."

There was silence in the kitchen as he turned to meet his brother's eyes.

"Care to explain what that means?"

"I requested an official leave of absence. And I'm considering making it permanent."

Startled, Rafe set down his mug of coffee. "Does this by any chance have something to do with losing your partner so suddenly? I know you were close to Joe Grisham, but do you really think he'd want you to—"

"Joe's death was a body blow, but it doesn't have anything to do with why I'm leaving the bureau." Pacing across the kitchen with the smooth deliberate gait of a federal agent at ease with his own strength, savvy, and skills, Travis took a seat at the table where he'd shared countless meals with his parents, his brothers, and his sister. For a moment, it almost seemed as if he could hear their voices all at once, teasing, laughing, arguing with each other over big country breakfasts, quick lunches, and hearty suppers.

With an effort, he shook off the ghosts and reeled his thoughts back to the present, meeting his brother's intent gaze.

"Joe's heart gave out. It might have happened anytime; it just so happened that he got hit with that heart attack in a hospital while waiting to interview some scumbag human trafficker who'd been shot by another agent on our team. Even the doctors on-site couldn't save him. It was too fast, too devastating."

His voice was low. The grief still sat on his chest like a fifty-pound anvil. "I still think about Joe's wife, the way she looked when she got there." Travis's mouth tightened as he remembered Caroline's eyes, dazed with grief, how her small, sturdy body seemed to fold in upon itself as he kept her from crumpling to the spotless hospital floor.

"They'd been married thirty-seven years."

Rafe nodded. "And you've been partnered with him for the past six."

"Yeah." It was a vastly inadequate response. But Travis had no words to express what Joe Grisham had meant to him. His heart felt leaden with the same weight he'd borne when his parents died. Joe had been more than his partner. The tall, grim-faced agent, always fighting a paunch, always quick with a story about the old days, had been his mentor, his friend, his ally from almost the first week he'd joined the bureau. And Caroline—she'd become like a second mother to him.

Which was why he'd spent nearly every off-duty moment of the past month helping her sort through all the legal and financial matters bombarding her after Joe's death. Why he'd tried to be there for her whenever he could while still following every lead to tie up the last case he and Joe would ever work together.

"I miss Joe," he said gruffly. "But that's not the reason I'm thinking of moving on from the bureau."

"And that would be . . . ?"

Travis frowned. "Too many suits. Breathing down my neck for too many years. Tight-assed, pencil-pushing supervisors on power trips. Sometimes, big brother, a man can only take so much red tape crap. It's time for a change."

"Maybe you're ready to roll up your sleeves and do some real work. Come into the horse ranching business with me." Rafe grinned. "Maybe we'll kidnap Jake from the rodeo life and rope him in, too."

"Haven't you heard? Kidnapping's a federal offense." Travis spread his big hands on the table. "Besides, I've got another idea circling in my head."

He laid out for Rafe what he was thinking. First about settling down in Lonesome Way, fixing up his cabin. And then his business idea. Starting up his own private security company, designed solely to protect individuals, corporations, and organizations.

The notion of being his own boss had started appealing to him six or seven months before. He sure as hell knew enough former FBI, Secret Service, and military personnel to power ten companies. He had the know-how, the contacts, and the experience to make it work. And he could do it all from the comfort of a rented office in town and a home office he intended to build on his two hundred acres of land just north of Sage Creek.

Rafe gave a low whistle. "Maybe I should think about going into business with *you*," his brother joked. "Guess my wife isn't the only entrepreneur in the family."

"Speaking of Sophie—she call yet? Any word on Aiden?"

Travis's sister-in-law had whisked his nephew to the pediatrician early this morning. The little boy had been under the weather for the past few days and today had started running a fever.

"He has a double ear infection. Sophie's picking up a prescription right now at Benson's Drugstore. They'll be back soon."

"Aw, poor kid. I heard him crying in the middle of the night—he sounded miserable. He's plenty cute, though, bro." Travis cocked a brow. "Good thing he got his mom's gorgeous looks. The boy's going to break a few dozen hearts in a couple of years."

"Why not? Runs in the family," Rafe drawled.

Travis eyed him across the table. "You got something you want to say? Seems to me you did your share of heart-breaking in your younger days."

"I was an amateur compared to you and Jake."

"Bullshit. Jake's a serial heartbreaker. He has a different girl every month. I only . . ." He stopped.

"Broke one heart? That what you were about to say?" Rafe took a slow sip of coffee.

"Why are we talking about this?" There was an edge to Travis's voice.

"No reason."

"You got something to say, bro, spit it out."

The dogs began to scratch at the kitchen door and Starbucks let out a single bark. Rafe pushed to his feet, let them in. The moment they were inside they rushed toward Travis, clamoring for his attention. Rafe watched in amusement as Travis scratched both mutts behind their ears.

"Mia still lives in town, you know." Rafe spoke casually. "She teaches fifth grade at the middle school."

The words made Travis's back go up. He stopped petting the dogs and they pattered to their water bowls and drank.

"So?" he asked in his most indifferent drawl.

"So . . . I saw how you looked at her at my wedding. It was pretty funny—a grown man, one who women seem to find attractive, though I can't for the life of me figure out why." Rafe's eyes gleamed with amusement. "And yet, this beautiful woman you used to date wouldn't give you a glance, let alone the time of day—much less her cell phone number."

"Let it go, Rafe."

"Just trying to get things straight." His brother shrugged. "Does Mia have anything to do with why you're back in Lonesome Way?"

"What if she does?" Now why did he say that? He could have just said *Hell no.* But that would've been a lie. He'd been thinking about Mia ever since the wedding. Maybe not every minute, but steadily, relentlessly.

Picturing her in that red dress. Curvy, sophisticated, sexy as hell. Her full mouth and thick-lashed amber eyes a combustible combination of sexy and sweet. Hard to believe she was even more beautiful now than she'd been in high school. But she was probably a completely different person from that sixteen-year-old girl, just as he was no longer that eighteen-year-old jerk who'd left her high and dry.

They didn't even know each other anymore. And yet . . . at the wedding, seeing her, something had happened to him.

He hadn't been able to get Mia—the petite, gorgeous, self-assured woman Mia was now—out of his mind.

She wasn't the reason he was back. Not the sole reason, at least. But a part of him had to admit, the idea of returning to Lonesome Way, of starting a business in the town where he'd grown up, where his family lived, where he had roots, had seemed even more appealing because he knew she was still there.

And still single.

It hadn't taken an FBI agent to determine that. Lissie, now and then, seemed to enjoy catching him up on the goings-on of the town and that had included mentioning Mia. She always made it sound casual, but he wondered if there was more to it. Knowing his sister, there was.

"If you still have feelings for Mia Quinn," Rafe said, "I wouldn't sit on my butt too long if I were you. She almost married Zeke Mueller a while back. They had a wedding date picked out and everything. Changed her mind all of a sudden."

"And why was that?"

Rafe shrugged. "Who knows? Lissie and Sophie might have some idea, but all I know is that she gave him back his ring. Mueller was plenty pissed, too, from what I heard. But now he's married to Deanna—you remember Deanna Scott—she used to work afternoons at her dad's gas station on Route 5. They've got triplets on the way. So that could have been Mia, you know—pregnant with another man's kids."

The knot that tightened in Travis's gut felt like a block of caked clay. It took all of his training to keep the sudden tension inside him from showing in his face.

"And you know what else?" Rafe stood, ambled over to the coffeepot and topped off his cup, and then Travis's again, as he kept talking. "Just last month, I overheard Boyd Hatcher from the Lazy Q Ranch running his mouth over at the Double Cross. He was ogling Mia out on the dance floor, saying he wished he'd had a teacher who looked like that when he was in school, and he wouldn't mind getting to know her better." Rafe continued on as if he hadn't noticed the almost imperceptible bunching of muscles in Travis's neck. "Actually, he said he wanted to get her in the sack. Or words to that effect."

"Is that so?" Travis managed to keep his tone even. He and Hatcher went way back. They'd never gotten along, even in third grade when Boyd had gotten his kicks shooting spitballs at Lissie on the playground. Until the day Travis punched him in the nose, and then they'd both been marched down to the principal's office.

"She was dancing with Coop Miller at the time—Mia and Coop dated on and off a few months back," Rafe explained casually. "But Hatcher wasted no time hustling over there to ask her for the next dance."

"Mia has every right to dance with whoever she wants." But Travis heard his own voice. The words had come out in a kind of growl. "I've got a kid to take care of and a business to get up and running. Mia and I were over a long time ago."

"Right." Rafe tried to hide a grin, and Travis had a feeling his brother could see right through him as no one else in the world could—except maybe Lissie or Jake. He and his siblings all knew each other too damned well.

"Keep telling yourself that, bro. Next thing you know, you could be seeing Mia at another wedding—*hers*."

No chance of that, Travis thought. *Not a chance in hell I'd be invited.*

He heard light footsteps treading down the stairs. Ivy, Rafe's thirteen-year-old daughter by his irresponsible ex-wife—was still at a friend's sleepover party, so it had to be Grady finally up and about.

His gaze softened as the boy appeared in the kitchen doorway. Grady was still a little small for his age, but time would take care of that. Grady's biological dad had been tall and rangy. And Val was five foot seven. The boy hadn't hit his real growth spurt yet, but he was a good-looking kid with even features, shaggy brown hair, a dusting of freckles, and those long-lashed serious green eyes under slanted brows. He'd be handsome by the time he reached his teens. This morning Grady had ditched his pajamas for jeans, a light green T-shirt, and athletic shoes. His longish hair flopped over his eyes. But the sullen look was still firmly entrenched on his young face.

"First time we go to town, we're buying you some boots, buddy." Travis smiled. "You must be hungry. How about some scrambled eggs before we head out to the cabin?"

"Sure." Grady hovered near the refrigerator, looking uncertain.

"Come on in, take a seat," Rafe said easily. Taking out a plate from the cupboard, he sliced off a hunk of the banana bread Sophie had baked that morning while he was busy changing Aiden and trying to give him a bottle. "You can start with this while your dad rustles up those eggs."

He watched as the boy leaned down, a smile breaking across his face for the first time as the dogs rushed to him, scrappy little Tidbit and the strapping Starbucks both competing to see how many times they could lick his face.

"You have a dog at home?" Rafe asked.

Grady shook his head. "My mom's allergic to animals. She let me have a hamster once, but Drew made me get rid of it when we moved to L.A."

Travis turned from the stove where he had sausage sizzling in a skillet alongside the eggs. His gaze met his brother's briefly, then shifted to his son's face.

"We've got tons of animals around here—two new barn cats, two dogs, and a whole bunch of horses," Rafe said. "You can pick out the horse you want to ride. There's at least three or four that should be right about your speed. I think Pepper Jack would be a good fit for you, but you need to decide if you like him."

"Pepper Jack?" For the first time, eagerness lit Grady's eyes.

"He's a lot of horse, but I think you can handle him if your dad starts you off slow." Rafe poured the boy a glass of orange juice from the white pitcher on the table, then glanced out the window as Sophie's Blazer rolled down the long driveway.

"They're back." He strode swiftly into the hall and was out the door in a flash.

"Can I ride Pepper Jack after we go to the cabin?"

"Sure." Travis carried the skillet of fried eggs and sizzling sausage to the table and heaped the food on Grady's plate. "Once we get a good day's work done, we'll come back and go for a ride."

"Yes!" Grady dug into the food as if he hadn't eaten in a week. He only stopped to look up as Sophie breezed in, little Aiden in her arms and Rafe right behind her.

"Good morning, Grady, Travis."

Travis thought his sister-in-law looked as gorgeous as always, though tired and distracted. The slight shadows under her eyes indicated she hadn't gotten much sleep the night before—he'd heard Aiden crying more than once through the walls of his old bedroom, down the hall from Jake's old room, now the nursery.

The little boy was fussing in her arms right now, making small unhappy sounds. Whew, his ears probably hurt like hell, Travis thought with sympathy. He remembered when Grady had an ear infection. It was a few months after he'd met the boy, while he and Val were dating. The poor kid had been miserable.

"Sorry," Sophie murmured as Aiden let out a wail. "He's not going to feel much better until the antibiotics kick in tomorrow."

Rafe dug the prescription bottle from the diaper bag and studied it, then took his son from his wife's arms. "Let's get you some meds, big guy," he said gently. "Show this rotten infection who's boss."

"Do you need anything?" Sophie glanced from Travis to

Grady after Aiden choked down the liquid medicine with a wail of outrage. "I'm going to try to get him down for a nap. Think I'll grab one at the same time."

"You do that," Travis told her. "Don't worry about us. I'm only sorry we dropped in on you with such short notice."

Gently, he swept his big hand across his nephew's tufts of fuzzy, golden brown hair and smiled into his sister-in-law's eyes. He'd known Sophie almost all his life. She and Lissie had been friends since they were no bigger than a couple of chipmunks.

"I promise Grady and I will be out of your hair as soon as we get the cabin fit for the two of us."

"Hey, there's no hurry," Rafe said.

"We'd love for you to stay, both of you. Aiden will be better in no time and he's going to want to get to know his uncle and his big cousin." Sophie's smile was genuine and warm, directed first at Travis, then at Grady. The boy didn't even look up, just kept eating his breakfast, eyes on his plate.

"There's an apple tart in the pantry and a blueberry pie in that white bakery box on the counter. Feel free to help yourselves," she called over her shoulder as she brushed a kiss against Rafe's mouth, then hurried upstairs with the baby.

Rafe left shortly after, for a meeting in town with a horse breeder, but not before taking Grady out back to introduce him to his foreman, Will Brady, and a few of the other wranglers.

Travis watched his son trailing after Will toward the barn as the dogs—not allowed in the horse barn—romped in the pasture behind the corral.

The boy trudging after the foreman was a far cry from the child he'd first met at Valerie's apartment in Phoenix.

That Grady had been a happy-go-lucky toddler who had grown into a gregarious little boy, but now, on the precipice of adolescence, he was a very quiet kid. Too quiet.

But at least he hadn't seemed to hate being surrounded

by family. It was hard to tell just what Grady was thinking, though. *He's had a lot of practice keeping things to himself. But it comes out in other ways,* Travis reminded himself grimly. *Like picking fights. And failing a class.*

One of his biggest concerns was the possibility that Grady might have to repeat fifth grade. He raked a hand through his hair and concentrated on cleaning up the kitchen. One thing at a time, he told himself. He needed to get to know his son again, to spend the next month or so trying to rebuild what had once been an easy, loving relationship, then deal with the crap that had gone down.

And what about Mia? a voice inside him asked.

What about her? He had no right to feel anything about Mia anymore. And even if he did try to get her to just *speak* to him, which she hadn't done in years—always somehow avoiding him on the rare times when he was home for a visit—what good would it do?

He'd already hurt her once. They'd both moved on, so . . .

So it was best to leave things that way, not even try to stir something up when he didn't know how the hell it would end. Mia could get hurt again. He'd be damned if he'd risk that.

Stay away from her, he told himself as he headed upstairs for a shower. *You have enough on your plate right now without bringing her into the mix.*

Grady had to be his first priority. And whipping the cabin into shape and setting up the new business would take up a whole lot of his time.

His years as a special agent had taught Travis to compartmentalize his thoughts and his life. To keep facts and emotions separate, orderly, and in perspective.

Right now, he had to do just that—and stay focused on what was in front of him. No getting distracted by anything outside those perimeters.

Like the past.

As the spray from the showerhead hit his bare flesh with

stinging heat, he welcomed the needle-like sensation. He turned the showerhead nozzle full force and let it clear his brain.

Mia Quinn was off-limits. No if, ands, or buts. He dunked his head beneath the spray and tried to drown out all other thoughts.

Chapter Five

⌢

"Britt didn't tell you *anything*?" Samantha sounded worried, and Mia could picture her taking deep cleansing breaths as she'd been trained to do in her twice-weekly yoga classes.

"She claims she needs a break. And she does seem really stressed, Sam, but so far I've no idea why."

Mia was driving down Squirrel Road, going forty-five. There was no traffic unless you counted the doe and two fawns she'd just passed, half hidden by sagebrush and juniper.

"All I can tell you is that she begged me to let her stay for the summer."

"The *summer*?" Sam's shriek made Mia wince and shift the phone away from her ear. "The entire *summer*? No way."

"It's perfectly okay with me. She's welcome to—"

"Are you kidding me? She's just acting out to get back at me for getting married again and—oh, I don't know—going off on a honeymoon and leaving her behind. For God's sake, it's only three weeks! She can stay with her father and then I'll be back and—"

Samantha broke off, drew in a long, shaky breath. "Why does she have to pull this crap right now? She used to be such an easygoing kid, even when she hit her teens. Maybe she just hates Alec. But he's so nice to her, Mia, I swear—and she always *seemed* to like him—"

"Sam, honestly, I'd love to have her stay for the summer. The two of us will have fun—and you and Alec can leave for Corfu tomorrow without having to worry about her every minute while you're gone."

"What would she do in Lonesome Way all summer long?" her sister demanded. "Except for you, she doesn't know a soul."

"She promised to get a job."

"A job? And what if she can't find one?"

Mia braked for a rabbit scampering across the road. After it disappeared into the brush she accelerated again along the rough country lane.

"You know, I can probably help her out with that. Sophie hires high school kids all the time to work at the bakery, especially in the summer. She has loads of part-time shifts. I'm sure she'd be willing to hire Britt—and Britt could make some friends that way. The bakery's definitely a hangout, just like Roy's Diner used to be when we were in high school. It could work out, Sam."

Seconds ticked by as she waited for her sister's response.

She pictured Sam, skinny as a doe in winter, filled with nervous energy as she wound her dark blond hair around her fingers and pursed her lips the way she did whenever she was weighing something in her mind.

"Are you sure about this? You want a sixteen-year-old hanging around all summer? Tell me right now if you're only being nice—"

"Since when am I ever nice to you?"

"It's been known to happen."

Mia laughed. "Really, Sam, it's no big deal. It seems pretty important to her to have a little break right now from life in Butte. Once she settles in, I'll try to find out why."

Finally her sister caved. Thanking Mia a half dozen times, she promised to call Brittany in a few hours to tell her she could stay *if* she found a job and *if* she didn't cause her aunt any trouble.

"Don't worry about a thing." Mia managed to get a word in finally when Sam wound down. "You just go and have a spectacular honeymoon."

"I'll try, damn it." Her sister exhaled. "It's my third one. I'd better have a handle on it by now, don't you think?"

Mia decided to make one stop on her way to Winny's cabin. She veered off Squirrel Road and onto the long wide drive leading to Sage Ranch, hoping Sophie would be home.

Ever since Aiden's birth, Sophie had begun doing quite a bit of the baking for A Bun in the Oven right in her own kitchen. There was a good chance she'd have some of her special cinnamon buns at home, or else brownies or a pie Mia could mooch to bring to Aunt Winny.

After all, what was supper without dessert? she thought as she pulled up behind a black Explorer she didn't recognize.

Hurrying to the front door, she knocked lightly in case Aiden was asleep.

How many times did I stand at this door, waiting for Lissie or her mom to welcome me into this house? she thought, a smile lifting the corners of her mouth.

She and Lissie and Sophie had all spent hours running around the ranch as girls, playing hide-and-seek in the barn and hayloft, tramping through the woods, hiking all the way to Sage Creek and back, then trailing in, exhausted, to flop into kitchen chairs while Mrs. Tanner served them pecan cookies and milk.

Having grown up living near town, it had been a treat

every time she visited the ranch. She'd felt inexplicably happy here, connected somehow not only to all the Tanners but to the valley itself, to the horses, the creek, the wide pastures and meadows riotous with wildflowers—or, in winter, cloaked in mounds of snow.

Not that she hadn't loved the house where she grew up. It was home and it was hers—small, neat, and absolutely charming, with its eggshell blue walls and hickory floors and six high, curtained windows facing the backyard and garden. Larkspur Road was also conveniently close to town and to the middle school where she taught.

But Sage Ranch had always felt like a second home.

She knocked once more, rapping slightly harder than she'd intended on the solid oak door.

The baby might be asleep. Sophie, too, she realized in chagrin when there was still no answer and she turned quickly away. *Aunt Winny will just have to get by without dessert. . . .*

When the door behind her whooshed open she spun back, an apologetic smile on her lips. "Please tell me I didn't wake . . ."

The words turned to dust in her throat.

It wasn't Sophie or even Rafe who stepped out onto the porch.

It was Travis.

Travis Tanner.

A towering six feet, one inch of rough, hard-bodied male.

And he was naked from the waist up.

This is so not fair, Mia thought desperately as every word in her vocabulary seemed to erase itself from her brain.

Fate was playing a nasty trick on her. Not only was Travis in town—and why the hell hadn't Sophie *told* her that?—but she'd obviously interrupted him in the midst of a shower. His dark hair glistened with water and small droplets of it clung to the hair on his very broad, very ripped chest. He smelled deliciously of soap and leather and man.

She felt her breath catching in her throat. He was wearing jeans. *And nothing else.*

Unless you counted that sexy, oh-so-male smile tipping up the corners of his mouth. A mouth whose taste and shape and texture were embedded in her memories, even after all these years. . . .

"I . . . dragged you out of the shower, didn't I?" she heard herself mutter inanely as if from a great distance.

"What was your first clue?" Travis grinned.

Don't you grin at me, Travis Tanner. Not now. Not ever. That's dirty pool.

Whenever he'd come to town over the past years, she'd reminded herself that she wasn't attracted to him anymore. That he was history. Old, buried, irrelevant history.

It was so much easier to believe that when she didn't actually have to *see* him. Up until now, she'd managed to avoid him just fine.

But now, here he was right in front of her. Tall and tough-looking, with the brawny build of a lumberjack, his jet-black hair glinting in the sun, his eyes keen and intent on hers.

And he isn't wearing a shirt.

It took all of her willpower not to drink in the sight of that lean, tanned torso or to stare at the bulge of muscles in his arms and chest.

Don't look at his body. Look at his face.

Under normal circumstances that would be a pleasure. Except that looking into Travis's face was every bit as dangerous as looking at his body. The man was hands-down gorgeous. He'd been handsome even as a boy, but he'd grown into a man with the kind of ruggedly dark good looks that could make a woman forget what day of the week it was, where she lived, and even her middle name. That strong jaw, the dark brows, and intelligent, penetrating eyes the color of gun smoke drew you in. Against your will.

For most women, staring into Travis Tanner's face would be a pleasure. But for Mia, it was torture.

She couldn't possibly still have feelings for him—not after all this time. It was just that when Travis looked at her, something seemed to quake inside her.

It's only some crazy reflex, she told herself. It had been that way since the first time he'd spoken to her in the hallway of Lonesome Way High School. She was wandering around lost, searching for her locker, a shy freshman, bewildered and a little intimidated, when in the rush of students stampeding down the crowded corridor, a pack of girls had bumped into her and accidentally sent her tumbling into a wall. She'd nearly lost her balance and had dropped her algebra book and her backpack.

Travis had appeared out of nowhere at her side, asking her if she was all right. He'd handed her the book, lifted up her backpack, grinned at her in a slow, easy way, a way he'd never had when she and Lissie were little girls playing with their Barbies at Sage Ranch.

The same way he was grinning at her right now. And she felt her heart trembling.

Come on. You're so over him, she reminded herself. *You're hardly sixteen anymore.*

But she felt the pull. And a deep, buried hurt stirred inside her.

Damn it, no. Get a grip.

"How've you been, Mia?"

"Great. Never better. You?"

Travis fought the urge to step closer to her. She looked a whole lot better than great. She looked as beautiful as the first day of spring. And every bit as sexy as an exotic dancer in those tight-fitting jeans and that skimpy little tank top that hugged her breasts.

But her tone was cool. Just this side of sarcastic. Actually, it was in danger of sliding over the edge.

The teenaged girl he'd known long ago had always been warm, honest, and as sweet as his grandmother's ginger cookies.

Well, what do you expect? he asked himself impatiently. *Especially after the way you treated her. She's different now. And so are you.*

But at least, he told himself grimly, unlike at Rafe and Sophie's wedding, she was speaking to him.

Sort of.

"I'm terrific now that I'm home," he told her and saw the flicker of surprise in those luminous amber eyes that had continued to haunt him over the years. "Looks like I'm going to be sticking around for a while."

"Sticking around?" Her petite, insanely curvy body went rigid, further accentuating the swell of her breasts beneath that pale blue tank top. Her eyes were locked on his. But not in a good way.

"You're . . . moving *back* here?" She said it as if he'd told her he was planning to rob a bank.

"Don't look so thrilled. It might go to my head."

Instead of earning him the smile he'd hoped for, she frowned. For some reason he couldn't explain, this irritated the hell out of him.

And the federal agent known for keeping his cool under the most extreme pressure couldn't contain the words that came out next.

"Worried you might have to actually talk to me now and again if we run into each other in town?"

"I'm not *worried* about anything. And I don't know what you mean by that."

"You avoided me at Rafe and Sophie's wedding. I tried to talk to you, to catch your eye, but you pretended not to see me."

"*You* were at Rafe and Sophie's wedding? I'm afraid I didn't notice."

Bemused, he stuck his hands in his pockets. "Well, I noticed you."

She *had* changed. The girl he'd loved years ago had worn

her heart on her sleeve. This woman, all grown up, was meticulously self-possessed and kept hers under wraps.

Maybe that was partly his fault. From the little he'd heard from Lissie over the years, he knew he wasn't the only man who'd let her down. Still, that didn't let him off the hook.

"A man would have to be dead not to notice you," he said quietly and for a moment, a breath, he thought he saw something in her eyes. She looked startled, open, and vulnerable, and he had the almost overpowering urge to take her in his arms.

Then she shut down, stepped back—and at the same time there was a commotion from behind the house. The dogs started barking like hounds escaped from hell. Will Brady's voice rumbled from the direction of the barn.

"Dad!" Grady shouted, racing toward them. "Mr. Brady let me pet Pepper Jack and he's going to show me how to brush him. Can I ride him now? Please? I really want to!"

"Whoa, Grady. I want to introduce you to someone. This is Ms. Quinn." He hoped his voice sounded steady. What the hell had happened a minute ago? What in hell was wrong with him?

"Hi." Grady looked up at Mia with a shy smile, then turned right back to Travis. "Can I? Can I ride Pepper Jack now?"

"We have to go to the cabin first, remember? Get started on the work there. When we come back later, I promise we'll spend a couple hours with the horses."

"But I want to ride now." Impatience flashed in the boy's eyes.

"First things first, son," Travis said evenly, and at that moment Sophie stepped out onto the porch.

"Mia, I thought I heard your voice." Her gaze flew from Travis to Mia, a look of concern touching her face, but Mia spoke quickly, moving toward her, breaking the tension.

"I hope I didn't wake you or Aiden. I didn't know you had company."

"Yes, Travis and Grady coming home was the one *good* thing that happened yesterday." Sophie managed a tired smile. "Aiden has an ear infection," she explained. "It was a pretty rough night."

"Oh, no. Sorry. I *did* wake you, didn't I?"

"I was only dozing." She cast another searching glance between Mia and her brother-in-law. "Come on in. I've got coffee."

As Mia hurried inside, telling Sophie she needed a favor, something to do with her aunt Winny, Travis had to force himself to turn away. To go down the steps and focus on Grady. The boy still looked bummed that he couldn't go riding that very moment.

"I'll be ready to roll in five." Travis placed a light hand on his head. "After we check out the cabin, we'll drive into town, get whatever supplies we need. Pepper Jack will be right here waiting when we get done. You'll have later today and the whole summer to ride him."

Grady stared at the ground, saying nothing, but Travis sensed the tension in him. Anger and frustration, probably. Suddenly Travis felt like a bad guy.

He'd spent most of his adult life being tougher than the toughest bad guys, putting them away, being in charge. But Grady wasn't a bad kid and he needed something different from him. The boy needed a firm but gentle touch.

Grady was hurting inside, and Travis didn't know why yet. He only knew he damn well wouldn't add to the boy's pain and sense of isolation. But neither did he want to reward sulky behavior or give in to impulsiveness. Children needed structure, a sense of self-discipline. And they also needed love. He sensed that guiding Grady along would require the right balance between the two. He'd have to feel his way along that particular tightrope. He suddenly wished he had more experience at being a father.

His own father had done a great job of being fair and

loving and instilling a sense of responsibility in him and his brothers. Travis only hoped he could do half as well.

Passing through the hall, he caught a glimpse of Mia and Sophie in the kitchen and was treated to the highly distracting sight of Mia's cute little rounded behind encased in snug-fitting denim. He paused.

Damn. She looked as drop-dead sexy in those jeans and that tank top as she had in that slinky red dress that had been stuck in his mind for the past year and a half.

And maybe even twice as beautiful.

Just the sight of all that shiny blond hair twisted atop her head made him long to undo that tiny white clip and watch it all spill down around her shoulders in a golden waterfall.

She'd worn it short and lusciously sexy the last time he'd seen her, at Rafe and Sophie's wedding, but now it was long again.

And he had no trouble at all remembering how those thick, silky blond strands had felt sifting through his fingertips. Particularly that winter day years ago when they'd made out on a blanket in the bed of his pickup as fragile snowflakes drifted down around them.

It was December and Mia had been wearing a white down parka. Snow had melted on her eyelashes. Her full, sweet mouth had tasted of pink lip gloss when he kissed her.

And her hair—her hair had brushed as soft as a wish against his skin. . . .

He suddenly felt an almost irresistible urge to touch it again. To touch *her* again.

But every grain of common sense he possessed shouted at him that it was too late to make things right. To go back. He had to find a way to shake off all the feelings for her he'd never quite been able to forget, even after he walked out on her.

Still paused in the hallway, he saw her move toward the counter with a grace that would draw any man's eye. She lifted the lid of the white bakery box Sophie held out toward her and was so engrossed in their conversation, he realized, that for her, he'd probably already ceased to exist.

No doubt she'd already even forgotten he was back in town.

His jaw clenched. He told himself it was better that way. That the past was done and gone.

Then he turned and took the stairs two at a time.

Chapter Six

"He's gone now," Sophie murmured. "He went upstairs. I'm sorry you had to find out that way about Travis being back—I should've called you,"

"Makes no difference to me if Travis is back—," Mia began, setting the bakery box on the kitchen table, but Sophie cut her off.

"Oh, please. I knew you way back then, remember? I was at your house that day fifteen minutes after he broke up with you—after he left." Her eyes brimmed with concern as she gave Mia a quick hug. "I'm sorry I didn't think to warn you he was on his way home. I've been so distracted with Aiden being sick that I completely forgot to give you a heads-up—"

"You don't have to 'prepare' me for Travis coming home. Travis and me—all that—it was a million years ago." Mia waved an airy hand. "But do we have to talk about him? I'd rather not."

Instead of replying, Sophie studied her. Mia suspected her friend could see right through the blithe indifference she was trying so hard to project. It was impossible to hide much from Sophie or from Lissie—and normally she wouldn't even bother to try. But over the years, the topic of Travis had always been pretty much avoided by all three of them by unspoken consent.

That had been easy to do while he was away at college and then living in Arizona, far from Lonesome Way. It might be a bit more tricky, Mia realized with a sinking feeling, now that he was back.

If he really *was* back.

"Of course we don't have to talk about him." Sophie turned to slice two generous wedges of banana bread from the loaf beside the coffeepot. She set one slice on a pretty yellow plate for Mia and the other on a plate for herself. "If I wasn't so wiped out, I'd know to just stay out of it."

"Nothing to stay out of." Accepting the plate Sophie offered her with a smile, Mia slipped into a chair and popped a bite of warm banana bread in her mouth.

"I'm a big girl, Soph. All grown up. Not that lovesick kid who cried like a baby for three days after Travis broke up with me. Considering my divorce from Peter and that mess when I ended things with Zeke, what happened with Travis was a mere blip in the grand scheme of things."

"You're due for something good to happen. For someone new to come into your life."

"Someone has. In a way." Mia smiled. "Guess who's spending the summer with me? Here's a hint. She used to call you Aunt Soapy."

"Brittany?" Sophie looked astonished. "I thought she was staying with her dad while Sam's off on her honeymoon."

"Apparently Brittany loathes that idea. I'm still not sure why. But Samantha wants her to find a summer job. So I was wondering . . ." She shot her friend a hopeful glance. "Do you by any chance have any openings at A Bun in the Oven?"

"Since two of my high school kids up and quit the day

before yesterday, I actually do." Sophie sank into a chair, shaking her head. "Those two seemed to think all they'd have to do to work at a bakery was eat brownies, drink coffee, and flirt with every guy under thirty who came in the door—not actually, you know, *work*. When Gran let them know otherwise, they walked. So Brittany can start tomorrow, if she'd like. Eight thirty A.M."

"I owe you, Soph. Big time." Polishing off the last crumbs of her banana bread, Mia carried her plate to the dishwasher and leaned down to set it inside. Much as she'd like to stay and chat with Sophie, she had places to go—and a grumpy old woman to see.

And Travis could be coming back down those stairs any minute now.

"Are you sure you don't mind my taking that pie for Aunt Winny? Let me pay you for it."

"Don't be an idiot." Sophie scooped up the box and thrust it into Mia's hands. "Maybe some pie will sweeten her up. Honestly, I don't know anyone who's ever seen Winona Pruitt give so much as a hint of a smile when she's come to town. Martha Davies told me a few months back that she was beautiful when she was a young girl. And wild . . . wild as one of those mustangs in Coldwater Canyon, she said."

"Was she? Really?" Mia stared. Mia and Sam had never found so much as an old photograph of Winny when they'd pored through their grandmother's things. Martha Davies, the owner of the Cuttin' Loose hair salon and the treasurer of Bits and Pieces, apparently knew more about Mia's great-aunt than Mia ever had. "I knew Martha and Gram were friends," Mia said slowly, "but Martha's never mentioned Aunt Winny to me."

None of Gram's friends ever had. No one ever seemed to talk about her. Except to comment on how unneighborly she was, having nothing to say to anyone in town, never pausing to speak to a soul on the rare occasions she drove into Lonesome Way.

"I think half the time people forget about her—she comes to town even less these days than she used to. And now with the accident and all . . ." Sophie shook her head. "Between poor Winny and Brittany, you have a lot on your plate right now, don't you?"

"Not as much as you do." Mia glanced at her friend sympathetically as the wail of a crying infant burst from upstairs. Sophie jumped up, her face tense, and rushed into the hall.

"Give Aiden a kiss for me," Mia called after her. "I hope he feels better soon."

Sophie was already racing up the steps.

On the front porch, as the summer sun slanted down, she paused at the sight of Grady gathering sticks near the edge of the woods. Travis's son glanced at her, then quickly away, back to his task as the dogs dashed in circles all around him, trying to grab the sticks he was collecting.

He looked to be about nine or ten, close to the age of most of her students. With his slight build, tousled light brown hair, and solemn eyes, he looked nothing at all like Travis, but then, they weren't biologically related, so why would he?

She knew Travis had married a woman in Phoenix and adopted her young son. She'd also heard they'd later divorced.

None of it was any of her business.

And neither was this lonely-looking boy.

But the divorce might explain that moment of tension she'd sensed between Travis and his son. Grady had wanted to ride Pepper Jack right that minute. And had clearly resented it when Travis said no.

Of course, Grady was nearing those ever-so-tricky tween years, the time when kids started inching toward independence, pushing their boundaries. That was probably all it was. She dealt with children that age from September until June, and she knew it was a time of emotional ups and downs, a long season of push and pull.

She waved to the boy when he glanced up again as she

started toward the Jeep, but he returned the gesture half-heartedly and immediately went back to trying to pry a stick away from Tidbit.

There was a melancholy twist to his mouth even as he played with the dogs. Backing out of Sage Ranch's long paved driveway and back onto Squirrel Road, Mia refused to let herself wonder why.

⌒

Travis yanked on an old navy blue T-shirt and swiped a comb through his hair. It was clear Mia had been anything but thrilled to see him, and she'd seemed to have no difficulty forgetting he was even at the ranch the instant Sophie showed up.

Still . . .

In all his years at the FBI, Travis had learned to trust his instincts. And now, as he sat down on the bed and pulled on his boots, those instincts told him that whatever had once been between them might not be gone for good. He'd felt something the moment he looked into Mia's eyes. And he'd be damned if she hadn't felt it, too.

Not that she'd ever admit it.

He couldn't blame her. After what he'd done . . . and the way he'd done it . . .

Hell. He never wanted to hurt her again. He needed to be damned careful. And sure. Sure of how he felt, sure of where things were going. If they got going at all.

Part of him still thought it best to just steer clear. Another part couldn't forget how good it had felt to actually be close to her and talk to her again.

Hearing the sound of a car's engine revving, he strode to the window in time to see her Jeep backing out of the drive below. He stared down at her profile, at those high sharp cheekbones and her delicately sculptured jaw, his gaze drawn to the firm set of her beautiful, kissable mouth.

He wanted to watch until she disappeared, but then he

caught sight of Grady, sprawled on the grass near the front porch, throwing sticks for the dogs to catch and retrieve.

Waiting for him.

Travis strode to the door and tried not to think about the girl he'd left behind, as he went downstairs to join his son.

Chapter Seven

Mia turned off Sweetwater Road and drove slowly along the lumpy heap of gravel that passed for a driveway leading to her aunt's cabin. Parking a dozen yards from Winny's ancient Ford pickup, she gazed at the tiny log dwelling practically teetering on the hillside.

Could her aunt possibly have found a lonelier spot? Surrounded by towering peaks and ponderosa pines, the cabin was a humble speck on the hip of the mountain. A hawk circled through the sapphire sky above, its cry the only sound piercing the silence. The closest house, old Abner Floyd's place, was at least four miles down the road.

In winter, it would be impossible to get in or out of here without a snowmobile. Good thing Winny hadn't taken this tumble in January.

Straightening her shoulders, Mia stepped down onto the gravel and drew out the basket of food and the pie. She started toward the cabin, noting in surprise the pretty row of lilac bushes abloom alongside the cabin and the pink and white hydrangeas and rosebushes planted in front. She'd never been out here in summer before, and if not for its weathered, ramshackle appearance, the cabin looked almost charming framed by those colorful blooms. She was so caught up in the pretty play of colors and the scent of the lilacs that she gave a small, startled cry when a small, almost feral-looking orange tabby suddenly lunged from the brush, darted up the porch steps, and beat her to the front door.

As she followed it, the cat arched its back and glared at her.

"Don't look at me like that. I come in peace," Mia said.

The tabby emitted an ear-piercing screech. But when no sound came from within the cabin, and the scarred door remained closed, the creature whirled with a huge swish of its tail and, without another glance at Mia, leaped off the porch, past the glowing roses, and disappeared into the brush.

Don't even dream you're getting rid of me that easily, Aunt Winny, Mia thought.

She shifted her weight on the creaky front porch, noticing the loose board that had caused her aunt's fall and making a mental note to call Denny McDonald, who owned a construction firm with his father, to come out and fix it.

"Aunt Winny? It's Mia. I heard about your accident. Ellis Stone told me this morning. Please open the door—I'd like to help."

Silence as deep as a forgotten canyon greeted her words. Mia felt a stab of worry.

"Aunt Winny, are you all right?" she called again, more urgently.

The faded floral curtain at the front window moved. It was only a tiny, almost imperceptible flutter, but she knew suddenly that Winny was there, listening on the other side of the door, as stubborn and aloof as ever.

"I was sorry to hear about your fall," Mia called again. "I've brought you some supper. Please, won't you open the door?"

The curtain hung motionless. An almost eerie silence settled over the clearing. With the rough grandeur of the mountain and the vivid color of the flowers, it was actually a lovely spot, marred only by the rusted mailbox leaning sideways toward the road, and the old dank leaves from the previous autumn still matted beneath the tree trunks.

"Aunt Winny, there's a fresh blueberry pie here with your name on it. Please open the door. I've brought roast chicken. A salad, too. And . . . did I mention the pie? I'm not leaving until I know you're all right."

"Since when am I not all right? And what do you care anyway, young lady?"

The barked words rang with surprising force from behind the closed door.

"I do care." Mia spoke quietly in contrast to her aunt's harsh tone. "And if you'll open the door, I'll show you. Please let me help."

"Get off my land."

"I just—"

"Go away. And take that food with you. I've no use for your pity or your charity."

Mia closed her eyes a moment. Injured or not, Winny was always the same. Gruff. Ill-tempered. Gram had been so sweet—determined and strong-willed, yes, or she never would have finished such a wide array of intricate quilts— but also gentle and kind and wise. Her sister, on the other hand, had never seemed to possess an ounce of sweetness or a kind bone in her body. But Mia knew nobody could be all sour anger and vinegar.

Not for the first time, she felt curiosity pricking at her. What had gone so terribly wrong between two sisters separated by less than two years in age? What could have caused such a rift, that the younger daughter of Louis and Abigail Sullivan had shut herself off from every other member of her family?

"All right, if that's what you want, I'll go. But this basket is staying on the porch. If you don't want it, that's fine—the cat will have it. Suit yourself. But call me if you need something. A ride to the doctor's office or . . . anything. I'm writing my cell phone number down, and leaving it in the basket, so put it somewhere safe."

She might as well have been speaking to the clouds. Reaching into her purse, she dug around for a scrap of paper. She knew she had a notepad somewhere in her bag. . . .

There. Ripping off a sheet of pink-and-white-striped paper, she scribbled her cell number and stuck it under the plate of chicken. She left the basket and the bakery box on the porch chair, a relic of sturdy wood and peeling blue paint.

There was still no further sound from inside the cabin.

"I'm going now, Aunt Winny. But you know how to reach me. And I'm not promising that I won't be back."

She waited a moment, listening, but apparently her aunt had used up her maximum number of words for the day. Mia headed to the Jeep. The orange cat was hiding not five yards away. Lurking in the brush, wary, silent, and still.

Well, at least I tried, she told herself as she slammed the Jeep's door. *I did my best.*

So why did she feel so guilty about leaving? It was what her aunt wanted. To be left alone. Apparently it was what she'd always wanted.

Reminding herself that she had a runaway niece sleeping in her guest room who'd probably be starving when she woke up, Mia backed up the rough gravel drive and headed toward home.

⌒

Winny waited until the sound of the car's engine faded away. Then she waited some more, her back straight, pressed against the cabin door, the cane the doctor had given her gripped in one spider-veined hand. Her once plush and perfectly shaped mouth was set in a harsh line.

She didn't want the damned food. Didn't need it either. Didn't she have perfectly good soup and ham in her refrigerator? And a loaf of bread she'd baked herself yesterday morning?

She had milk and eggs and cat food. She'd gone to Livingston only last week and stocked up.

Besides, if she *did* need something, she'd call Abner, not that great-niece of hers. Alicia's granddaughter.

Not for the first time, she wondered what Alicia had told her granddaughters about her all these years. Wondered what she'd told everyone. Did everyone in Lonesome Way and their children and their children's children know what she'd done? What they *thought* she'd done?

Not that it mattered. She didn't care. Not anymore. It had been more than half a century ago. She'd been ashamed then, and furious, and had wanted nothing more than to put as many miles between her and her family as possible. And now . . .

Her mouth twisted into a grimace.

Now it was much too late to ever set things right. So what difference did it make if the girl knew? Maybe she *should* know.

Then she might stay away and not drive out here bothering people with picnic baskets and pies.

The girl who'd come knocking on her door today was no more family to her than the cat who happened by now and then.

She didn't give a care about either of them.

Or about that letter at the bottom of her dresser drawer. It had been there for the past five years now, and she hadn't been tempted to open the seal even once.

All it would do was stir up the hurt all over again.

Still, something made her ease open the cabin door and limp out onto the porch with the aid of the cane. She brushed a hand over the wicker basket her great-niece had left perched on the old chair.

Slowly tears filled her eyes.

She shouldn't have ever come back here. She'd left Lonesome Way once—way back when it all happened—and she should have just stayed away.

There was no point in thinking about any of it now. Lifting the basket in one hand, she hobbled back inside. She set the basket on the small kitchen table and limped back out for the pie.

Against her will, she had to admit it was a lovely pie. A bright circle of berries and golden crust, resting in a white box with red printing that said A BUN IN THE OVEN on the top and the side. A Bun in the Oven. That pretty little bakery everyone in Lonesome Way—even Abner—jabbered about all the time.

She'd never stepped inside. Too many people. Some she knew from way back when, but she considered all of them strangers. Strangers who stared at her . . .

These days she usually drove all the way to Livingston for her groceries and quilt supplies and whatnot so she wouldn't have to see a soul in Lonesome Way.

The pie did look wonderful, though. And the chicken smelled like heaven, if heaven smelled like lemon and garlic and oregano.

She hadn't eaten a bite since last night's supper, before she took that spill.

But the cat was there, a small shadow at her door.

"Here, I've got your food," she muttered, and she left the pie and the chicken on the table while she dug out the cat food bag. She rattled pellets into the bowl she kept on the corner of her old counter.

The cat shot to the base of the porch and stood stock-still, watching warily as she limped outside and set the food down near the top of the steps.

By the time she clumped back over the threshold, the orange tabby was up there, gobbling it down.

Winny saw there was still water left in the other bowl

she put out for the creature. She didn't know why she bothered.

Maybe, she realized as she sank down onto a kitchen chair and stared at that bright, fresh blueberry pie, it was because next to Abner Floyd, who never bothered her by speaking more than about a dozen words a year, that pesky cat was the closest thing she had to a friend.

A half hour later, she had polished off every bit of the chicken, washed and dried her plate, and sat at the kitchen table savoring a slice of pie with a hot cup of tea.

Then, feeling better for no reason she could explain, she hobbled into her bedroom, set down the blasted cane, and sank down at her sewing machine with the Jubilee quilt she'd begun the week before. She pulled the colorful squares of calico onto her lap and, for the first time since her fall, experienced a small sense of peace. Blocking out the past, the memories, and the rest of the world, she set to work.

Chapter Eight

One week later Mia combed through racks of jeans and shorts at Top to Toe on Main Street as Brittany scanned the shelves piled with folded tank tops and T's.

"Don't worry, Aunt Mia, I promise I'll pay you back from my next two paychecks," Britt murmured, examining a turquoise tee with a paisley heart stitched on the center. Her sunglasses were perched on top of her head. "This one's cute, isn't it?"

Setting down the khaki shorts she'd picked up, Mia glanced at her niece. "Wouldn't it be easier to drive home and just pack up some more of your clothes? I don't mind going with you. We could make a day of it. Have lunch on the deck of that nice restaurant we all went to for your birthday last year and—"

"I'm not going all the way back to Butte for some clothes." Brittany's voice rang through the store and she quickly lowered her tone as several other customers and Erma Wilkins, the owner, turned to stare. "I'm s-sorry." She bit her lip. "I didn't mean to sound rude. But we'd just be wasting gas to drive to Butte, wouldn't we? Besides, I only need a few more things to get through the summer."

Flushing a little, she hurried to the sales counter and deposited a pink V-necked top and a pair of white shorts, as well as the turquoise tee, a purple tank, and a couple of colorful wispy thongs and bras.

"I have my jeans and the top I wore yesterday. I'll do my laundry every few days. It's no big deal."

What teenaged girl doesn't want her entire wardrobe of clothes at her disposal? Mia wondered, trying to study Britt's face, but the sixteen-year-old whirled away from her and snagged another tank top, a skimpy white one.

"Brittany . . . ," Mia began in a low tone, "come on. There's some reason you don't want to—"

"Please, Aunt Mia." Brittany's suddenly pleading expression tore at Mia's heart. "I need to get back to the bakery really soon. There's only five minutes left on my lunch break. You don't want to make Aunt Sophie sorry she hired me, do you?"

Without waiting for a reply, she turned toward Erma, who was arranging some new tops in the window display. "We're ready now, can you help us, please?"

"Well, to be sure, I can." Erma bustled over, beaming, and began ringing up the clothes.

"A little birdie told me you're staying for the whole summer, young lady." Carefully folding all of the merchandise, the store owner began stuffing each item into a large bag. She'd opened Top to Toe the year before Samantha had entered middle school and she knew every soul in town as well as all of their tastes and sizes. "Isn't that nice for you, having such lovely young company?" She flashed Mia a smile as she worked.

"And not just any company." Mia handed over her credit card. "My favorite niece."

"The spitting image of her mother, too—and that's a

compliment, young lady," Erma told Brittany. "I heard your mom's going on her third honeymoon. All the way to Corfu, imagine that. Well, you know what they say. The third time's the charm."

"I thought they said that about the second time." Britt took the bag the older woman handed her.

"No, it's the third." Erma flashed a grin as she returned Mia's credit card. "But who's counting? Now, what about you, honey?" She shifted her hawkish gaze to Mia, who was just turning toward the door. "I heard Travis Tanner's back in town."

Of course you did. Erma wasn't the first person to mention Travis's return to her—she must be at least the seventh or eighth. Lonesome Way's gossip hotline would have no trouble holding its own against TMZ.

"He always was a *mighty* handsome young man. But then, you'd know that better than I would. If I were a younger woman . . ." She winked at Brittany, then turned back to Mia. "Now, I know it was a long time ago, and far be it from me to stick my nose where it doesn't belong, but everyone always said you two were the perfect coup—"

"I'm afraid we have to hurry, Erma, or Brittany's going to be late for work." With a wave and a smile, Mia made a beeline for the door and escaped onto Main Street before Erma could finish the sentence.

It was a warm, brilliant afternoon, and the sun glinted in a blinding dazzle off the long row of storefront windows. Behind her, Brittany slid her sunglasses down across the bridge of her nose.

A dozen or so people strolled along Main, enjoying the bright flowers planted in trim window boxes along the storefronts, the view of the park, the peaceful, picturesque atmosphere of the town set in the shadow of the mountains. A woman and two little boys about eight and five years old were sitting on the wooden bench outside of Benson's Drugstore, licking ice cream cones. A gray-haired ranch hand in a plaid shirt and faded jeans whistled as he loaded grain into the back of a pickup outside Tobe's Mercantile. Inside the Cuttin' Loose hair salon, Hannah Berg, owner of the day care center, was getting a manicure, while Martha Davies snipped away at her friend Dorothy Winston's squirrel gray hair.

"Travis Tanner, hm?" Britt grinned at her as they walked across the street. "He's your old boyfriend? Is he related to Aunt Sophie?"

"Yes, her husband's brother. And once upon a time, way back in the Stone Age, he was my boyfriend. That's the problem with small towns, Britt; people don't ever forget anything about your life—ever." Pausing, Mia held out a hand for the Top to Toe bag. "I'll take this home for you. You'd better hustle back to the bakery or you'll be late for the midafternoon rush."

"I know—it got crazy in there yesterday. Sophie's grandmother was the only one who stayed calm when that tour bus stopped in front on its way to the Half Moon Campground." She shook her head. "We sold out of cinnamon buns and chocolate chunk cookies in ten minutes flat." Britt thrust the shopping bag into Mia's hand and started to turn away, then impulsively turned back and threw her arms around her aunt's neck. "Thanks for the clothes, Aunt Mia," she whispered. She squeezed tightly for a moment, as if reluctant to let go. "I'll pay you back. Every single penny. For everything. I promise."

A little worried at the thick emotion in her niece's voice, Mia watched her race off toward A Bun in the Oven. Just as Britt was about to open the bakery's door, it opened from the inside and a lanky, red-haired boy of about seventeen or eighteen appeared, to let her in. He grinned and said something to her that made her laugh.

Mia recognized him. Seth Dalton—one of Sophie's most reliable teenaged employees. He'd rung up Mia's order last month when it was her turn to bring scones to the Bits and Pieces meeting.

As she studied him, Seth glanced over and saw her.

"Hey, Miz Quinn. Guess what! I got an A on my English lit final this semester," he called out.

"That's great, Seth. I always knew you had it in you."

"Well, my mom says it's all because of you. You made me read books in fifth grade and I got hooked."

"Tell your mom hello from me, will you?" she called.

"You bet!"

He turned back to Britt and Mia saw her niece reach up and brush his hair back from his eyes as they lingered, talking, in the doorway. Seth had been a challenging student in her English class. He'd clowned around most days, and she'd had to send him to the principal's office at least once a week for talking out of turn during class. But he'd always been unfailingly polite and irresistibly likable, despite waiting until the last minute to do all of his assignments. He'd turned them in just under the bell and managed to pull an A every single time.

Seth was smart, and he'd grown into quite a responsible young man.

At least it looks like Britt has made a friend, Mia thought with a tug of relief.

Her niece's mood had improved considerably over the past few days. Perhaps Seth was the reason. Sometimes when she didn't realize Mia was looking at her, Mia still caught that glimpse of worry in Britt's eyes, and that nervous hunch of her shoulders Mia had never seen before, but overall, most of the time Britt seemed happier, even cheerful.

She's a teenager—it's normal for her to be stressed now and then. Here she is with a new job, in a new town, trying to make new friends, while her mom is half a world away with a new husband.

But still . . .

Something had made Brittany want to spend the summer in Lonesome Way, miles from her home and her friends.

And so far, Mia was no closer to finding out what that something might be.

Turning toward her car she noticed another boy—a young man actually, since he looked to be about twenty—also watching Britt. He was tall and burly, handsome in a tough kind of way, with short sandy hair, and he was standing outside of Ponderosa Earl's Camping Outfitters at the far end of the block with a large bag of purchases, including, by the looks of it, a sleeping bag. But for a moment he stood stock-still, gazing toward the bakery—and Britt.

No surprise there, Mia thought, amused. Her niece was an extraordinarily pretty girl. It was only natural young men would take notice. She'd never seen this boy before and guessed he was a tourist passing through on his way to some campground or one of the national forests. As Seth grabbed Britt's hand and pulled her inside and the bakery door swung closed, the young man started to turn away, then met Mia's gaze, flashed her a friendly grin, and strode off in the opposite direction.

Mia forgot all about him as she heard a familiar voice call her name. Turning, she saw Lissie and Molly walking toward her from the park.

"Just the person I wanted to see." Lissie looked as fresh and pretty as a scoop of sorbet, in a lemon yellow tee tucked into crisp khakis. "Molly, look who's here—it's Aunt Mia! Tell her where we're going."

Mia was already stooping down, holding her arms out to the little girl, and Molly rushed into them. "Badery!"

"Bakery," Lissie corrected, but Mia laughed in delight and hugged the child.

"Are you going to eat a chocolate chip cookie?"

"*Two* cookie," Molly said eagerly.

"One for now and one for tomorrow," Lissie interjected firmly.

"Tomowwow." The little girl nodded solemnly, then planted her chubby hands on Mia's cheeks. "You cookie?"

"You eat one for me, okay?" Mia grinned, lightly tapped Molly's nose with the tip of her finger, and stood. "What's up?" she asked Lissie. "I heard Aiden's all better."

"He is. Sophie even got a solid night's sleep the past two nights. So she's ready to party. And after we pick up our cookies, Molly and I are headed to Benson's for streamers, poster board, and markers."

"You're making an art project?" Mia glanced down at the little girl, who was studying Mia's sandals and pink-polished toes intently. "Are you going to draw me a picture, angel?"

"Pixture for Daddy!"

"You forgot, didn't you?" Lissie stared at her accusingly, shaking her head. "Tommy's birthday party. Saturday night? At the Double Cross? Don't even tell me you forgot!"

Mia's eyes widened. She *had* forgotten. Completely. Lissie had told her about the party for her husband's birthday weeks ago. But somehow she'd neglected to mark it in her calendar and what with Brittany turning up and Aunt Winny's tumble down the steps and the Bits and Pieces meeting tonight—not to mention Travis showing up in town—it had totally slipped out of her brain.

"I confess. I'm a moron." She held up a hand appeasingly.

"Mo-won," Molly repeated, smiling up at her.

"That's someone very silly." Mia leaned down and smoothed the little girl's curls back from her face. "I forgot about your daddy's party."

"You're still coming, aren't you?" Lissie had that determined gleam in her eyes that seemed to be a Tanner characteristic. All of her brothers had it and Lissie had inherited the identical gene.

"Big Billy told me I'm free to decorate the Double Cross all I want—and Ivy's going to help us make Happy Birthday signs this afternoon." Lissie's eyes narrowed. "Don't even think about not coming because of Travis."

"I couldn't care less about seeing Travis," Mia retorted.

For all the good it did. Lissie's slender brows rose and her face was a study in skepticism.

"Will he even be there?" Mia blurted out a second later, despite being nearly certain of the answer. It was most likely the primary reason she'd blocked Tommy's party from her mind.

"He claims he wouldn't miss it." Lissie scooped Molly up into her arms. "You're not going to chicken out, are you?"

"Of course not. Unless you need a babysitter?"

"Nice try. Ivy's babysitting Molly."

Rafe's daughter by his first marriage had just turned thirteen. She was levelheaded, a good student, and responsible. So there went that excuse.

"Sophie's mom and Mr. Hartigan are babysitting Aiden and Grady," Lissie added with a smile. Sophie's mother had married their former high school geometry teacher last year. "So please don't even think about using that as an excuse."

"I'll be at the party, no fears."

Her friend's eyes suddenly softened with quick sympathy.

"There's going to be a fairly big crowd. You probably won't even run into him, much less have to talk to him."

"I told you—"

"Yeah, yeah, I know what you told me." Like Sophie, Lissie had been there all those years ago when Travis had dumped her. She'd been furious with her brother.

But it was all ancient history now. Why didn't anyone get that?

"The party's going to be a blast. I promise. Only . . ."

"What?" Mia saw the slight frown in her friend's eyes.

"There's just one more thing I need to warn you about." This time Lissie really did sound regretful. "Deanna Mueller cornered me at Tobe's yesterday—she heard me talking to Sophie on my cell about the party and . . . she sort of invited herself. And Zeke."

"You've got to be kidding me."

"Can you believe it? She just suddenly burst out with a promise to drop in and wish Tommy a happy birthday. There was nothing I could do."

"It's not a problem." Mia bit her lip. "Don't worry about it."

Great. Her love life really *did* sound like a disaster when her friends worried about her coming to a party and having to encounter both her ex-boyfriend *and* her ex-fiancé and his pregnant wife. But she hoped that had more to do with Deanna Mueller than with her.

In high school, Deanna had run against Mia two years in a row for the office of class secretary. Deanna had always gone after what she wanted, no holds barred, and if she didn't get it, she was known for complaining about how it wasn't fair and she'd been wrongly cheated out of what should have been rightfully hers—all of which was vociferously relayed to anyone and everyone who would listen.

She hadn't taken it well when she'd lost to Mia not once, but twice. So maybe when Mia broke up with Zeke last year and Deanna snagged him for herself, she could be excused for telling everyone in town who would listen that Zeke had dumped Mia for her.

Deanna had been a freshman in high school when Zeke was a senior, and he'd barely noticed her, but that hadn't stopped her from letting her crush on him become public knowledge. She'd stared at him in the halls, invited him to every school dance, and waited by her locker even after the bell rang for class, pretending to fidget with her lock just to be close to him when he walked by.

To his credit, he'd never laughed at her when his friends all did—but he'd always turned down Deanna's dance invitations and ignored her stares and phone calls. Rumor had it he thought she had good taste but he'd been turned off by her whole stalker act.

They'd never dated in high school or after.

But a year and a half ago, shortly after Sophie and Rafe's

wedding, Mia and Zeke had started seeing each other. They'd gone out to long, comfortable dinners, to drinks at the Lucky Punch Saloon, and to the movies over in Livingston. She'd invited him over for barbecued chicken and lasagna and Gram's famous chocolate frosted brownies, and he'd taken her to the rodeo and to a quilt show in Bozeman. Zeke was easy to be around, honest, and dependable, not to mention blond, nice-looking, and flatteringly eager for her company.

Getting engaged to Zeke after a little more than six months had seemed to Mia like a good idea at the time. Her biological clock was ticking on overdrive and her friends all had husbands and babies, and she could see herself having a future with him: children and family dinners and good times. Zeke was solid and kind. He had a big sweetheart of a dog. And just because he laughed at jokes she didn't find funny and her heart didn't race when he walked into a room, that didn't mean they couldn't be happy together, did it?

But two months after she accepted Zeke's ring, she handed it back. Something was missing. She knew with each passing day that the engagement was a mistake. It wasn't a case of cold feet.

Just cold truth.

Much as she wanted to, she didn't love Zeke. Not even a little.

Marrying him wouldn't be fair—to either one of them.

He hadn't taken it well. Not at first. But after a few weeks he'd come to terms with the fact that she wasn't going to change her mind. And less than a month later, noticing Deanna having a drink at the Double Cross, he'd asked to join her. They'd started dating, and from that moment on, Deanna never missed an opportunity to crow to everyone in town that she'd snagged the man of her dreams, the man Mia Quinn couldn't hold on to.

Mia had ignored her, unwilling to dignify any of it with a response—or to give the town gossips more to talk about. But Sophie had lost it once and told Deanna off in the middle of the town library, and ever since then, the air had been frigid as the snow on the Crazy Mountains whenever Deanna Mueller and Mia Quinn found themselves in the same room.

"Saturday should definitely be an interesting night," Mia muttered.

"You think?" Lissie's laughter rang out on the sunlit street.

"Cooookieee, Mommmeee." Molly jabbed a soft finger into her mother's cheek. "Pwease!" Setting her down, Lissie grasped her daughter's hand and started toward A Bun in the Oven.

"See you Saturday," she called over her shoulder.

"Counting the minutes," Mia called back. She could hear Lissie's muted laughter behind her as she headed toward her Jeep.

Chapter Nine

Travis set his paintbrush in the metal tray as the front door opened and Grady trudged into the cabin.

"Hey, buddy. Ready to call it a day?"

It was pretty much a rhetorical question. The boy's Diamondbacks T-shirt and jeans were coated with grime. He'd spent the last couple of hours scrubbing years' worth of dead insects and mud from the outside cabin windows and his face was flushed with sweat and streaked with dirt. Despite this, he looked almost happy.

"More than ready," he answered emphatically, wiping his filthy hands on his jeans. "Can I have a Coke, Dad?"

"You bet. You did a great job out there. The good news is," Travis added, with one last glance at the sage green paint he'd just finished carefully applying to the tall living room walls, "another few days, a week at most, and we might actually be able to move into this place."

"Why can't we just hire someone to do the rest of it?" Grady swiped an arm across his sweaty face as Travis stepped over the drop cloth covering the floor. "You work for the FBI. They must pay you pretty good. Don't you have money?"

"Not a matter of money. Sometimes elbow grease is good for the soul."

Grady shot him a skeptical glance. "In L.A., my mom and Drew hire people to do *everything*. Plant the gardens, clean the pool, cook all the food when they have parties . . ."

"Well, this isn't L.A."

"That's for sure," the boy piped up, but a slow grin seeped across his face. He stared down at his filthy hands with a kind of pride. "It was sort of fun to get all dirty and stuff. If Mom were here, she'd be yelling at me right now to get into the shower."

"Yeah, well, she'd be right." Travis laughed. "Now that the water's turned back on and the bathrooms have been scrubbed down, we can start bringing over some clean clothes and towels so we can shower and change here before going back to the ranch. That'll make it easier not to mess up Aunt Sophie's nice clean house."

"That'll work." Grady bobbed his head in agreement and trooped after Travis toward the kitchen, where soap and rolls of paper towels waited on the granite counter.

"I'm kind of hungry. All that work, I guess," he added, trotting past wide windows looking out onto rolling grassland backed by a forest of ponderosa pines and a spectacular view of the mountains.

"Do you know what Aunt Sophie's cooking for dinner?"

"Heard something this morning about steaks on the grill." Travis began scrubbing paint off his hands. "Thought I'd rustle up some double-baked potatoes and corn on the cob, too."

"Awesome!"

For a second there, if Travis wasn't mistaken, his son almost looked—and sounded—like a perfectly happy kid. He was seeing glimmers of smiles these days. Even a laugh now and then.

But too much of the time, Grady still clung to the reserved and slightly sullen attitude he'd exhibited on their drive from Arizona.

The first day they'd driven over to work on the cabin, Grady had seemed surprised upon seeing the place. Apparently he'd been expecting a shack, not a roomy two-story house tucked away in a wide clearing that was as pretty as any Travis had ever seen.

His cabin was surrounded by miles of open land and graceful cottonwoods, and it was close enough to Sage Creek that in the hush of night, if you listened real hard, you could hear frogs and crickets chirping away, owls hooting, and the whisper of rushing water.

There were three big bedrooms, three and a half baths, a dining room that could easily seat ten, and a good-sized kitchen, but Travis had it in his head to add on—maybe another bedroom, a game room with a pool table, an office for when he got his company up and running—possibly a Jacuzzi in back on a wraparound deck facing the woods.

He hadn't opened up the place in a couple of years so it had been sorely in need of sweeping, scrubbing, sanding, and paint, but after a good part of all that was done, he'd discovered that the hickory floors were still in great shape and that the drop cloths on the furniture had protected the fawn-colored leather sofas and the chocolate armchairs. The floor-to-ceiling walnut bookshelves in the library had been smothered in dust but now they, too, gleamed like the floors.

Not a bad week's work, he thought as he and Grady finished cleaning up and he handed the boy a can of Coke and a snack bag of pretzels. They let themselves out the kitchen door and trekked toward the winding, tree-lined driveway.

In four or five days they could most likely move in, start settling down, Travis thought. That would give them even more one-on-one time together.

Who knows? Travis told himself as he and Grady piled

into the Explorer. *This place might even start to feel like a real home. . . .*

An image popped into his brain as he backed out of the drive. For a split second he saw himself sitting on the deck with Mia—the deck that wasn't even built yet. It was almost dusk, and he saw Grady catching fireflies near the woods and the sun going down over the mountains in a splash of fiery color. Mia's head was resting on Travis's shoulder, and she was cuddled close against his side. . . .

Where the hell did that come from?

He blinked, and almost swore aloud.

He hadn't seen Mia since the day she'd come to borrow a pie.

And not because he didn't want to. He just didn't think it was a good idea. For either one of them.

There was plenty on his plate right now—including getting the cabin whipped into shape so he and Grady wouldn't need to impose on Sophie and Rafe the entire summer. And getting his new business up and running.

He had about a hundred phone calls to make, starting with a dozen or so to his former co-workers—retired FBI field agents, all of them top-notch—and expanding to a list of buddies who'd retired from the military and might be interested in a private security gig. He also needed to read through and sign the rental agreement for the office he'd found on Oak Street in a building three blocks off Main, and he had to start reaching out to potential clients. . . .

Coward, a voice inside his head mocked.

You've taken on serial killers and white supremacists. Terrorists and kidnappers. Not to mention the scum who deal in human trafficking and arms smuggling.

And you're scared of a woman.

Not exactly scared. And not just of any woman.

One particular woman. A stunning, sexy-as-hell blond schoolteacher who no doubt hated his guts. And he couldn't much blame her.

He remembered how she'd looked at the ranch in that skimpy tank top and jeans—lush, tanned, and gorgeous, her hair piled on her head, her shoulders and throat and arms gleaming golden. And those incredible amber eyes a man could get lost in, so cool and steady on his.

She'd looked as delectable as an ice cream sundae on the hottest day of the year.

He'd been trying to erase that image from his mind ever since, but it wouldn't go away.

Not good, Tanner, not good.

Suddenly he noticed Grady staring at him.

"Hello-o-o—Earth to Dad."

"Yeah. Dad to Kid. I'm here." With a grin, he reached over to the passenger seat and ruffled the boy's hair, pleased when Grady smiled.

Concentrate on your kid, Travis reminded himself, realizing he was damned lucky he wasn't on a case right now, where losing concentration—thinking about Mia as if the two of them could ever actually be together again—could get him fired, or killed. Of course, he'd already fired himself, he reflected as he watched a hawk soar high above the pines.

"We should just about have time before supper for a quick horseback ride."

"Can we go back to the creek?"

"Again? Don't you want to head into the foothills for a change?"

"Nope. I like Sage Creek. So does Pepper Jack."

"Then the creek it is."

Grady had proven to be a natural rider, and a hard worker once he got started. He didn't complain or try to slack off, and he'd done a damned good job washing the windows, sweeping the floors, and helping Travis clear away all the old leaves and brush that had piled up around the porch, the perimeter of the house, and the grounds.

"So why don't you tell me some of what happened at

school last year?" he asked conversationally as Grady swallowed the last of the pretzels.

"What do you mean?"

Just like that, the tension was back in the boy's tone. Resentment stiffened his shoulders.

Travis kept his voice even. "Your mom told me she's worried about you. She's pretty upset about those grades you got in earth science and English. According to your teachers, you weren't even trying."

Silence filled the space between them. The boy twisted toward the passenger-side window suddenly, his face hidden from Travis. He appeared to be studying the sky, where a western meadowlark swooped against an expanse of hard-edged blue.

"I know you're smart, Grady," Travis continued matter-of-factly. "Your mom's smart and your dad was, too. He was a doctor. That takes a lot of smarts, so I know you have it in you."

Suddenly he had Grady's full attention. "You . . . *knew* my dad . . . my *real* dad?"

The boy sounded amazed. And eager. Glancing at him, Travis saw a kind of hunger in his eyes. Damn, hadn't Val ever told him anything about his biological father?

"I never met him, but your mom talked about him when we first got to know each other. He was in line to be chief of staff at the hospital where he worked when he came down with the cancer. If he hadn't gotten sick, he'd have been one of the youngest chiefs of staff in the country. Your mom must have told you that."

Grady shook his head. "She told me he was a doctor and helped people. That was it. Mom doesn't like talking about him. So I stopped asking."

What the hell? Val, what's up with that? Travis chose his words carefully. "Sometimes when people are sad about something they try to avoid talking about it."

He hoped to God he was handling this right.

"But it's usually easier to just talk about it, get it out. You can always ask me about your father, anything you want, and I'll tell you what I know. But you should try asking your mom again, too. Now that some time has passed, she might be ready to talk about him and answer your questions—"

"Mom doesn't want to talk about anything. Not in front of *him*."

"Him? You mean Drew?"

"Who else?" Grady was staring straight ahead now down the road.

"Things aren't so good between you and Drew, huh?"

Grady looked down. "We rub each other the wrong way—that's what Mom says. But I . . . Dad, can I tell you something?" he burst out.

"You can tell me anything, buddy."

"I can't stand that guy!"

"Yeah? What's wrong with him?"

"He's a jerk. He bosses me around and yells at me all the time, even when I don't do anything wrong. He yells at Mom, too. Sometimes she tries to stick up for me, but he doesn't ever listen. He just gets mad at her, too." Grady shook his head, seemed about to say more, then suddenly changed the subject. "I still don't understand why you think I'm smart. Kids don't always get their parents' brains, you know. Sometimes they just get their athletic ability or their singing voice or their ears that stick out, and that's it."

A half smile broke across Travis's face, despite the tension that had started searing through him the moment Grady began confiding about his stepfather. "Don't forget I've been spending a lot of time with you since we came to Lonesome Way. And I've noticed things—like what you just said to me about what kids inherit from their parents. That was a pretty smart observation. And then there's how quickly you catch on to things."

"I do? What kind of things?" He felt Grady staring at him with an eagerness that ripped at his heart.

"I only had to show you once how to saddle Pepper Jack, remember? And how to cinch the bridle, adjust the stirrups, all that stuff. You picked it up quickly, and you remembered how to do it every time. Same for how to pitch hay.

"And," Travis added, "the other night when you played Scrabble with Ivy, you came close to beating her. Ivy's smart as they come and she's almost three years older than you. You have a good brain, Grady."

"Yeah, well, try telling that to my teachers. I suck at school."

"Why is that?"

"I'm no good at memorizing stuff out of books. It's boring to just sit around and study. And what difference would it make?" His face darkened. "Drew says I'm dumb."

"Drew's wrong." Travis fought to control the surge of anger banding across his chest. What the hell right did Drew Baylor have to tell his boy he was dumb?

"What else does Drew say?"

"Nothing."

"It's okay, Grady, you can tell me. I've met guys like him before; nothing you can say will surprise me. What does he say?"

"He says I'm lazy." Grady's voice was a low mumble. "And a loser. He said he can tell I'm headed for trouble."

"That's a load of crap."

As the boy glanced quickly at him, Travis saw uncertainty in Grady's eyes.

Damn that asshole. He'd never met Baylor, but what he knew was bad news. Any man who went off on a kid, basically told him he was worthless and would never amount to a hill of beans, was a son of a bitch. Why in hell did Val put up with it?

They were almost at the ranch. Pines whipped by as he chose his words carefully. "The only place I see you headed, Grady, is where *you want to go*. Wherever that might be. You're in control of your life. You have it in you to achieve whatever you set your mind to. And don't let Drew or any-body else tell you different."

"But . . . in a way, he's right, isn't he?" Grady sounded miserable. "I messed up last year in school and I . . . I got into fights and stuff. And now it's too late. Everyone thinks I'm stupid and a troublemaker. I can't fix it. No one can. That day Mom put me on the plane, I overheard her on her cell. She told her friend Annie that I'm going to flunk fifth grade."

He hunched back toward the window, and Travis couldn't see his expression any longer but the hopelessness in the boy's tone hit him in the gut.

"So I'll have to repeat the whole stupid year, while all my friends . . ." His voice quavered and he gulped. "I really only had one friend. One real friend. His name's Scott. And he's gonna be a year ahead now. Everyone will be, for the rest of my life. They're all going to think I'm stupid. A loser."

Travis tried to remember what it had felt like to be ten. To feel that kind of peer pressure, where what everyone else thought and said and did was the end all and be all. It was hard to fathom—he didn't remember worrying about what everyone thought when he was young.

Maybe because he'd always had his brothers and Lissie and his parents to back him up.

Sure, he and Rafe and Jake had fought plenty among themselves, but no one had better put down any of the Tan-ner boys or their sister, or they'd all band together as solid as a wall of iron spikes.

The boy on the seat beside him had no one to back him up, apparently, except maybe this kid Scott and, for what it was worth, his mother.

Until now.

"Hey. I'm only interested in what *you* think." He glanced over at Grady. "Do *you* think you're stupid? Or could you have done better if you'd tried harder?"

"I guess so."

"Would you work your butt off, if you had another chance?"

"Sure, but—"

"All right then. There's hope."

"What do you mean? What kind of hope?"

"Might be something you can do about having to repeat fifth grade."

"Like what?" Grady looked so doubtful that Travis had to fight to keep from shaking his head. The boy was too young to have such a dim view of the world. A kid should feel like anything is possible. Not like his future is written in stone, that if you make a mistake or two, there's no chance in hell it's going to turn out okay in the end.

"Let me check into a few things, and I'll get back to you soon. I promise. In the meantime, how about we take that ride?"

His son's face lit up again for the first time since Travis had raised the subject of school. "We can still ride to the creek?"

"Sure. I'll meet you at the barn in a few minutes and we'll saddle up. I need to make a quick phone call first."

After parking the Explorer in the driveway, and watching Grady race toward the ranch house with Starbucks and Tidbit bounding out from the pasture to meet him, Travis yanked out his cell. He punched in Lissie's number. She picked up on the second ring.

"Trav, can I call you back later? I'm in the middle of fixing supper—," she began, sounding busy and distracted, but he interrupted her.

"This will only take a minute. I need a tutor for Grady. Give me a name. The best teacher in Lonesome Way."

Chapter Ten

That night the brightly lit basement of the Lonesome Way Community Center was packed with women. Women of all shapes, sizes, hair colors, and coffee preferences. They ranged in age from twenty-three to eighty-six.

Aside from all of them living in Lonesome Way, one other thing united them. They were quilters. Some were beginners, some had been piecing and stitching and appliquéing for more than half a century—but all of them were drawn together by the lure of creativity and the desire to make something of lasting usefulness and beauty.

Every one of the Bits and Piecers leaned forward in their chairs to watch intently as Evelyn Lewis, the recording secretary, shared a video from the quilt show she'd attended in Cody, Wyoming, the previous month.

"That quilt is similar to the one I'm making for the exhibition," Karla McDonald, the newly elected treasurer, murmured to Mia as a quilt of redwork sweetheart blocks with flowered borders flashed onto the screen and the audience murmured appreciatively. "But I'm going to try some ribbon borders on mine."

"That sounds beautiful," Mia whispered back.

A striking batik quilt came up next on the video, which occasionally jumped from one colorful quilt to the next a little too wildly for her stomach.

As a lovely old-fashioned patchwork quilt in orange and green filled the screen, she realized she hadn't given much more than a passing thought to her own Starry Night quilt in days, not since she'd finished her design and figured out her yardages. She'd decided to use a whole-cloth background and do appliqué for the stars. But she'd need to get sewing—and soon. Leaning back in her chair, she made a mental note to head out to the quilt shop in Livingston tomorrow and stock up on supplies.

The exhibition weekend in July would be here before she realized it and she needed to set aside the next week to make a start. This would be the fourth year she'd be sewing an exhibition quilt without Gram working beside her, sharing her ideas and advice.

She knew she ought to be used to it by now, but in some ways she wasn't sure she'd ever get used to it.

Shortly before the meeting ended, Karla rose to her feet, holding the delicate silver box that usually contained spare change, cash, and checks from member dues, and which, after the quilt exhibition, would hold a single slip of paper containing the total amount of money raised from ticket sales and the quilt raffles. At the end of the day Karla would tally up the donations and write the total on a note inside the box—a box Gram had once used to hold hair clips and ribbons, and which she'd donated to Bits and Pieces in place of the old cardboard cigar box that had been used for the past thirty years. Then Becky Hall, Mia's cochair in charge of the quilt exhibition, would step to the podium and thank everyone for coming and for their contributions, and Mia would stand beside her to open the box and read the total aloud.

"Don't forget, everyone," Karla said, holding the silver box aloft, "we want to raise more money this year than any other." She looked around the room. "There are so many women and children in need. Let us all make beautiful quilts and make a beautiful difference."

There was a quick smatter of applause and a ripple of excitement and determination surged through the room.

Then the meeting ended and the women all came to their feet, chattering and eager as they headed toward the stairs. Mia spotted Martha Davies carrying her cardboard coffee cup in one hand while clutching the fat quarters she'd won in the drawing tonight in the other.

Remembering what Martha had told Sophie about Aunt Winny, she began weaving her way toward the owner of the Cuttin' Loose, but found herself waylaid by her cochair. Becky wanted to fill her in about Tobe's Mercantile, which had all but agreed to purchase a square on the community quilt they'd be raffling off. Becky was to confirm with them in a day or so. She then asked Mia if she planned to exhibit any of her grandmother's quilts at the fund-raiser. By the time Mia promised to select one, Martha was already halfway up the stairs.

Mia darted after her, skirting others with a hurried smile. She finally managed to catch up with her in the community center parking lot.

The salon owner, whose short bob of hair was dyed a rich shade of bordeaux this month, was trying to remember where she'd parked her car.

"Martha, I see it. It's right over there. Look, next to Hannah's Taurus."

"Well, don't you have eagle eyes, dear? It pays to be young, that's for sure." Martha beamed at her. Beneath the nearly full moon, she appeared closer to seventy than eighty. Her dangling gold earrings with citrine stones glistened in the moonlight as other quilters began to stream into the parking lot, calling soft good-byes to each other.

Martha headed briskly toward her car once more and turned her head in surprise as Mia fell into step beside her.

"Do you have a minute, Martha? I wanted to ask you about my aunt Winny. I heard you knew her years ago."

The older woman stopped short and glanced at her, making a tsking sound. She immediately resumed walking. "Well, of course I did. We went to school together. She was a year behind me."

As she reached her car, she peered sideways at Mia. "It was a long time ago," she added with finality and opened her car door.

"Was Winny a friend of yours back then?"

"Well, no. I wouldn't call her a friend. Aside from your dear grandmother, her own sister, Winny didn't have many friends. Not girlfriends, anyway. She had plenty of boyfriends," she added, her lips puckering.

"Why only boyfriends?"

"Mia, dear, what's the point in talking about this? What's done is done. In my experience, there are times when it's best to leave the past alone."

"But someone in this town must know what happened between Winny and Gram." Mia searched Martha's eyes. "Do you?" she asked softly.

The other members of Bits and Pieces were nearly all gone now, the parking lot practically deserted. Only the distant sound of country music floating from the Double Cross Bar and Grill broke the quiet of the night as Martha peered into Mia's eyes and hesitated, biting her crimson-painted lips.

"You *do* know, don't you?" Mia said slowly.

"The point is, if your grandmother wanted *you* to know, I think she would have told you, dear."

"Gram might have had her reasons for keeping it to herself—but that doesn't mean I don't have the right to know. Gram's gone, Martha. She's been gone for three years. But Aunt Winny is *here*. She's family, and she's alone. She doesn't want me coming anywhere near her and I don't have any idea why."

As the older woman drew in her breath, looking trapped, Mia pressed on.

"Samantha and I are the only relatives Winny has left. We have a right to some answers about our own family. To know what happened."

For a moment the other woman looked like she was planning to refuse again. To simply climb in her car and go home. But then she searched Mia's face once more, and slowly, she nodded.

"I don't know everything that happened." Her voice was low, resigned. "Alicia wouldn't speak much about it and neither would her parents. I only know one thing. There was a horrible falling-out and Winny destroyed something before she ran away. Something precious that belonged to your grandmother. It was only a few weeks before Alicia married your grandfather. And there was no turning back after that."

"What?" Mia felt her breath catch in her throat. "What did she destroy?"

With a sigh, the older woman whispered the words that struck Mia like tiny swords.

"She burned up your grandmother's good luck wedding quilt."

Chapter Eleven

Brittany was curled up with Samson on the small sofa in the den, eating the last crumbs of a macadamia nut cookie from A Bun in the Oven and watching a rerun of *The Gilmore Girls*, when she heard a car's engine in the driveway. Her heart skipped a beat at the same moment that Samson leaped off the sofa and raced in a blur toward the front door. He was barking like ten big dogs instead of just one tiny one, as if he knew whoever was out there was trouble.

Panic chilled her blood. She jumped off the sofa so fast she almost knocked her Coke can off the coffee table. But she didn't follow the dog. Not yet. Her heart was lodged in her throat. As much as she wanted to know who was there, outside, she could only stand frozen, fear knotting in her chest, making it hard to breathe.

It isn't him. He doesn't know you're here. No one from home knows, except Laura. And she'd never tell. . . .

She'd emailed Laura just that morning from Aunt Mia's

laptop and asked her if she'd told him anything. Laura had written back two words.

No way.

Britt swallowed and fought the fear. *It's probably just Aunt Mia. It must be. Her meeting must be over by now.*

But Samson never barked when Aunt Mia arrived home. He somehow knew the sound of her Jeep or sensed it was her. He was definitely barking now, frantic, high-pitched barking that blared in her ears like alarm bells.

Slowly Brittany forced herself to tiptoe down the hall, into the living room. She edged to the window and ever so slowly inched the curtain back to peek out.

The car parked behind her convertible was definitely not Aunt Mia's Jeep. It was bigger, an SUV, a dark bulky blur in the night.

It isn't him. He doesn't drive an SUV, she thought with a burst of relief. But her heart was still racing. The memory of Wade's expression the last time she'd seen him swamped her with fear.

Wade was as smart as he was short-tempered. He could have borrowed a car. He could have *stolen* a car. She wouldn't put anything past him.

She ducked back, then stood perfectly still as she tried to tune out Samson's barking and prayed the doorbell wouldn't ring. No way was she opening that door. Not to anyone she didn't know. Not unless she was sure it wasn't Wade, or someone he might have sent to scare her.

What if whoever's out there saw me peeking through the curtain? Panic rushed back. Samson was barking so loudly—maybe he'd scare whoever it was.

Fat chance, a voice inside her yelled. Samson was a pip-squeak. An adorable pipsqueak, but still a pip—

Someone knocked on the door.

Don't open it. Don't open that door.

"Everything okay in there?" A man's voice. But it was older, deeper than Wade's. A strong voice, even and calm.

Don't answer, she told herself even as a measure of relief flooded over her.

Still, she stood motionless as Samson finally turned and stared at her expectantly, then gave another bark as if to make sure she knew someone was out there.

"You must be Mia's niece, Brittany. My sister-in-law, Sophie Tanner, mentioned you were here for the summer."

So he *had* spotted her when she peeked out. But he knew her name, and he knew Sophie. If Sophie was his sister-in-law . . .

It suddenly dawned on her that this must be the guy Erma was talking about. Aunt Mia's old boyfriend.

She was panicking over nothing. This was Lonesome Way, where everyone knew each other, not some big city full of strangers.

She was letting Wade turn her into a paranoid coward.

"Who are you?" she called, just to be sure. Her voice almost sounded normal. "What's your name?"

"Travis Tanner. I'm a friend of your aunt's."

She let out a sigh of relief. Travis Tanner. All right then. She wanted a look at the guy. Erma had talked like Aunt Mia was still in love with him. But Aunt Mia seemed like she couldn't care less.

Cautiously, Brittany opened the door on the chain, which only slid back two inches.

"Are you okay?" Travis Tanner asked as Samson barked again like a maniac and ran in circles around her.

Brittany gaped at the man on the other side of the screen door. He was tall and handsome, wearing a flannel shirt with the sleeves rolled up, jeans, and boots—ordinary clothes. But there was nothing ordinary about him. He was definitely the hottest guy she'd ever seen. She couldn't speak for a moment as she stared into his strong, tanned face. He had muscles like a football player and silver-blue eyes. Of course, he was way too old for her, probably in his thirties, but he had what Laura would call the whole package.

Aunt Mia didn't want to get back together with *him*?

"Sorry, I—I was just watching a scary movie. It freaked me out and then the doorbell rang." Her fingers a bit unsteady, she unhooked the chain, eased open the door. "Aunt Mia went to her quilting meeting, and she isn't home yet but she should be back any minute. You can come inside and wait for her, if you want."

"Thanks. I really need to speak to her tonight."

Travis studied the girl who stepped aside so he could enter the house. She definitely looked shaken. Her skin was pale, and he saw uneasiness still hovering in the depths of her eyes.

Must have been some scary movie, he thought.

"Good move, being careful about opening the door to a stranger. Even here in Lonesome Way. Though you do have this fierce watchdog here to protect you."

She managed to laugh as he stepped into the hallway. He knelt down to scratch Samson behind the ears. The dog jumped up, placing his paws on Travis's knee, his tail wagging furiously.

"Tough guy, huh? You protecting this place?"

"His name's Samson. Aunt Mia found him in the road. Someone threw him away. Can you believe that?"

"Ah, unfortunately I can. She should have named him Lucky." Travis stood and closed the door behind him. It had been a long time since he'd been in this house, and Mia had obviously made some changes over the years, but it still felt incredibly familiar. The cherrywood chest in the corner, the cozy L-shaped living room with its matching plump chintz sofas, and the tall windows looking onto the street all brought back memories of another time. A time when he and Mia meant everything to each other. A time of first love and boundless hope and a feeling of complete happiness.

Up until the day he'd come here, stood on her porch, and told her in the coldest way possible that they were done.

"You sure you're okay?" he asked the teenager, reminding himself he was here for Grady's sake, not for a stroll down memory lane.

Mia's niece still looked nervous. In his line of work, Travis had seen a lot of people who were afraid—and not of something that was happening in a movie. This girl looked nearly as on edge as half the crime victims he'd seen.

"I'm fine. I . . . I guess I have an overactive imagination. Can I get you something to drink? We have some cookies—"

"Thanks, but you don't need to entertain me. I'll just wait here. If you want to go back to your movie, that's fine with me—"

The words were barely out of his mouth when they both heard another car in the driveway. The teenager spun toward the door, her eyes wide.

"That's most likely your aunt, isn't it?"

Brittany visibly relaxed, but before Travis could ask her exactly what scary movie she'd been watching, Mia came through the door fast and the little dog flung himself at her as though she'd been gone for a year.

"What are *you* doing here?" she demanded, staring at Travis.

The dog jumped on her, his tiny paws flailing at her white capris, begging her to notice him, but she just stroked his head, keeping her gaze firmly trained on Travis's face.

"Sorry to come by without calling first," he said evenly, "but I need to discuss something with you. It's important. I came to ask for your help."

"I can't imagine how I could possibly help you with anything."

"Only because you haven't heard what I have to say yet."

Mia started to snap a reply, but she clamped her lips shut as she noticed Brittany watching her and Travis—a wide grin spreading across her face as her fascinated gaze flitted back and forth between both of them.

Oh, no, not you, too.

She frowned at her niece.

"Um, going now," Britt said lightly. "I really need to get some sleep. Have to be at work early tomorrow." Her slender figure edged slowly toward the hall. "It was nice meeting you, Mr. Tanner."

"Call me Travis," he said, his gaze still glued to Mia's face.

"G'night, Aunt Mia."

"Don't forget to set your alarm, Britt."

Mia heard the fading sound of Britt's flip-flops on the wood floor as she padded toward the guest room, heard the click of her door closing. Samson had given up trying to get Mia to notice him and was lying down on the rug, looking dejected, his chin on his paws.

She felt the tension in her shoulders and tried to relax. Okay, so she'd acted like a shrew, but it had thrown her, seeing Travis standing in her living room like that.

She'd been thinking about Aunt Winny destroying Gram's wedding quilt all during the drive back from town. She'd heard a great deal about that quilt—and had even seen an old photo of it once. It was hand pieced and hand quilted, with a double wedding ring pattern and exquisite scalloped edges. According to family lore, the quilt had been passed down through the women in her family for at least four generations and was originally believed to bring all the brides it was gifted to good luck. But that luck had certainly run out after it was burned to ashes only weeks before Gram's wedding.

She'd been trying to figure out why no one had ever told her Winny was responsible for that. And even as she'd turned onto Larkspur Road, she'd been struggling still to wrap her head around the idea that Gram's own sister could have done something so terrible.

The last thing she'd expected when she reached home was to find Travis's car taking up half her driveway, and Travis in her living room talking to Britt. Even more disconcerting was that he looked just as good with his clothes on as with half of them off.

How was she supposed to act cool and indifferent when he stood there all gorgeous, relaxed, and at ease while her heart was skittering all over the place? She didn't want to look at hard, rugged features that were embedded in her heart, or at his tall, buff frame. And she certainly didn't want to gaze into blue eyes that still held the power to unsettle her.

"Fine, since you're here, you may as well sit down," she said with what she hoped was an indifferent shrug. She knew she sounded rude. But seeing Travis here in her house, after all these years, was throwing her off her game.

"After you."

"Always the gentleman," Mia muttered under her breath, but he heard her. One dark eyebrow shot up.

Travis had always had impeccable manners. He'd even come to her door and broken up with her politely all those years ago the night after his prom. Short and sweet.

I can't do this anymore. Good-bye and good luck. Slam, bam, thank you, ma'am.

Her jaw set, she sank down on the sofa. Immediately, Samson leaped up, landed in her lap, and began licking her cheek. Gently, she stroked the soft fur under his chin as Travis took the armchair, stretching his long legs out in front of him.

He looked big and powerful in this small, cozy house. If she was a bad guy, she definitely wouldn't want to tangle with him in a dark alley. But she suddenly noticed the tension in his neck and the worried look in his eyes. Concern immediately edged out the shock she'd felt at seeing him in her home.

"What's this all about?" she asked quickly.

"A favor. It's not for me," he added grimly. "It's for Grady."

"What sort of favor?"

Travis kept his gaze trained on her face, wondering why she always had to look so damned adorable. Her hair was swept up into a ponytail. Her mint green scoop-necked tee hugged her breasts. With her shapely legs encased in white capris and her toenails glistening shell pink in those delicate white sandals, Mia looked good enough to devour in one slow, delicious bite.

Or, he thought, in a thousand tiny nibbles. He tried to concentrate solely on her heart-shaped face, but it was equally distracting. Even without a touch of makeup except for a trace of lip gloss, her skin glowed creamy and he had to be careful not to let himself get drawn in by those darklashed amber eyes watching him so seriously.

"I need you to tutor Grady in English and earth science."

She looked startled. And the instant she opened her mouth to reply, Travis knew she was going to refuse.

"This is a kid who used to love to read," he continued before she could get the words out. "And now he's flunking fifth grade. His school in California wants to hold him back and force him to repeat the entire year. The only way to prevent that is for him to pass a proficiency test. A tough one."

He hurried on, keeping his tone firm, professional, as it was when he laid a case out before an FBI supervisor or a federal prosecutor.

"I've already been in touch with his school district in Los Angeles and they've agreed to email me the curriculum requirements and textbook information. Lissie tells me you're the best teacher in Lonesome Way. Hands down. So here I am." His gaze held hers. "I'm desperate, Mia. And I'm throwing myself on your mercy."

"Travis, I'm sorry about Grady." She bit her lip. "You seem to have been very busy trying to help him."

"Not busy enough." Travis's eyes were grim. "Some of this is my fault. And I need to fix it."

Regret as well as worry flickered in his face. She searched his eyes, thinking how once, long ago, she'd been able to look at Travis and understand everything he was thinking and feeling. But not anymore.

"I know you're worried about him, but I'm afraid I can't help. I'm not a tutor. The good news is, I know several people who are."

Rising, she started toward the kitchen where she kept a notepad and pen. "I'll give you some numbers. You should start with Mary Carnes. She's a wonderful tutor. She—"

"I don't want Mary Carnes." Travis sprang out of the chair and reached her in two swift strides. His fingers closed around her arm, gently but firmly turning her back toward him.

"I want *you*."

For one awful moment, the double meaning of those words seemed to hang in the air between them. Mia felt her cheeks burning.

"You know what I mean," Travis said quickly.

"I know exactly what you mean. But I'm not available." *For tutoring or anything else.*

"You could be, if you wanted to, couldn't you? Look, Mia, I know you don't owe me a damned thing. I'm sorry for what happened between us all those years ago. I was a jerk. Young and stupid. And I treated you like crap. You deserved a whole lot better. But we were kids then, and this is now, and you're a teacher. A boy needs your help. Can't you forget that he's my son?"

For a moment his quiet, insistent tone and the desperate look in his eyes sent a twinge of impossible-to-ignore compassion stabbing through her heart.

He was still holding her arm and the warmth of his fingers was distracting. Unnerving. Just like his nearness.

She'd nearly forgotten what this was like—standing so close to Travis. The intense chemical attraction that had been set off the first moment they spoke in the halls of Lonesome Way High School was still there. It licked through her, hot as a stray spark from a campfire. He was standing so close to her she could see the sexy five o'clock stubble trailing along his jaw, the glint in his seen-it-all eyes. She was intensely aware of the sheer force of will of this man who had kissed her years ago with a hunger and tenderness she'd never been able to forget.

But Travis was no longer that high school boy she'd loved. He was a man, a formidable one. An FBI agent, accustomed to forging his way through a world that was bigger, harsher, and more dangerous than anything she'd ever encountered. He knew what he wanted and he went after it with single-minded purpose.

But he was doomed to disappointment in this case, Mia told herself. Just as he'd changed, she had, too. She wasn't the impressionable girl she'd been back then, naïve and in love. She was every bit as strong willed as he was now. And he'd just have to deal with that.

If he thought an apology and the touch of his hand on her arm would turn her into a mass of Silly Putty, he was wrong.

"This has nothing to do with you and me. Mary Carnes is an excellent tutor. I'm a *teacher*," she explained firmly.

"True. But you offered to tutor Ivy when she started sixth grade, didn't you?"

So. Lissie had told him that. *Thanks, Liss*. She sighed. "That was different."

"Different how?"

"I've known Ivy since she was born. She seemed uneasy about starting middle school, and I was only trying to make her feel more comfortable, more confident—" She cut herself off. "I don't owe you any explanations, Travis. There are plenty of competent tutors in this town. Any one of them can help your son—"

"Competent doesn't cut it. I'm not taking chances with Grady's future. If you're the best—and according to my sister, you are—then it has to be you."

He released her arm and paced toward the window, scraping a hand through his hair.

"Look"—he wheeled back toward her—"Lissie told me

you really care about kids, that you go to bat for them, stay after school to help, that they trust you. I can't believe you'd turn away a boy who desperately needs a helping hand. And believe me, he does need it, Mia. Grady's in trouble, in more ways than one. He needs a win here. He needs to know he can work hard and make a positive change in his life. This kid has a lot of catching up to do. It's going to take the best to get him through."

An image of the boy she'd seen at Sage Ranch flashed through her mind. The loneliness and joylessness in his face as he threw sticks for the dogs, unsmiling and alone.

She felt a wavering inside her. *No. No, no, no.*

"What other kind of trouble is he in?" she heard herself ask even as a part of her shouted to just stay out of it.

"He's been screwing up in a lot of ways. I'm not making excuses for him, but . . . he's been through a lot. Can we just sit down for a minute and talk?"

She hesitated, fighting a battle with herself. And losing. Taking a breath, she nodded, knowing this was probably a big mistake. But she couldn't say no. She walked to the sofa and he followed, seating himself beside her.

"I'm listening," she murmured, against her better judgment.

"Grady's had a lot going wrong in his life lately." Travis shook his head, a gesture filled with regret and coiled frustration. "First there was his mom and me getting divorced. And then Val remarried. The guy's from L.A., a big-shot corporate type, owns a chain of luxury hotel properties around the world. Within a few months, he convinced Val to sell her house and he moved her and Grady out to La-La Land."

"Any move to a new city can be rough on a child," she agreed.

"And in this case, it definitely was. But it's not only that." Travis's mouth twisted. "I let him down. I haven't been as involved in his life over the past few months as I used to be.

As I *should* have been. I was too damned busy chasing bad guys for the bureau."

"I'm sure you did your best." Even as the words came out of her mouth, she wondered why she was defending him, reassuring him. Probably because he looked so dejected, so full of regret.

"Don't sugarcoat it. I should have done better. A whole lot better. Especially since Grady and Val's new husband don't get along. I just found out recently that Grady was getting into fights at school. He stopped doing homework and let his studies slide over the last few months before the semester ended. I'm no psychiatrist," he muttered, leaning back on the sofa, his face tight, "but I'm guessing he's acting out because he can't stand his stepfather—and from what I've heard he has good reason."

"And that is?"

Travis's gaze hardened. "The guy seems to put him down nonstop. Tells him he's a loser, he's stupid—stuff like that."

"Emotional abuse." Mia felt a clutch of dismay. "Travis, that can be as harmful as physical abuse."

"I know. I'm going to deal with it, believe me. Going to deal with Val and that asshole, too. Whatever it takes to protect Grady. But in the meantime, he needs to do something this summer, too. He needs to work on passing that test. If he can somehow turn this around, get accepted into sixth grade through his own hard work, I think it'd go a long way toward building up his confidence."

"You're right," she said slowly. "He needs to believe in himself again."

"And he needs to believe in me."

This time as his eyes met hers she saw not only regret, but an ironclad determination.

"This kid feels defeated. These last months must have seemed like the whole world was lined up against him. That's no way for a ten-year-old to feel."

Mia felt an ache deep in her heart. For the boy. And for the man.

This was the Travis she knew. The Travis who wanted to right the wrongs of the world. The Travis who'd taught his younger brother, Jake, to be a protector, as he'd been, on the playground. Travis had always displayed a sense of decency and fairness, even back in high school when other kids only cared about belonging to the right cliques, the right clubs, being the best at this or that. . . .

Her throat felt dry. "What you're trying to do for Grady— it's a wonderful thing. He's . . . very lucky to have you."

"I can't help him alone. He needs you, too, Mia."

She looked away.

What was she getting herself into? Her better judgment warned her to stay out of this—away from Travis and his son. But something else was pulling her in.

A young boy needed help. What Grady accomplished this summer—or didn't accomplish—could mark a vital turning point that might affect him over the course of his entire life.

It could make a difference for him in everything that followed.

And that was what teachers did—and always hoped to do. Make a difference.

Could she really walk away from him? Turn her back on a child? *Travis's child,* she thought, and her heart constricted.

She knew the answer.

She stood up, paced away a few steps as she braced herself.

"All right, I'll do it." She turned back, returning to stand before him. "We'll start with two-hour sessions four times a week, and see how it goes."

"Whoa, thank you." Grinning, Travis surged to his feet and without thinking reached for her and scooped her up into his arms as if she weighed no more than a puff of air.

With a whoop that set Samson barking, he whirled her in a circle, his grin widening as she gasped and then began to laugh. He laughed, too, and then with one final spin, set her back down on her feet with a soft plunk.

But she was so dizzy with laughter she swayed, and his strong arms quickly slid around her waist, steadying her.

"Whoa, again," he said softly.

A rush of sensations enveloped her.

For one breathless moment she just leaned against him, her arms lifting to slide around his neck.

For stability, she told herself. *Nothing more.*

She breathed in the clean leather-and-soap scent of him, intensely conscious of the hard steel of his body pressed against hers. Even Travis's muscles seemed to have muscles. His eyes gleamed into hers and she couldn't look away.

This feels good. Dangerously, crazily good, she thought, and knew she should pull back, put some distance between the two of them. Right now.

But she couldn't. Not just yet. . . .

"Sorry about that. I got carried away." But Travis didn't look the least bit sorry. He looked pleased with himself and with her—and he still had his arms clasped firmly around her waist. He smiled down into her eyes.

"Thanks for helping my son. I won't ever forget it."

"Grady's lucky to have you in his corner." She hoped her voice sounded steadier than she felt. She drew in a breath and tried to lasso her emotions back under control.

"Lissie has my email. Tell her to forward me the curriculum requirements and the textbook info. If you or your ex-wife can contact Grady's teachers and find out the areas where he was weakest, that would be a big help. Bring him by on Monday at two. I'll make sure I study the requirements by then and . . . and I'll map out some initial lesson plans."

"We'll be here." His gaze was locked on hers.

She hoped he hadn't noticed that her voice was a little too breathless to be completely businesslike.

"I owe you, Mia. Big-time."

"No, you don't," she said quickly. Too quickly. "I'm doing this for Grady . . . not for you."

"Yeah, teach, I think I got that."

She laughed then. She couldn't help it. Travis had always had a way of making her laugh. As his eyes glinted down into hers, she felt her heart lurching into dangerous territory.

Fortunately, her sense of self-preservation kicked in and she did step back then. Away from his touch. Out of the circle of his arms.

It seemed to her that he released her reluctantly, then hooked his thumbs in his pockets, watching her as she pushed a loose strand of blond hair from her eyes.

"Tell me what the going rate is for tutors. I'll double it."

"I don't want your money, Travis."

A frown creased between his brows. "Sorry, if you think you're doing this for free, think again."

"Not for free exactly. I have a better idea."

He lifted a brow.

"Whatever you were planning to pay me, why don't you make a donation in that amount instead? I'm cochair of the fund-raising committee for Bits and Pieces. Our quilt exhibition is next month. All of the money is going to the Loving Arms shelter. It would be great if you'd contribute to that."

"You've got yourself a deal."

He smiled at her suddenly, and Mia finally fully woke to the fact that Travis Tanner was here in her house, smiling at her. That same smile she remembered so well—only—if possible—even more devastatingly sexy.

It was a smile that made a woman want to smile back.

And if she were being honest, it made her want to do a whole lot more. Like grab him by the shirt collar, pull his head down, kiss him until neither of them could stand it anymore and they both had to tear off each other's clothes and fall on the floor and . . .

She drew in a breath and headed resolutely to the door. None of that was going to happen. Ever.

There was nothing further to discuss and she wasn't at all sure where they went from here, so he needed to leave. Immediately. She needed time to figure out how to handle this new apparent truce between them.

As she opened the door to the summer night, she fought back a rush of something that bordered on panic. She'd managed to avoid him for all these years and now in the space of an hour she'd agreed to tutor his son, and everything between them seemed to be shifting.

It scared her. She needed him to leave so she could think. Process. Get her equilibrium back.

Both he and Samson had followed her and, without a word, Travis pushed the screen door, holding it open for her.

She led the way out into the quiet June darkness, Samson scampering at her heels as she was met by the vastness of a purple Montana sky glittering with stars. On both sides of the street, the houses were dark. Quiet.

Samson raced eagerly down the porch steps and onto the grass, turning to look expectantly back at her just as a breeze tinged with the sweet scent of sage wafted gently down from the mountains.

"I had no idea you were into quilting," Travis said, coming down the steps behind her.

"What? Oh . . ." She spun to face him. "That's because you don't know anything about me anymore."

He moved deliberately toward her, closing the gap between them. "Maybe there's something we can do about that."

"*Maybe* we shouldn't push our luck."

His slow grin sent her pulse racing. She felt her breath catching in her throat as he stood before her, all tall, dark, and dangerous. If she were Superman, Travis would be her kryptonite.

"Something tells me it doesn't need much of a push," he said softly.

Run. Inside. Right now, a voice inside her ordered. But heat fired through her and she felt rooted to the spot. Travis's gaze was locked on hers. Then, before she could do the smart, sensible thing and leave, he pulled her into his arms and slowly lowered his mouth to hers.

She could have pulled away. Could have told him no. But she didn't. Colors and sparks exploded inside her as he kissed her searchingly. She kissed him back, craving the taste of his mouth on hers, needing it.

She cupped his face, touched her tongue to his, her body taking over, moving against his tall, muscled frame, soft curves against hard steel, her heart racing, needing, wanting.

The kiss they shared was slow and intimate. As heady as the summer night. It had every nerve in her body electrified as she tightened her arms around his neck, never wanting to let go.

As if reading her mind, Travis tugged her closer still against the length of his body.

He took the kiss deeper, slowing it down, savoring it until her heart was pounding. An ache filled her, sweet and hot, roaring through her blood like thunder.

The night seemed to tilt around them.

Travis meant to take his time. But it didn't work out that way. Once he tasted her mouth, then her tongue, exploring its texture, he couldn't stop breathing her in and wanting more of her. *All of her.* She tasted so sweet, as sweet as candy and as sexy as musk. Incredibly sexy. Her lips against his were soft and eager, their shape and taste exactly as he remembered from a lifetime ago.

To hell with slow. She all but melted like candle wax in his arms and he felt consumed by everything about her, the softness of her skin, that little moan in the back of her throat, the way her tongue flirted against his.

Mia. She kissed like no other woman he'd ever kissed. Made him feel like no other woman had ever made him feel.

He drew her closer still, his hands sliding downward

along the curve of her hips, then gripping her bottom as she fitted herself against him. Their mouths were hot and welded together, waging an escalating battle in a secret language that was theirs alone.

It felt familiar and yet new . . . brand-new. Hotter even than before. He couldn't tear himself away from her and he was glad as hell she didn't seem to want him to. Her arms were wound tight around him and her velvety mouth clung to his as if she were clinging to life and breath itself.

"Travis," she gasped, trembling against him.

Cradling her face, he found himself wishing her hair wasn't in a damned ponytail so he could stroke his fingers through it. He bent her head back, his mouth taking and giving with a single-mindedness that left them both shaken.

They might have been alone on the highest peak of the Crazies—hell, alone on the planet. There was only the starry vastness of the night, the sage-scented air, and the two of them, him and Mia.

And the dog. The damned midget of a dog.

Samson barked, nudged against Travis's leg. He barked again, and kept on barking as he jumped up, bracing his paws against Mia's knee. She seemed to waken from a trance and froze, then jerked back, her lips parting suddenly—not in passion but in shock.

She stared at Travis for a moment as if he were a vampire who'd materialized from the grave and flown like a bat into her front yard, then she scooped the dog up into her arms.

"This wasn't supposed . . . to happen," she whispered unsteadily, and without waiting for him to reply, she bolted up the steps and disappeared inside, slamming the door behind her.

Chapter Twelve

Brittany grabbed up her cell phone Saturday night, then quickly set it down again on the nightstand in the guest room without opening the new text message.

Don't look at it. Don't even think about looking at it, she told herself. But nervousness twisted inside her like razor wire. Wade had sent her two other texts today and she'd deleted both of them unread.

But he was relentless. He just didn't let up.

What was he writing this time? Was he begging her to get back together, or threatening her? Promising he'd never hurt her? Or hinting that if she didn't take him back, she'd be sorry.

He's never going to leave me alone, she thought in despair.

He won't give up. Ever. Oh, God, what am I going to do?

For a moment, she had to struggle against the tears squeezing from between her eyelashes.

Maybe I should tell Aunt Mia, she thought. She already

felt guilty for not having told the truth in the first place. If only she'd told her mom. . . .

But her mom had been so happy and excited getting ready for her honeymoon. Britt hadn't wanted to spoil that.

Since meeting Alec, her mom was happier than Britt had ever seen her. Alec was the nicest guy in the world, and he treated her mother like she was someone special. Britt knew if she'd told her mom Wade was sort of stalking her, she'd have canceled her whole honeymoon and probably called the police and who knew what else.

Staring glumly at her reflection in the tall oval mirror in the guest room, she tried to calm the fears building inside her. *You can handle this,* she whispered to herself for the thousandth time. *He hasn't hurt you or anyone yet. So chances are he's not going to.*

But he'd threatened Tate. Her half brother, only three years old. He'd sworn if she didn't meet him to talk over their relationship he'd get to Tate. Scare him. Maybe even hurt him.

The idea of that adorable little boy who called her "Bwitney" and who had the sweetest little giggle in the world getting hurt or even scared on her account made her want to die.

She'd actually agreed to meet Wade at Starbucks that day. Anything to keep Tate safe. But when Wade showed up, he'd said they had to leave Starbucks, go someplace else to talk. He wanted her to go for a ride with him alone up into the mountains, where they could talk about getting back together without all these people around.

Brittany wasn't going anywhere alone with Wade. She'd left, run back to her car while he was busy at the counter ordering more coffee.

That was the day she'd decided she had to disappear. She hastily packed a few things, told her mom she was having a sleepover at Laura's, and then left Laura's house at five in the morning to drive to Lonesome Way.

Laura was the only person who knew how bad things were with Wade, and she'd sworn she'd never let on to him that she had any clue where Britt had gone.

Until this morning, Britt had almost started to believe he really wouldn't find her. That by the time the summer ended, he'd have forgotten all about her or landed a new girlfriend, and would be ready to leave her alone.

But this morning everything had changed. Because Wade was here. *In Lonesome Way.*

He'd found her.

The photo he'd sent to her cell phone proved that.

He'd sent it from a different cell phone, not his own. One with a number she didn't recognize—otherwise she wouldn't have opened it.

But the instant she saw the photo, she felt a clutch of fear. It could only be from him.

The shot had been taken early this morning when she'd stepped onto the porch to pick up the *Lonesome Way Daily* for Aunt Mia. In the photo, she was wearing the gray tank top and pink sleep pants she'd worn to bed last night, and her hair was still all mussed from sleep, not even brushed yet.

Britt knew this was Wade's way of telling her that he was here in Lonesome Way. Close by. He was trying to scare her.

Somehow he'd found out where she'd gone when she left home, and he'd been hiding outside Aunt Mia's house early this morning, watching her, snapping that photo to show her she hadn't gotten away.

Fear pumped through her, but so did anger. What had she ever seen in Wade? He was cute, sure, and pretty hunky. Not to mention smart. He'd been nice at first and funny, with that kind of sarcastic edge that appealed to her, but underneath it all . . . she'd always sensed something. Something a little bit off.

He always wanted to know what she was doing when she wasn't with him. And he didn't like her talking to any other guys, even her guy friends, the ones she'd known forever.

He picked fights over the stupidest little things, like when she didn't tell him she'd made plans with Laura and their friend Tracy to go shopping downtown without checking with him first to see if he wanted to hang out. He'd started acting like he *owned* her—and that's when she'd broken things off.

Her hands shook a little as she pulled on her cute new T-shirt from Top to Toe, the one with the heart. It looked perfect with her khaki shorts, all crisp and new. Taking a deep breath, she slipped into the silver wedge sandals her new friend Lacey from A Bun in the Oven had lent her to wear to Jackie Kenton's party tonight.

But her skin felt like ice and she wasn't as excited any-more about going with Seth to Jackie's house. She was scared. And she wasn't sure what to do.

She dug her peach lip gloss from her purse and swiped it on. As she ran a brush through her hair one more time and let it fall in loose curls around her shoulders, she could hear Aunt Mia in her own room, opening and closing draw-ers, getting ready for the birthday celebration at the Double Cross Bar and Grill.

If I tell her what's going on, it'll spoil her whole night. She'll stay home and she'll make me stay home, too. She'll probably even make me call Dad and tell him.

He'll force me to go back home—and keep me under lock and key for the whole summer.

She wanted to stay *here*. She liked living with Aunt Mia, she liked working at the bakery—and she liked Seth. He was sweet and easygoing and funny. He made everyone at the bakery laugh, and she hadn't met a single person who didn't want to be his friend.

Seth actually was everything Wade wasn't. As in, *normal*.

And what good would it do if she did go back home? Wade would get to her there, too.

And he'd be closer to Tate. . . .

I can handle this by myself, she told herself, dropping
the lip gloss back into her purse and taking a deep breath.
*There's no reason to tell anyone yet. It's only a photo.
Wade's being a jerk and a creep, yeah. But he's just trying
to pull my chain.*

You don't have to let him, she decided as she met her
reflection in the mirror.

Hearing the doorbell, she dashed to the window, and
smiled in relief and anticipation as she spotted Seth's Chevy
truck parked out front.

*I won't let Wade ruin my summer. And he's not going to
spoil tonight.* She snatched up her purse and headed down
the hall.

Aunt Mia was already opening the front door, greeting
Seth. Britt stifled a wince. Oh, God, it was so embarrassing.
She was telling him to drive carefully tonight.

If she only knew. . . .

"Hi, I'm ready," Britt called out, skidding to Seth's rescue
just as he promised to drive nice and slow.

"You look *great*." Seth's glance skimmed over her cute
new clothes and long legs. Britt loved that he actually
blushed a little. Then he smiled into her eyes.

"He's right, honey. You look beautiful." Aunt Mia
brushed a kiss against her cheek. "Have fun, you two. Be
good. Remember, Britt, home by twelve."

"I know." Britt gave her aunt her sunniest smile and tried
to ignore the knot of worry as tight as a spool of tangled
thread in her chest. Walking out to the Chevy hand in hand
with Seth, she was grateful Aunt Mia didn't know that Seth's
driving speed was the least of her problems.

Chapter Thirteen

Cruising into town, Mia heard Vince Gill's voice blasting from the jukebox before she even neared the parking lot of the Double Cross Bar and Grill.

A few clouds had just begun to drift across the night sky, nearly obscuring the moon and stars, but there was enough misty light to see that the lot was even more crowded than usual and she knew it was due to the turnout for Tommy's party. She recognized his and Rafe's trucks in the lot, along with a half dozen other vehicles, including Zeke Mueller's police cruiser, but as she headed toward the door, her gaze sweeping over the parked cars and trucks, she didn't see Travis's Explorer.

A cold sensation settled in the pit of her stomach. Travis hadn't arrived yet—maybe he wasn't coming at all. Maybe he'd had second thoughts ever since their kiss and wanted to avoid her.

Which would be just as well. She was having second thoughts herself. And third thoughts.

She didn't know what had come over her the other night. But whatever it was, she was ready to obliterate it. *Travis not only back in town, but back in her life?*

No. That wasn't happening. It was only one kiss, one little kiss. Well, she thought, memory flooding back, maybe not so little. And maybe not just one.

But none of it meant anything.

We were swept up in the moment and now we're back to point zero, she told herself as she crossed the lot.

Travis had found out her email from Lissie and sent her the information she needed from Grady's school district himself. But he'd added only the briefest of notes.

"Here you go. Will get you the textbooks. Thanks."

So romantic.

And for all she knew, he'd probably just drop his son off on Monday and drive away. Go someplace where he could kill time until the tutoring session was over.

It will be better that way, she assured herself as she pulled open the heavy double doors and a roar of noisy merriment—along with the smells of beer and chili burgers—swept over her.

If she *did* see Travis tonight she'd just pretend that kissing business never happened.

No problem.

And there was always the possibility he wouldn't even show up.

As comforting as that thought seemed on the surface, deep in her heart, she doubted that would happen. It was his brother-in-law's birthday, after all, and the Tanners were all about family and celebrating every milestone together. Lissie had told her that Jake was competing in a major bull-riding event at a rodeo in Tulsa tonight, with a huge liquor endorsement deal riding on it if he stayed on the meanest bull on the circuit for eight seconds, so he wouldn't be making it to Tommy's party.

But Travis? Travis would be here.

She'd known that as she dressed tonight. As she brushed her hair and let it flow long and loose in smooth curls that tumbled past her shoulders. As she slipped into her favorite topaz silk sweater and black pants and stuck her feet into sexy black stilettos.

After dressing, she'd hunted through her jewelry box for the small diamond studs her parents had given her when she graduated from college. While scooping them up she'd accidentally knocked her engagement ring from Peter onto the floor.

The ring was a marquise-cut diamond, big, bold, and flashy—so very Peter. At the time of their engagement he'd been flush; that was before his business wheelings and dealings went sour and his little real estate kingdom came tumbling down around his ears. Mia had offered to give the ring back to him right after the divorce—right *before* she discovered that he'd cleaned out their joint savings account. He'd breezily insisted she keep it—and she'd never been sure if that was due to pride or arrogance. Peter Clancy had more than his share of both.

Looking at the ring as she snagged it and set it back inside her jewelry box, she'd suddenly had the surreal feeling that her marriage to Peter had existed not only in another lifetime but almost in another dimension. Peter Clancy had no more bearing on her life now than a road marker on a nearly forgotten trail.

But Travis, of all people, was back in it. Marginally, perhaps, but still . . .

Those kisses were anything but marginal, a voice inside reminded her. She felt herself growing warm at the memory.

But she wasn't going to think about Travis. If he didn't want to talk to her or deal with the mistake they'd both made the other night, that was fine with her.

There were plenty of men in this town who might want to dance with her tonight. And she would dance when she felt like it. She'd laugh and have fun. She'd drink a beer and have a good time.

Even if it killed her.

Edging her way through the throng of cowboys and the women in short sparkly tops and tight jeans who were flirting with them, she passed chattering tourists wearing stiff new cowboy hats and boots they'd purchased at Ponderosa Earl's. People were lined up three deep before the crowded bar.

Then she spotted the huge Happy Birthday signs and banners strung up all along the back half of the restaurant and began inching her way in that direction as the jukebox blared a Carrie Underwood tune and couples swayed close together on the dance floor.

One of those couples, Mia noticed with a slight jolt, was Deanna and Zeke. Their arms were locked around each other and they were grinning goofily into each other's eyes like a couple of lovestruck teenagers.

Unfortunately, at that exact moment, Deanna happened to glance over and her gaze fell on Mia. She immediately turned back to Zeke, stood on tiptoe to give him a big sloppy kiss, and then inched even closer against him—about as close as she could get with her cute little baby bump. She rested her head on his shoulder and smiled a beatific smile straight at Mia.

Give me a break, Mia thought, but something twisted painfully inside her.

She was glad for Zeke—he seemed genuinely happy. But the sight of him and his smugly pregnant wife made her feel strangely empty inside. Not jealous—not of Deanna. But sad. Mia envied what the two of them had found together, envied all they were about to share—babies and birthday parties, noisy game nights and vacations. A laughing, busy, happy home, with a family to grow and nurture.

Something she hadn't ever managed to achieve, she reflected wistfully. And who knew if she ever would. . . .

A couple of older ranch hands in Wranglers and checkered shirts headed toward the pool table, blocking her view of Deanna's smug smile. She wove her way toward the back of the bar, dodging waitresses wearing short red skirts and skimpy black sequined tops who bopped between tables with trays of food.

"Mia!" Lissie's voice reached her above the din of music and talk and laughter. She was waving her arm back and forth near a cluster of long tables a few yards from the dartboard. Tommy was seated beside her, holding a beer, deep in conversation with Rafe, Sophie, and Lissie's cousin Decker and his wife, Leigh. A score of other friends chattered at surrounding tables, along with Tommy's parents and his sister Susie with her husband, Jack. But she saw that Lissie had saved her a seat beside her own.

"Well, don't you look all sexy and amazing." Lissie flashed her a welcoming grin.

"You're pretty spiffy yourself." Lissie was radiant in a low-cut pink silk top and dressy black capri pants.

"Hey, gorgeous." Shoving back his chair, Tommy ambled over, wrapping her in a bear hug that nearly cracked her ribs.

"Happy birthday, you." She squeezed him back.

"How's your aunt doing?" Sophie asked, pushing one of the baskets of barbecued chicken wings along the table toward her. She followed this with a huge family-sized bowl of the Double Cross's special Whooper Dooper salad as Mia slipped into her seat.

"Don't ask. She wouldn't let me in when I got to the cabin. Talked to me through the door."

"You've got to be kidding."

"I wish I was. All she kept saying was that she didn't want my charity."

A thoughtful expression came over Sophie's face. "My grandmother says Winny was always . . . different. But not even opening the door when you drove all the way out to her cabin? It's hard to understand, isn't it?"

"I'm not giving up. I'm going back tomorrow to check on her and give it another shot. But I did leave supper and your beautiful pie on her porch. I just hope she had the sense to go get them after I left."

"How about a beer, Mia?" Rafe interrupted. "Or would you like wine like my wife?"

"Beer sounds good, thanks." Mia used tongs to heap salad on her plate and snagged a couple of chicken wings.

As Rafe ordered her a cold one, Sophie eyed the big plate of salad. "Um, you might want to leave some room. We have nachos and guacamole coming any minute now. Pizza and steak burgers and fries to follow."

"Too bad you guys don't know how to order enough food for a crowd," Mia said with a laugh.

"Oh, that's nothing. Wait until you see the birthday cake Sophie baked." Lissie nibbled at a chicken wing and delicately licked sauce off her fingers. "Big enough for everyone in this entire place to have a slice. Devil's food with sour cream fudge frosting. Tommy's favorite."

"Oh, God. I need to save some room," Mia muttered. But the knot inside her was relaxing. Now that she was here, she was glad she'd come. It felt good to be with her friends as Johnny Cash crooned from the jukebox and a group at the bar started singing along. As all around her people she loved talked and joked and laughed. She almost forgot about how awkward it would be when Travis arrived . . . if Travis arrived. . . .

"Uh-oh, don't look now, but here comes lover boy," Lissie said suddenly. "Looks like he still has the hots for you."

Mia froze as for one insane moment she thought Lissie was talking about Travis. But of course it wasn't Travis. She just had Travis on the brain. Lissie didn't have a clue what had happened the other night between them—not unless Travis had told her, which was highly unlikely. Travis no doubt wished he could click an undo button just as much as she did.

Flicking a glance behind her, she saw that the man wending his way through the crowd straight toward her was Boyd Hatcher, a burly, red-haired wrangler who worked at the Lazy Q Ranch. She'd known him since grade school and had always felt a little sorry for him because his older brother, Lane, had been killed playing on the railroad tracks when Boyd was eleven, and Boyd had worshipped his big brother.

She'd always tried to be nice to him because of that loss, but the last time she'd come to the Double Cross, with Rafe and Sophie, he'd made a pest of himself. He'd obviously been drinking and had cut in while she was dancing with Coop Miller. Then he kept coming over, trying to buy her a drink and repeatedly bugging her to dance with him until she finally did, once, and then left.

He'd called her several times for a date in the weeks that followed. After turning him down the first few times, Mia had started screening her calls.

Her stomach dropped as she saw the intent smile on his rough-hewn face.

"Tommy, get up. Quick. Dance with Mia. Right now," Lissie whispered urgently.

But Mia shook her head as Tommy started to rise from his chair. "It's okay. One dance with the guy won't kill me."

Hadn't she promised herself she'd dance tonight? Boyd had nearly reached their table and she didn't want to make a scene. Not at Tommy's party.

"It's no big deal," she told both of them. "I'll be back in time to hog the nachos."

"And if you're not?" Lissie demanded.

"Then send the cavalry to cut in." She laughed just as Boyd clapped a hand on her shoulder.

"Hey, Mia. Long time no see."

She slanted a glance up at the man looming over her. With a quiver of unease she realized that he looked more than a little drunk. There was a bleary light in his close-set gray eyes.

Great, just great.

"They're playing our song." He winked at her. "How about it?"

Conway Twitty's cover of "I Only Have Eyes for You" wafted from the jukebox.

That's our song? Mia thought. *I don't think so.*

But it was only one dance, she reminded herself, and if she turned him down now it would be awkward for both of them, what with the entire table of guests looking on.

"Sure," she said lightly and stood up.

Dancing with a slightly inebriated Boyd Hatcher was about as much fun as cleaning an outhouse, she realized very quickly as he stumbled yet again and his booted foot stomped on her toes.

"Ouch."

He swore as she winced. "Crap. Sorry about that. My big stupid feet. I'm kind of clumsy when I'm distracted. You distract me somethin' awful, Mia, so it's actually your fault." His smile was sloppy, almost leering. "I think you're about the prettiest woman in this whole entire town."

"Will you think I'm pretty on crutches?" she asked with a forced smile, wondering when the damned song was going to end.

"Ha-ha! The lady's funny as well as beautiful. I like me a woman with a sense of humor. Not to mention a great pair of knockers." He gazed down at her chest with an appreciative grin spreading across his face like pancake syrup on a plate.

Classy, she thought. Boyd had never been offensive before. It had to be the liquor. But Mia had had enough.

"I need to head back to the party now."

Her tone left no doubt she was done. The song had come to an end anyway and a George Strait tune now blasted through the Double Cross as she started to pull away.

But Hatcher had other ideas and grabbed her arm, yanking her back.

"Oh, c'mon. One more little dance. What's your hurry?"

"I'm with friends. It's a party. People are waiting for me." She tried to pull away, but he tightened his grasp. "Boyd. Let me go."

He grinned and pulled her up against him. All around them couples were dancing; people at tables and booths were singing along. Between the music, the conversations, and the singing, the din was deafening.

Mia planted her feet, refusing to dance, straining against his grip. "Let me *go*, Boyd," she repeated, her amber eyes turning icy.

"Hey, c'mon. You don't fool me. I know your type, Mia Quinn." He winked at her, then bent his head close to hers as she struggled to break free. The smell of beer and Old Spice filled her nostrils.

"You always were a hot little number. Even in high school when Travis Tanner was doing you. You're just playing hard to get."

Anger darkened her eyes. He had one thick hand at her waist, and the other gripped her arm like a vise. He wasn't listening to her—either because he was too drunk or he didn't care.

"Someone should have taught you that no means no." She glared straight into his eyes as his hand began to slide downward from her waist, his fingers skimming over her bottom. "One more time. Let go of me, right now."

"Or what?" He laughed and nuzzled at her neck.

But his laughter choked off abruptly, turning to a yelp of pain as she rammed her knee into his balls with every ounce of her strength.

"Fuck!" he yelled at the top of his lungs. He let her go, staggering back, his face scrunching in pain as everyone in the Double Cross stopped talking and turned to stare. From a distance she thought she heard Tommy shout something as she stepped away from Boyd. Then she saw that Tommy was on his feet and Rafe had already sprung out of his chair.

She started toward them, back toward the table, hoping to head them off, but before she'd gone more than two steps Hatcher grabbed her arm roughly and hauled her back to face him. Anger glittered from his eyes.

"You little bitch, what the hell did you do that for?" he bellowed.

She yanked her arm free and nearly stumbled backward and that was when everything seemed to happen at once. Travis must have just come in, because he caught her from behind, strong arms steadying her. Then he moved around her fast, shoving Boyd away from her, slamming him up against the wall. An instant later Travis's muscled arm was wedged against the other man's throat.

"Now, that's a hell of a way to treat a lady, Hatcher. I think you'd better leave before I decide to break your face. And that would be just for starters."

Travis's tone was deadly calm but Mia could see the tightness in his jaw, the controlled fury in his eyes. She was terrified he really might hurt Boyd if the other man dared to open his mouth.

He was a good three inches taller and far stronger than Hatcher, and he looked like he might easily snap the red-haired wrangler in two at the slightest provocation.

"Travis. No." Quickly, she touched his arm. "It's all right, let him go."

"You should head back to the party and have a seat, Mia." He spoke quietly, without taking his eyes off Hatcher's reddening face. "I'll join you in a minute."

"Not until you let him go."

"Did he hurt you? Are you all right?"

"No, he didn't, and I'm fine." She swallowed, remembering it was Travis who had taught her that defensive move back in high school. He'd told her that if she ever needed to get away from any guy, kick or knee him hard in the balls. Made her practice ramming her knee upward until she dissolved in laughter.

"It was nothing, honestly. Let him go. I don't want anything to ruin Tommy's party."

Hatcher was struggling futilely, and he looked scared. Mia feared he'd pass out any second for lack of oxygen.

Frank Custer rushed over. He was one of the older Lazy Q ranch hands, and a nephew of Sheriff Hodge. "What the hell's wrong with you, Hatcher? Getting rough with Mia that way. Sorry, Mia." He threw her an agitated glance.

"He's just been drinkin', that's all," Frank told Travis. "He don't think sometimes. He keeps that up, he'll lose his job for sure. But I'll get him outta here, Travis, and drive him home."

"That's a good idea, Frank," Mia said swiftly.

Travis said nothing, just increased the pressure on Hatcher and watched him squirm. Then Deputy Zeke Mueller came ambling up. He'd left Deanna at their table and now eyed Hatcher with a frown. He might be off duty but he was still deputy sheriff of Lonesome Way and it was his job to keep the peace.

And he'd seen Hatcher grab Mia.

He planted himself right beside Travis as Frank stepped back a pace, then Zeke studied the man wriggling on the wall like a pinned bug.

"Evening, Mia, Travis, Frank."

"Evening, Zeke," Travis returned calmly, never taking his eyes off Boyd's face.

"You okay, Mia?"

"Zeke, I'm fine. Tell him to let Boyd go," Mia demanded.

"You h-heard her. Let me . . . go," Hatcher choked out desperately.

"You know, he's not looking too good, Travis," Zeke commented thoughtfully, his voice slow and calm, as if they were talking about the chances of rain on Tuesday. He shrugged. "I guess it's best if you do let him go."

"I'm taking it under consideration." Impassively, Travis surveyed the man caught in his grasp, who was no longer even bothering to struggle.

"You hear that, Hatcher?" Travis's tone was low and even. "Mia's worried about you. So's Frank. Deputy Mueller here thinks I should let you leave without a broken jaw or a black eye. So I'm going to respect that. Consider yourself lucky. I'm going to give you a break because they all asked me to. But that only holds if you walk out of here without saying another word. Not one word. Got it?"

Hatcher, red faced and struggling to breathe, managed a nod.

Travis waited another ten seconds before dropping his arm from Hatcher's throat. He stepped back, making sure he was positioned between Mia and the other man just in case.

He needn't have worried. Hatcher didn't have any fight left in him. He slumped toward the floor, coughing, but the deputy caught him by the arm and hauled him up.

"You shouldn't be driving in your condition." Zeke eyed him with a frown.

"I'll get him home." Frank rushed forward to grip Hatcher's arm. He practically dragged the other man toward the door.

"Much obliged, Frank. Drive careful, now." The deputy watched until the older wrangler had guided Hatcher outside.

"You have a nice night, Mia," her ex-fiancé said softly; then he met Travis's gaze in a brief silent look, lawman to lawman, before turning on his heel and returning to the table where his pregnant wife waited.

Mia hadn't noticed how quiet it had grown in the Double Cross until that moment. She'd been too focused on Travis's hold on Hatcher.

But suddenly everyone in the place started talking at once and it was bedlam as she stood there beside Travis in the midst of all the hubbub.

"Are you sure you're all right? He really didn't hurt you?" There was something like fear in his face.

She shook her head, her emotions tumbling.

"I'm fine. I told you. I'd handled it."

Their eyes met and for a moment the rest of the room faded away. She saw only Travis. Not the eighteen-year-old boyfriend who had left her behind so many years ago, but the man he had become during that intervening time. The man who loved his son and stood up for him. The man who'd just stood up for her even when she didn't want him to get involved.

Electric sparks streaked again down her spine. They might have been back in the front yard of her house again, beneath the night sky, alone except for Samson, and she could almost feel those strong arms around her, holding her close and tight. Safe.

She could taste the deep kisses they'd shared, feel the solid warmth, drink in the scent of him as he'd held her, touched her. . . .

It had felt so natural, that instant fire between them, neither of them holding back. . . .

And then Tommy and Rafe bounded up, along with Big Billy, the Double Cross's giant, tattooed bartender-owner, marching right behind them.

"Everything okay out here?" Big Billy demanded gruffly. "We had a problem in the kitchen and all of a sudden, all hell started breaking loose out here."

"Everyone's all right, Big Billy," Lissie assured him as she and Sophie breezed right around him and everyone else to stand on either side of Mia.

"Come on, let's go sit down." Sophie tucked Mia's arm in hers. "We saved you some nachos."

"Yeah, I think there's been enough fun-filled drama for one night," Lissie added.

"Only for one night?" Mia glanced back and forth between them. "For the year, is more like it."

As Big Billy lumbered back to the bar, Lissie turned to Travis and planted a kiss on his cheek. "Good job, bro. Wish you'd cleaned his clock, though. I always knew that spitball thrower was nothing but trouble."

A half hour later, Mia sat at one end of the table, finishing off a slice of pizza, and Travis was seated far at the other end, calmly eating a burger. He was seated beside Will Brady, Rafe's foreman, and across from Tommy's parents, who had driven in from Bozeman and were spending the night with Lissie, Tommy, and Molly.

"Was that an actual conversation taking place for a minute between you and my brother back there?" Lissie wanted to know.

"Not really."

"I could have sworn I saw a few sparks there."

"Lissie!"

"Okay, okay. But I know what I saw. "

Thankfully Sophie set the massive birthday cake, twinkling with candles, in front of Tommy just then and everyone joined in singing "Happy Birthday."

⟳

Travis bided his time.

While the birthday cake was sliced and served and eaten, while coffee and more wine and beer were served, he listened to Tommy's father's account of his childhood in Cody, Wyoming, and to Will Brady telling him how his brand-new Chevy truck got rear-ended in Billings a few weeks back by a pretty, red-haired woman in a Prius, and how he'd taken the truck-smashing woman to dinner two days later.

Travis nodded and made the appropriate comments. He joked and talked and watched and waited. His sister and Tommy headed to the crowded dance floor. They were laughing and talking, dancing with abandon beneath the Happy Birthday banners.

Rafe and Sophie were already out there in the thick of the crowd, arms around each other's waists, lost in each other's eyes.

Travis studied Mia, stunning with that knockout classic beauty as she leaned forward, deep in conversation with his cousin Decker and Deck's wife, Leigh. Then Decker and Leigh moved off to dance and he knew he didn't want to wait a moment longer.

He stood and started toward her with long strides. At that exact moment Mia happened to set down her coffee cup, lean back in her chair, and glance his way.

Her gaze widened ever so slightly as he approached, and he saw her entire body tense and straighten.

"May I have this dance?"

Brilliant amber eyes seared him. "Are you crazy?" she asked in an undervoice, glancing wildly around her. "People are already talking about us after what happened before."

"Good. Let 'em talk." Travis's grin was unconcerned. He held out his big hand. "Since when are you afraid of a little talk?"

"I'm not afraid of anything," she said sharply. But she shivered as she put her hand in his and rose from her chair. "We're both going to live to regret this," she warned him as he led her onto the dance floor, forging a path through the crowd.

"Speak for yourself. I won't regret one minute of it." Gently, he swung her into his arms.

⌒

Oh, God. What was she doing? It was one thing to kiss Travis in the dark privacy of her own front yard, with the entire block asleep and no one the wiser. It was quite another to dance with him in the Double Cross, with all of their friends and family around.

Lady Antebellum's "Need You Now" streamed from the jukebox. The song—and Travis's nearness—soaked into every inch of her soul.

His muscled arms felt so right around her. Strong and gentle and . . . arousing. His very touch, every glance made her feel like she'd been infused with fire. His big frame moved easily to the music, his eyes gazing straight into hers. The sad truth was she burned with wanting him. *Again. Still.*

Whatever. It was all insanity. And he'd started it when he'd come to Larkspur Road to plead with her to tutor Grady.

"What in the world are we doing?" She tipped her head back, narrowing her eyes.

"We're dancing. Getting to know each other again."

"And setting every tongue in this town wagging again."

"The only tongue I care about right now is yours," he teased. "And if we weren't surrounded by everyone we know—"

"Stop right there," she murmured, though she felt a flush rushing through her cheeks and a laugh rising in her throat. She couldn't choke it back in time and it burst out. Suddenly she couldn't *stop* laughing.

Travis's grin widened.

"Careful, people might think you're having a good time."

"I need to go home," she said, just at the moment the music ended. "It's late."

"I'll walk you out."

"That isn't necessar—"

"How do I know Hatcher didn't come back here and isn't waiting outside for you?" he interrupted.

"More likely if he *is* waiting outside, it's for *you*," she countered.

"I should be so lucky."

He looked like he actually wished Hatcher would come back for him. Mia sighed and shook her head.

Another song came on the jukebox and somehow they were still dancing. Despite her words, now that they were on the dance floor, hand in hand, their bodies touching, swaying, she wasn't certain she wanted to stop.

"You didn't bring me those textbooks," she reminded him, trying to steer the conversation back to neutral ground

as his big hand pressed warmly at her waist and she resisted
the urge to close her eyes and lean her head on his shoulder
like some lovesick fool.

"Sorry, I meant to. I got hung up on a few things." His
tone had turned serious. "Grady and I have been hauling
our gear over to the cabin—we're moving in this week. And
in the midst of all that . . ." He paused. "Val called."

The ex-wife. Mia watched his eyes darken with a controlled anger.

"I take it that didn't go too well."

"She wanted to talk to Grady, to see how he was doing.
Before I had a chance to discuss it with her first, he told her
that he was going to be tutored to help him pass that proficiency test. And according to Grady, she started sounding
all funny, said she wanted to talk to me. And then . . ." He
frowned. "You won't believe what she said."

"Try me," Mia said softly, worried about the tension she
saw in his face.

"She told me not to waste my time getting him a tutor.
Because she and Drew have come up with their own solu-
tion. My guess is it's really Baylor's decision and Val's going
along with it to please him. At least I'd like to think that,"
Travis added darkly.

Mia listened, bracing herself.

"They want to send Grady away to boarding school."

"What?"

"Drew's already made inquiries. He has a friend whose
son supposedly got 'straightened out' at boarding school.
In Richmond, Virginia, of all places. It's called Broadcrest
Academy. The perfect answer to all their problems. Grady
would have to repeat fifth grade, but he wouldn't have to
endure teasing by anyone about having failed. Because no
one enrolled at Broadcrest Academy would know. The staff
is excellent, according to Val, and the program is highly
structured, whatever the hell that means. Drew Baylor is
apparently making arrangements for Grady to get intensive

private tutoring and monitoring to prevent any further 'problems.' In other words they want to just ship him off and get him out of their hair. Needless to say, it ain't gonna happen," Travis added flatly.

"That's awful." Indignation seared her as she tried to take it in. "Boarding school for a ten-year-old? What's the matter with them? What kind of a mother—" Mia broke off, realizing she was out of line. "I'm sorry." She drew in a breath. "This is none of my business."

"It *is* your business. Because you're Grady's tutor and nothing is changing that. I told Val to go to hell, though not in so many words. But I made it clear that boarding school is out of the question."

"How'd *that* go over?"

"Val practically had a meltdown. Told me she'd talk to Drew." His mouth twisted as the song came to an end. "The woman I married was stronger than this. Ditzy sometimes, but she was totally devoted to her son. Val used to be a very committed mother. Now . . . she seems committed only to one thing. Pleasing the rich asshole she married." Travis looked down into Mia's eyes. "She doesn't know it yet, but I'm planning to have a few words with Drew myself."

"I wouldn't want to be him when that happens," Mia murmured.

"Drew won't want to be him either."

Mia realized the party was starting to break up. People were making their way to the doors and when she and Travis headed back to the table to say their good-byes, Lissie and Sophie both smiled widely at her. But neither said a word about her dancing with Travis.

Rafe winked at his brother. Decker gave Travis a thump on the back.

Mia felt herself tensing as Travis walked her out to her car.

"See what you started? I expect you're going to be grilled

like a scorched steak when you get home," she said with a half laugh as they reached her Jeep.

"Fine with me. I'm a hard nut to crack. And besides, I'm moving out in a day or so."

Her lips tilted in a smile as he opened the Jeep's door for her and they stood there together in the soft, cool night. Just looking at each other.

The sound of doors slamming, of people calling good night to each other, echoed through the parking lot as Travis smoothed a pale strand of hair that had blown across her eyes.

"It's going to be worse for you. I'd say I'm sorry about that, but I'm not. I enjoyed our dance, Mia. Dance*es*," he corrected with a grin.

Searching his eyes, emotions swirled through her. She saw fierce heat in those dusk blue depths. A heat and wanting that matched her own. She and Travis weren't touching, but he might have been stroking his hands down her body, caressing her breasts and exploring all of her intimate places, for the warmth that swept through her.

Time to take a step back, she thought, panic beginning to seep in.

"I enjoyed them, too. And . . . maybe the talk won't be so bad. Maybe everyone will realize . . . we're just friends now."

His hand gently snagged her arm. "Whoa. Is that what you think? That we're just friends?"

"Are you saying we're not?"

Travis smiled a slow, sexy cowboy smile that turned her heart upside down and inside out. "Word games," he murmured. "That's the English teacher in you. Me, I'd rather play kissing games."

He tugged her close.

She could have said no. Could have moved away.

But she didn't.

Her heart skipped several beats as his arms went snug around her and then she was wrapped in the warmth and strength and scent of him.

Every one of their friends and family were gone now, though the parking lot was still half full. And they were alone outside the Double Cross, alone beneath the pale twinkling of the stars. She ignored the warning voice in her head, lifted her arms to twine them around his neck, and tilted her mouth up to his as he bent to kiss her.

It was a long, slow, searing kiss that made her brain crash like a meteor slamming into the earth. His tongue teased and caressed hers and she felt her legs wobbling, her self-control flying off in the wind. Her hands slid through the thickness of his hair as she pressed closer, needing the heat and taste of him. No—needing more than that. Needing *him. Travis.*

She forgot where she was. She lost herself. In that kiss. In that moment. In Travis.

"Who won the kissing game?" she asked at last, shakily, when they broke apart, both of them breathing hard, staring into each other's eyes.

"I'd call it a tie."

She laughed, her whole body aching for him as she traced a finger along his strong jaw.

A tie. Equal. No winners, no losers.

It sounded so easy.

But Mia had lost before.

A rowdy group of people were bursting out of the Double Cross, singing and laughing, swarming toward them.

"I'll see you Monday," she said, feeling as if she were yanking herself out of a lovely dream; then, before she could change her mind, she pulled away from him and stepped up into her Jeep.

"Count on it." Travis closed the door.

She peeled out of the lot. In her rearview mirror she saw him, all tall and brawny and handsome, watching her drive away. His words echoed in her head. She could still taste his kiss on her mouth.

Count on it.

Could she? Could she count on anything where Travis was concerned? Anything other than that he could still make her heart race and her pulse tingle and her whole body come alive?

Proceed with caution. That's the answer.

But like most things in life, Mia thought, it was a lot easier said than done.

Chapter Fourteen

Early the next morning, Mia planted herself at the kitchen table with a cup of coffee and a bagel and pondered her Starry Night quilt design. She closed her eyes, imagining the midnight blues and the golden stars and swirls of light. If she did it right, it would be beautiful. Perhaps her best quilt ever. For a moment she wished Gram was there to see it and a flicker of loneliness washed over her.

Sometimes she thought that moving back into this house after her divorce had been a huge mistake. Yes, it was her childhood home and yes, she'd been happy here. Happy to open it to Gram and to share it with her in her last years. But now . . .

Now she occasionally felt that she was trapped in the past in some way, unable to move on. However warm and charming and cozy the house was, even with all of the renovations she'd done, she lately still sometimes felt that she didn't belong here anymore.

But if not here, she asked herself, setting down her pencil, *then where?*

For a moment she thought back to last night, when she'd stared into Travis's eyes after Hatcher staggered out of the Double Cross.

Standing there with Travis, the rest of the world forgotten, just as it had been the night they kissed in the front yard, she'd felt something she hadn't felt in a long time.

She couldn't put her finger on it. But it had opened a longing deep inside her.

A longing for Travis?

Not for the boy he'd once been, she realized. Or for the teenaged lovers they'd left behind.

For the man he was now.

A man who was harder, tougher in many ways, and yet gentler. Who just about set her body on fire whenever he looked at her, let alone when he touched her. A man who was a committed father, trying to be there for his son.

A man coming home out of the blue to settle again in Lonesome Way.

And *un*settling her heart.

She set down her second cup of coffee with a thump and narrowly missed spilling it all over the table just as Brittany padded in from the guest room. The girl was wearing gray cotton sleep pants and a faded red tank top and rubbing sleep from her eyes.

Britt had been home and out like a light when Mia returned from the Double Cross shortly after midnight. With a mumbled good morning, she headed for the fridge, and Mia had to smile when Samson stopped eating his kibble to run over and jump on her in greeting.

"Morning, sweetie. How was the party? Did you have fun?"

"Mm-hm. I guess." Lifting out a carton of orange juice, Britt poured herself a glass. Her hair hung in her eyes, hiding them, and Mia couldn't see her expression, could only hear the subdued tone of her voice.

"Everything okay?"

"Yep."

"How about some scrambled eggs? And a bagel."

"I'll just take a granola bar."

She plopped down with her juice and bit into an almond granola bar, pushing her hair out of her face, and for the first time, Mia saw that her eyes were red. She'd been crying.

"Britt . . ." Mia felt the stirring of alarm. "What's wrong, honey? Did something happen at the party?"

"It was . . . okay . . . well, at first." Britt set the granola bar down and stared at it.

Slowly she lifted her gaze to Mia's face and Mia plainly saw the misery there, a misery she was trying very hard to hide.

"And then what? Something happened. Honey, tell me."

A rush of concern filled her as still Britt said nothing.

"Whatever it is, you can talk to me about it. Was it Seth? Did the two of you have an argument?"

"*No*. Seth's great." Brittany's voice began to quaver. "He's really nice. It's just . . . I feel so terrible." She shoved back her uncombed hair and took a deep breath. "Someone spray-painted his truck last night while we were all in Jackie's backyard."

Her gaze slid away.

"Spray-painted his truck?" Mia drew a breath. Apparently she wasn't the only one who'd had a run-in with trouble last night. "Who would do that? What did they write?"

"They didn't write anything. They just sprayed all this purple and black paint all over, including the windows." Britt's tone was subdued. "They must have used up ten, maybe fifteen spray cans of paint. It was a huge mess."

She took another gulp of juice. "Seth was so upset. He said his parents would be furious." Her eyes filled with quick tears. "I feel awful about it!"

Mia reached across the table, took her hand. "I understand, but, honey, it's not your fault."

"I . . . know. I know it isn't . . . but . . ." She swallowed, for a moment looking wildly confused. "It's just that . . . we were all dancing in the backyard and the music was turned up really loud. Maybe if we'd just been paying more attention . . . we—someone—maybe *I* would have noticed that there was somebody out there on the driveway. . . ." Her voice trailed off.

Something that felt like fear turned over inside of Mia. Britt looked truly distraught. And also like she was holding something back. But what?

Unsettled, Mia walked to the coffeepot, thinking hard as she poured herself another cup. Lonesome Way was a pretty quiet town. Of course, teenagers everywhere acted out sometimes, and this town was no different. But here, misbehavior was usually in small, harmless ways. Without much destruction. Serious vandalism was pretty rare.

"I can't imagine who would do something like that," she murmured, her gaze resting on Britt's face. "Can you?"

"N-no." Britt grabbed up the half-eaten granola bar, took another bite, and hastily began to chew. "Seth can't either. We didn't know anything about it until Dan and Lacey went out to Dan's truck to head home—they were the ones who spotted it. No one could believe someone did that right in Jackie's driveway. Jackie's parents were totally freaked out. They called the sheriff and everything."

"So Sheriff Hodge came out? Did anyone see or hear anything? Does he have anything to go on?"

"I . . . I don't think so." Britt swallowed another bite of the granola bar. She didn't look like she was enjoying it much.

"Was anyone else's car spray-painted?"

Britt shook her head. "Only Seth's." She moistened her lips. "He . . . he was so upset. He said his parents will have to call the insurance company and everything."

"Well, I hope Sheriff Hodge catches whoever was behind it."

"So do I!" Britt's tone was so fierce, Mia stared at her.

The girl broke a tiny bit off the last quarter of her granola bar and fed it to Samson, who gently nibbled it, his tail wagging.

"I had an email from my mom and one from my dad this morning." Britt changed the subject abruptly.

"And?" Mia leaned forward. "How are the honeymooners doing?"

"Good, I guess. Mom said Corfu is beautiful. She sent me a photo of her and Alec on the beach—they looked really happy. She wrote that she bought me a present in a shop in some little village down the road from their hotel."

"Lucky you! I don't suppose she mentioned anything about a present for her wonderful baby sister?"

That earned her only a fleeting smile. "Nope. Can't say she did."

"And your dad . . . what's up with him?" Mia asked.

"He has to go to China and then Singapore for some tech conferences. The guy from his company who was supposed to speak at them was in a bad car accident, so Dad has to fill in. He's leaving tomorrow and won't be back for a couple of weeks. Around the same time as Mom. So," she added, biting her lip and trying to muster a smile, "I guess you really are stuck with me for a while. I couldn't go home to Butte now even if I wanted to."

"Not unless you wanted to spend some time with Gwen and Tate."

As Britt's shoulders stiffened, Mia said gently, "Not that I want you to go. We did plan on the whole summer, didn't we?" She set down her coffee cup and pushed back her chair as Samson trotted to the door and looked back at her hopefully. Following him, she opened the door and let him out.

Rain had moved in late last night and the world was washed clean, the sun gleaming across the bright grass and the lavender-gray peaks of the mountains.

"Since you're not working today, how'd you like to take a ride with me out to Aunt Winny's place?" she suggested, returning to her chair.

For the first time, Britt seemed to shake off her dejection. Interest brightened her sea blue eyes. "Really? You're going to see Great-Aunt Winny? I've always wanted to meet her. I heard all those whispers when I was little about how she and Gram got into a big fight and Winny ran away. I always wanted to know what happened. But Mom says Winny doesn't want anything to do with our family."

"That's what Winny says, too. But I'm checking on her whether she likes it or not. And I'm bringing her a Tupperware full of tuna salad and another of fruit. Thought I'd bake up some chocolate-frosted brownies, too. Gram's recipe."

"I'll go with you." For the first time today, Britt's smile looked genuine, even eager as she leaned back in her chair. "Do you really think she'll let us in?"

"Only one way to find out."

⌒

Three hours later Mia took a good look around but spotted no sign of the orange tabby as she and Brittany left the Jeep and made their way across the uneven gravel toward Winny's cabin.

Mia carried the containers of tuna salad and fruit—an assortment of apples, plums, strawberries, and green grapes. Brittany clutched the plate of still-warm-from-the-oven brownies covered in foil.

The desolate little clearing on the side of the mountain was silent but for the wind whining through the pines. It was a lonely sound.

"She really lives here all alone?" Brittany whispered. "It's kind of spooky out here. I'd be scared."

"Winny would have everyone believe she likes it. Maybe she even does." Mia kept her voice low.

Upon reaching the porch, she was pleased to see there were no longer any rotting planks or buckling wood. Denny McDonald had done a seamless repair job. Balancing the food in one hand, Mia knocked sharply on the cabin door with the other.

This time, unlike the last, Winny's gruff voice boomed through the door almost immediately. "I don't remember inviting anyone to my home."

"My mom always taught me that family doesn't need an invitation," Mia called through the door. "How are you feeling, Aunt Winny?"

"I *felt* pretty damned good before someone came down my road and disturbed me."

"Your great-grandniece wants to meet you."

There was silence.

"What's that you say? Who?"

"Brittany. My sister Samantha's daughter."

She looked over at Britt. "Say something," she whispered.

"Hi, Aunt Winny," the girl called out in a high-pitched, breathless tone. "Can we come in? We have brownies and . . . and some other stuff for you. I'm visiting Aunt Mia for the summer and . . . and I've heard so much about you—" She broke off suddenly, flushing. "Nothing bad, of course," she said quickly. "Just about . . . how you hurt your foot and how Aunt Mia's really worried about you."

"I'll just bet she is." The word was a harsh bark. The door remained closed.

"Aunt Winny," Mia tried again, her tone full of determination. "We only want—"

Without warning, the door swung open.

Winona Jane Pruitt stood there in faded yellow cotton pants, a pink and green print top, an old sneaker on one foot and the other wrapped in bandages that left her toes wriggling free. To Mia's surprise, her toenails were painted a glittery sparkling blue, her fingernails bright orange.

She was a slim, tall woman, a good four inches taller than Gram. Her features were sharper, more defined, Mia noticed. There were traces still of striking beauty, even at seventy-odd years. Winny's dark gray hair was still thick and straight. She wore it pulled back into a severe knot at her nape, secured with dozens of brown bobby pins, but it framed a face that had a timeless chiseled elegance.

But that face wore a frown. And there was mistrust simmering in her eyes, which were a deeper brown than Gram's—sable-colored, really—dark and intelligent. And wary.

"Come in then. But be quick about it, if you don't want to let all that hot air in."

She moved aside, her lips compressed tightly together, and Mia slipped past her before she could change her mind. Britt skittered in after Mia, eyes wide. The moment the girl was inside, Winny slammed the door.

The cabin had no air-conditioning and it was warm inside, but a table fan blew the warm air around the somewhat barren, but neat-as-a-pin living room. The furnishings were few—a curved old sofa with springs poking through the floral fabric on one end, floral curtains that once might have been rose colored but were now faded to a blush pink, two matching armchairs with pretty needlepoint cushions propped against their backs, and a small white wicker chest for a coffee table. A birdcage perched on top of a whatnot chest filled with books. Inside the cage a white pot brimmed with ivy, which trailed cheerfully through the bars of the cage.

To Mia's surprise, she spotted the tabby peering warily around the kitchen counter. The cat had looked almost feral the last time Mia had seen it, but now it appeared almost calm, and remarkably at home.

Someone has more of a heart than she's willing to let on, she thought with a glimmer of hope.

"You may as well put whatever you brought over there."

Winny waved a hand toward the kitchen counter and Mia set the tuna salad and fruit on its surface. Britt followed suit with the plate holding the brownies as the cat inched out from behind the counter, swishing its tail.

"Was it you who sent that McDonald boy out here to fix my porch?" Winny demanded, limping to one of the armchairs and sinking down on it with a grimace. Mia wasn't sure if the grimace was due to the pain of walking or their presence in her home.

"I guess you could say I'm guilty as charged." Without waiting to be invited, Mia walked to the sofa and sat down near one end, avoiding the places where the broken springs poked through.

Britt followed suit and perched on the opposite end, leaning forward, her flip-flops resting against the edge of an old blue and red needlepoint rug.

"Well, who asked you to stick your nose—and McDonald's—into my business?" the old woman bit out.

Mia's brows rose. "I didn't want you to trip and get hurt again. That broken board was dangerous. Believe it or not, Aunt Winny, you *do* have people in this town who care about you."

Her aunt snorted and narrowed her eyes. "That's a load of bunk and you know it, young lady. Abner Floyd is the only one in this town who gives a hoot about whether I live or fall off this mountain tomorrow. You're after something, aren't you?"

"You've got me there." Mia smiled. "I do want something. I'll admit it. I want to get to know you."

"So do I," Britt piped up. She looked pretty and flushed and nervous, but she spoke quickly, as if she needed to get the words out. "And my mom does, too. She's always saying we don't have much family left, except for Aunt Mia—and you. And I can tell it makes her sad sometimes—not knowing you, that is. My mom told me you ran away years ago, when you and Gram were young, but none of us know why. Not that we expect you to tell us," she added hastily. "I mean . . . we're curious, of course, but you . . . d-don't have to . . ." Britt's voice trailed off as Winny's cheeks darkened to a deep, mottled shade of plum, and her long slim fingers knotted in her lap.

"Is that what you think? That I ran away?" Winny gave a short laugh, a caustic sound in the tiny cabin. Mia detected sadness beneath it as well.

"We don't exactly know what happened," she replied carefully. "And you don't have to tell us, if you don't want to."

"I don't." Winny's lips clamped together.

"The only thing we care about now is making sure you're all right." Mia cast a reassuring glance at her niece. Britt looked like she was afraid to say anything else, and Mia felt a sudden tinge of worry. Maybe she shouldn't have brought Britt out here today. She'd been upset enough this morning—she didn't need any more drama right now. Despite having admitted them to her home, Winny's manner was nothing short of hostile.

"What does Doc Grantham say about your foot? Is it healing?" She shifted the conversation to what she hoped was a neutral subject.

"Healing? If that's what it's doing, it's sure taking its own sweet time. That doctor changed the bandage and told me to come back in about ten days so he can check things out again. Not that it's anybody's business," she sniffed, throwing Mia a glance that clearly said: *This means you, missy*.

Just then the cat streaked across the room and startled Britt, who gasped as the tabby leaped into Winny's lap and gave the loudest meow Mia had ever heard.

"Hush, you," Winny said absently, but she began to stroke the tabby's head with long, thin fingers. Mia noticed that her eyes had softened the moment the cat landed in her lap.

"I'd be happy to take you to your next appointment at the hospital." Mia leaned back against the sofa, which creaked at the slightest movement. It wasn't very comfortable and she guessed the furniture in the cabin was nearly as old as

Winny herself. "Just tell me the day and time and I'll come pick you up."

"Now, why would you want to do that?"

"Because family helps family."

Winny's skin flushed that deep plum color again. "I'm not part of your family. I was thrown out. Thrown away. Like so much garbage. Anyone ever tell you *that*?"

Mia caught her breath. Shook her head. Glancing at Britt, she saw that the girl's mouth had fallen open.

"No one ever told me anything about what happened. Samantha has no idea either. Gram never talked about it. Or about you. And she didn't tell our mother either."

Winny looked startled, but quickly recovered, wiping away all trace of emotion from her elegantly chiseled face.

"Whatever it was—whatever happened all those years ago—it doesn't matter anymore." Mia met her eyes. "Not to us. You're here, Aunt Winny, and so are we. You're family. We'd all like you to be part of our lives—if you want to be."

Silence as deep as a forgotten well settled over the old cabin.

For almost a minute there was no sound but the whir of the fan, and a clock ticking loudly from another room.

Britt sat as still as stone, a slender figure on the old sofa. Winny stared at Mia, her dark sable eyes seeming to sear into her face. Something flickered in them, something that looked like wonder. And sadness.

Or was it hope?

"You . . . mean that?" Winny asked at last.

"Absolutely. I'm ashamed I haven't tried harder before now." It was true. Guilt pricked at her as she faced the aunt she'd not even made an overture toward for far too long.

"You have your own lives. I can't see why you'd care to bother about mine."

"But we do care." Even as Mia spoke she saw Brittany lean forward.

"Maybe you can tell us some stories one day. About you and Gram when you were growing up."

Winny stiffened and seemed about to say something biting, but then she glanced into the girl's face and her expression softened.

Mia wouldn't exactly describe the way she looked as warm and fuzzy, but whatever sarcastic comment she'd been about to spew was swallowed back. Her long fingers stilled on the tabby's fur.

"Your gram was always the good one," she said at last. "She was sweet, obedient. Everyone loved her from the moment they met her. I was more trouble than a peck of rabid monkeys. And that's most likely all you need to know."

As her aunt wobbled to her feet, indicating the visit was over, Mia realized she now knew more about Gram and Winny than she'd known all the rest of her life.

"So about that doctor's appointment," she said, standing as well, and Britt popped up, too.

Winny eyed Mia skeptically. "A week from Friday. Eleven thirty in the morning." She shrugged. "I was going to reschedule, seeing as Abner was going to take me and I found out he and his brother are going fishing that week. Won't be back until later that night, matter of fact."

Mia smiled. "Not a problem. I'll be here at eleven. We can go to lunch at A Bun in the Oven after your appointment. Their sandwiches are as delicious as the desserts. Have you ever tasted their chicken Caesar wrap? Or the spicy turkey?"

Winny appeared floored by the offer.

"The ride will be much appreciated," she said after a moment. "But I don't want lunch. That bakery's too damned crowded. And I'm not much of a people person, as they say," she muttered.

Now, there's the understatement of the year. Mia suppressed the laugh that bubbled in her throat.

"Well, people person or not," she continued, heading toward the door, "if you'd like to come to supper one night, we'd love to have you. Anytime. Four forty-two Larkspur Road. Samantha always invites me to Butte for Thanksgiving and Christmas dinners and most years I go there for one or both. You're welcome to drive along with me anytime you want. I know Sam would love for you to join us, so I hope you'll keep that in mind."

"Don't be holding your breath. I'm not one for family get-togethers either." Winny looked like she'd rather shack up with a skunk than come to a holiday dinner.

"Think it over and if you—" Mia broke off as for the first time she noticed the wicker basket sitting atop an old brass trunk beneath the window. It overflowed with a pile of fabric scraps and some red and green calico quilt squares.

Stopping short, she whirled to stare at her aunt, who was limping along behind them toward the door.

"I never knew you quilted, Aunt Winny."

As the old woman's eyes locked on hers, Mia had the sensation that another wall was shooting up. Winny seemed to withdraw even more deeply into herself, as if gathering her secrets close, hiding them behind a stone facade.

Then she remembered. *Quilt.* Winny had burned Gram's wedding quilt.

I'm an idiot, she thought, wishing she could stuff the words back in her mouth, but it was too late for that.

"You can go on all you want about us being family, girl, but there's a lot more about me you don't know. Things you don't ever want to know. And you never will," her aunt snapped, immediately reverting back to her former prickly self.

Don't be so sure. But curiosity vied with sympathy as Mia cast one last glance at her aunt's unyielding face. She felt unexpectedly sorry for the old woman even as Winny slammed the door shut the moment she and Britt stepped outside, leaving them on the porch without so much as a good-bye.

"That didn't go so well," Britt whispered as they hurried toward the Jeep.

"Well . . . sometimes progress comes in baby steps. We'll see," Mia added as they left the windswept clearing and pulled out onto Sweetwater Road. "I think we may have inched a tiny bit forward today."

"Really? How can you tell?" Britt switched on the radio and Faith Hill's rich voice filled the Jeep. "Aunt Winny is so . . . so . . ."

"Recalcitrant? Secretive? Skittish?" Mia suggested.

Britt broke into her first real grin of the day. "*D.* All of the above."

Chapter Fifteen

✥

Leaning back in his desk chair on Monday, Travis held his cell phone to his ear and listened to his old friend Marcus Belmont bullshitting about how he deserved a half-million-dollar finder's fee for referring five guys who would be ideal recruits for Tanner Security. Outside the window of Travis's Oak Street office, it was a busy afternoon in Lonesome Way.

A few boys about Grady's age played catch in the park. An elderly couple shuffled from the Toss and Tumble Laundromat with a basket of folded laundry clutched between them. Chatty young mothers pushed their babies on swings near the rock garden in the park.

Three blocks down, on Main, he could see people flowing in and out of Benson's Drugstore. He heard ranch hands calling to each other in greeting as they paused outside the hardware store or parked their trucks down the street from Tobe's Mercantile.

Through the open window he saw Sheriff Hodge amble out of Pepper Rony's Pizza with a carry-out box, and a bunch of teenage boys jostling and shoving and goofing off outside the Lickety Split Ice Cream Parlor.

He was sure that, a few blocks over, A Bun in the Oven was bustling with people munching on cinnamon buns, sour cream coffee cake, and fresh baked cookies as they sipped specialty teas and cappuccinos.

He'd be headed there himself soon to pick up Grady. He'd left him sitting at one of the smaller booths in the rear of the bakery with his backpack, a comic book, a handheld video game, a roast beef sandwich on sourdough, and a peanut butter cookie.

Sophie and her grandmother, who helped her run the bakery, and Brittany, who'd been working the cash register and mentioned something about Mia spending the morning preparing for the tutoring session, had all promised to look after him.

Glancing at his watch, Travis realized it was almost two. He needed to get Grady over to Mia's house pronto.

"Yeah, yeah, in your next life," he interrupted Marcus, unable to keep from grinning. Marcus Belmont, a forty-one-year-old, six-foot, four-inch former Navy SEAL who'd retired from the Secret Service the previous February, was a master at the art of bullshitting. "Tell them to call me and I'll set up a video meeting. If I hire even two of them, I'll buy you dinner at the Golden Fox the next time I make it back to Georgetown. Maybe five, six years from now. At the earliest."

He laughed at Marcus's reply. The guy should get a medal for being able to string that many four-letter words together in a single sentence.

"Yeah, more than a dozen clients lined up already. Some real heavy hitters," he told Marcus, one eye on his watch. "So I need guys who can get off to a running start by the end of the month. One client is headed to Greece for that economic summit and needs round-the-clock protection for six weeks minimum. I'll let you know the details tomorrow.

Sure thing, get back to me in the morning. Anyone you think is up to it, have them fax me their resumes."

Ending the call, Travis glanced around the office space he'd rented. He only had two desks and office chairs so far—one here in his own office, with a view that included Oak Street and a section of the park, the second set in the reception area. The rest of the furniture and all the computer and video-monitoring equipment would be delivered by the end of the week.

In the meantime, he had his fax, his laptop, and his cell phone—and it was enough for now. Things were coming together very quickly in a short space of time. Word had gotten out that he was hiring and wanted only the best. His contacts in the military and the Justice Department had been referring clients to him right and left. He was interviewing for an office manager tomorrow, but for the rest of today, it was all about Mia and Grady.

He was praying his son would take the tutoring as seriously as he needed to.

Locking the office door behind him, Travis sprinted down the stairs and stepped out onto Oak Street, crossing quickly toward Main.

When he entered the bakery, the delicious scent of fresh-baked bread and pastries filled his nostrils. Sophie's grandmother, Ava Louise Todd, peered at him from the cash register with a welcoming smile.

"Hello again, Travis. Your young man's right back there where you left him—hasn't made so much as a peep." She chuckled. "He's all caught up in that comic book of his. Just let me know if either of you needs anything else."

"I'd love a dozen or so of every cake, pie, and cookie in the place, Mrs. Todd, but then you'd be out of business before closing time."

"Goodness, no, I can whip up more before you blink." She chuckled, then slanted him a sparkling glance. "I heard you and Mia Quinn were dancing it up at the Double Cross the other night." The keen glance she sent him was full of equal parts kindness and avid curiosity. "Folks are saying you two might be getting back together. Is that true?"

"Mrs. Todd, you know a gentleman never tells." Travis's eyes gleamed at her. "Guess you'd have to ask the lady."

A smile spread across her gently lined face. "I might just do that," she told him with a nod. As Travis turned toward the booths in the back of the bakery he swore he could feel her vibrant green eyes piercing into his back.

The town matchmakers must be having a field day, he thought. Mia was *not* going to be amused. Somehow the idea only made him grin.

Most of the tables and booths were full, but he had no trouble spotting Grady in the last booth, his nose still in the comic book. The boy hadn't even looked up when Travis entered.

As he moved toward the back, Brittany breezed out of the kitchen carrying a fresh-baked cherry pie in an open white bakery box.

"Hi, Mr. Tanner—I mean, Travis," she said as she passed him. "Your son is so cute. He hasn't budged once from that booth." She rushed past him toward the front counter.

But as he reached Grady's table he heard a shriek and a loud thump from the front of the bakery, and a gasp went up among the customers even as Travis wheeled around.

It was Brittany who'd shrieked. She'd dropped the pie on the floor and it had spilled out of the box. Bright cherry filling and juice and pastry oozed in a red gooey puddle across the previously spotless floor.

She stood beside the disaster but she wasn't looking down at it. She was staring instead at the smiling young man coming through the doorway of the bakery.

"Geez, I'm sorry. I didn't mean to startle you," he said, his voice full of contrition as he approached the counter.

Travis had never seen him before but he looked to be about nineteen. Twenty at most. He was clean-cut, with a husky build, fair hair, long jaw. He wore flashy cowboy boots. Expensive looking, Travis thought. In contrast, the kid had on a plain gray T-shirt and a well-worn pair of jeans.

He looked pleasant enough, but for some reason Mia's niece stood frozen and, oddly, she couldn't seem to tear her gaze from him.

"I'm sorry," the guy said again, his smile turning more concerned. "Can I help you clean that up?"

But Mrs. Todd bustled forward.

"Never mind, young man, I'll take care of it. Brittany, dear, don't you worry. I've dropped a few pies in my day, too—and so has Sophie. That goes for Karla McDonald, too—and for that matter, Seth, and everyone else who's ever worked here. It happens now and then. You just go ahead and wait on this young man."

"I'm s-so sorry, Mrs. T-Todd," Brittany stammered.

"Not a problem. Now, if you start getting the dropsies twice a day, that's a different story." The white-haired woman laughed and patted the girl's arm before heading in back for a mop.

"Dad, can I have another cookie?" Grady asked as Ava Todd disappeared into the kitchen. Travis dragged his gaze away from Brittany and the guy at the counter to glance down at his son.

"What did you say?" He was still distracted. Something about what had just happened struck a strange chord somewhere in his gut. He couldn't quite put his finger on it.

"I really want another cookie. Please?"

"Oh. Sure." He ruffled Grady's hair. "Peanut butter again? How about we get you one for the road?"

Brittany was talking to the kid at the counter. He was pointing at something in the display case, a smile still on his face. Their interaction seemed perfectly normal, but . . .

I've been on the FBI payroll too long, Travis told himself. Mia's niece was obviously just the jumpy sort. She'd been on edge the night Travis first met her, too.

Stuffing his gear in his backpack, Grady slid out of the booth. "I just hope it won't be too hard," he said in a low tone, looking worried.

"Hope what won't be too hard?"

"English and earth science. The tutoring." Grady sighed. "All the homework and stuff."

Travis studied the uneasy expression in his son's eyes. "It might be hard," he told the boy steadily, "but I know you can handle it. You want this, don't you?"

"I want to pass into sixth grade more than anything."

"Then you'll make it happen." Travis hated the self-doubt he saw in Grady's face. "Just take your best shot. Don't waste it. Grab it and make the most of it."

The same could be said, Travis realized, about his relationship with Mia.

Not that he and Mia actually *had* a relationship. *Yet*.

But he was working on it. He wasn't exactly sure what it was, or where it was going . . . but they were feeling their way. He knew, though, that he could only afford to take things day by day for so long. Whatever happened, he didn't want to hurt her ever again. He'd have to figure it all out soon—before one or both of them got in too deep.

He needed to give it *his* best shot. *If* they were starting over—and not just getting each other out of their systems once and for all. . . .

As they moved up the aisle between the tables and booths, his attention shifted to the husky kid leaving the bakery. Travis watched him lope off down the street with a white pastry sack in his hand.

"We'll take another peanut butter cookie to go," Travis told Brittany, noting that she looked upset.

Her hand trembled as she reached for the cookie and stuffed it into a bag.

"You okay?" Travis asked. "You know that guy who just left here? Did he say something to upset you?"

Her eyes widened. "N-no. I'm just having a bad day. I

think I had too much caffeine or something." Her smile looked forced. "I didn't get much sleep last night."

If you say so, Travis thought. Something was off. He didn't press her, though, not now, while she was at work. He made a mental note to mention it to Mia later when they had a moment alone.

If they had a moment alone.

He hoped like hell they would. Actually, when it came right down to it, he hoped they'd have a whole lot more than a moment.

Chapter Sixteen

❦

"I have to read this book by *when*?"

Mia pushed the copy of Louis Sachar's *Holes* closer to Grady. She'd checked it out from the Lonesome Way library so he could get started right away.

"Next Monday. A week from today. And write a two-page book report on it."

She couldn't help but smile at the shocked expression on his face. Grady dragged a hand through his hair in a gesture so much like one she'd seen Travis use that she almost laughed out loud.

"Oh, man," he groaned.

"According to your dad you used to love to read."

"I did . . . I do. But now I like riding horses, too, and working in the barn and stuff." He set his elbows on the table, his long-lashed green eyes intent. "Uncle Rafe's going to teach me how to start a horse. I have to just watch for a while first. That means I need to spend a whole lot of time in the corral with him or Will so I can see how they do it—"

He broke off and peered at Mia with a hopeful smile. "Are you *sure* I have to finish the whole book by Monday?" he asked. "*And* do all that science homework?"

"Are you *sure* you want to pass that proficiency test?"

A slow grin spread across his face. "Positive."

"Then I guess you know the answer to that question. How about some more lemonade?"

"Sure. I mean . . . thanks," he added.

Mia moved to the counter and brought the lemonade pitcher to the kitchen table, refilling his glass as birds sang outside the open window, almost as loudly as the shouts coming from across the street. It was after four and Ellis Stone's twin grandsons were playing catch in her front yard, laughing and hooting over every dropped ball or bad throw.

She'd found herself surprised when Travis dropped Grady off earlier. She'd seen little today of the lost-looking boy who'd barely glanced up the first time she met him at Sage Ranch. The boy Travis ushered into her house two hours ago was surprisingly pleasant—and more talkative than she'd expected. He'd asked her several rapid-fire questions about Samson after the dog raced over to him when he walked in the door. And he'd sat patiently, even attentively, at her kitchen table during the first hour as she'd reviewed with him the names and characteristics of all the planets—the first section of the core fifth-grade earth science curriculum he needed to master.

"Can I *see* any of these planets when I look at the sky?" he interrupted at one point.

"Several of them—if you look at the right times. Venus, Jupiter, and Mars are three of the brightest. You can also see Saturn and Mercury with the naked eye."

Mia had smiled at the excitement in his face.

"Maybe your dad will show them to you one night. And if he doesn't know where they are, I can point them out to both of you. But once you learn, you'll always know how to find them in the sky."

"Cool." Grady's eyes lit up. "You know what would be fun? To ride way up into the mountains one night and be really high up. You know, closer to the planets, and see them from there. With no buildings around, or other people or anything . . . just the sky."

"That *would* be cool." Mia smiled. Travis's son might not have been born in Montana, but he had the soul of a cowboy. "I bet your dad would take you up into the mountains for a camping trip sometime if you asked him."

"Yeah, he told me he would. He promised me we'd go camping before I have to go back to L.A."

The face he made showed clearly what he thought of that idea.

"Do you miss your friends there and your mom?" Mia asked lightly.

He shrugged, looked down. "I don't have that many friends and . . . yeah, I miss my mom sometimes. But I don't see her too much anyway. Not like when we lived in Arizona. She's always going out someplace with my stepdad— or getting *dressed* to go someplace. Or shopping for clothes to go someplace. We have a housekeeper, Mrs. Landen. She's okay. She watches TV a lot in her room. So I just play video games or watch my own TV. I have a big flat-screen in my room—fifty inches."

"That must be nice." But a fifty-inch TV was no substitute for family time. Or attention, Mia thought.

Her heart went out to this little boy with the long eyelashes and an innate sense of curiosity. Grady had a love for horses and dogs and the outdoors. He was smart and sweet and just a little bit young for his age. There was a vulnerability about him that suddenly struck her like a dart to the chest and made her more determined than ever to ensure he passed that proficiency test.

Travis had better be able to talk his ex-wife out of sending Grady away. The boy loved the outdoors too much to be cooped up in a boarding school night and day, with corridors full of other kids, and pranks and pressure, and little chance to just be a kid himself.

If Grady found out his mother and stepfather intended to send him away . . .

She closed her eyes a moment at the thought. Her throat ached imagining the effect it would have on him.

Travis was right. Grady wasn't a child who didn't want to learn. He was a child who'd flourish with the right guidance, someone taking the time to nurture him, encourage him. All he needed was someone to show an interest.

Travis will convince Val not to do this. He has to.

And at that moment she heard his Explorer pull up into the driveway.

Ever the faithful guard dog, Samson hurled himself toward the front door and Grady bolted from his chair. Boy and dog raced for the front door and, amused, Mia followed them.

Grady wasted no time flying across the lawn to greet his father.

"I've got tons of homework," he announced. "But I'll do it," he added quickly, with a glance over his shoulder as the screen door banged shut behind Mia and, smiling, she walked across the porch.

"What's going on at the cabin?" the boy asked as Samson dashed in circles around Travis, his tail wagging furiously. "We're still moving in tomorrow, right, Dad?"

"If our beds and the new fridge get delivered on time."

"All right!"

Travis grinned at his son's enthusiasm, then his gaze shifted to Mia. He felt something clench in his heart at the sight of her in that sweetly sexy yellow sundress, her shoulders bare, her hair loosely twisted atop her head.

"How about the three of us going out to dinner?" he said.

Surprise flashed in Mia's eyes but before she could reply, Samson began to bark again and two skinny figures bounded onto Mia's front lawn.

Evan and Justin, Ellis's twin grandsons, screeched to a halt. Evan threw himself to his knees in the soft grass to pet Samson while Justin said, "Hi, Ms. Quinn."

"Hi, Justin. Hi, Evan." She smiled as the boys eyed Grady with friendly curiosity. There weren't any other kids their age on the street. She introduced Travis first, then his son.

"Want to come over to our grandma's house and play ball?" Evan asked Grady as Samson licked his face, ears, and neck.

He turned eagerly to Travis. "Can I, Dad?"

"Is your grandmother at home?" Travis asked the boys.

"Yeah, she's on her laptop, working on her blog," Justin said.

"She likes us to play outside while she's writing. So we're out of her hair," Evan added.

Travis turned back to Grady, saw the hopeful gleam in his eyes. He remembered that back home Grady said he had only one friend. Scott. One friend could be plenty if it was a good one, but right now he had a shot at two.

"Sure, go ahead. I'll call you when it's time to head out." He was rewarded by a huge grin. An instant later all three boys were running back across the street, whooping just for the fun of it.

"How'd it go?" he asked Mia, coming up to join her on the porch. Somehow they ended up sitting side by side on the swing. Samson had looked like he wanted to run across the street with the kids, but in the end decided to chase a butterfly around the lilac bush instead.

"Not bad. Not bad at all. Grady was a little shell-shocked at the amount of homework, but he's so smart, Travis. And very sweet. I contacted his English teacher and according to her, he was doing great in English all year long and only got that D because he didn't turn in half of his assignments during the last month of school—and then there was that little matter of skipping class several times a week. Which in turn helped get him suspended. Up until that point, Mrs. Larson said he was pulling mostly A's and a few B's."

"And earth science?"

She sighed. "I'm guessing he failed that class in part because he hated his teacher. He told me Mr. Fracken was so boring he could put a rock to sleep. I think I'll be able to make things a little more exciting for him."

A slow smile tugged at the corners of Travis's lips. "You only have to look at me and I get excited."

"Give me a break."

"The lady thinks I'm kidding." He captured her hand in his, closing his fingers snugly around hers.

His hand felt warm and strong. *Solid,* she thought. *A hand to hold on to.*

"I've never been more serious," he insisted.

"And I've got a stake in a gold mine up in Wild Bull Basin I want to sell you," she shot back. *Keep it light,* she told herself. *He's flirting with you. It doesn't mean anything. It doesn't have to mean anything.*

And she didn't want it to, she told herself. But it would be so much easier if she didn't yearn to kiss him every time they were within a dozen yards of each other.

"Did you speak to Val yet? Or Drew?" She deliberately changed the subject.

The smile faded from his face. "Tried to, but it was a bust. For now. Val blew me off. Said they were still busy getting ready for this party they're throwing, and claimed Drew was far too swamped to talk to me. She said it would have to wait. It sounded like she was on the verge of telling me something else, too, but then she seemed to change her mind."

"I'm sorry."

His booted foot absently pushed the swing. The gentle rhythmic movement felt relaxing as Travis held her hand in his and the sun sparkled across her daffodils and peonies.

"Don't be. This is a battle that hasn't even started yet. I'll give her a few more days and then I'm going to get Drew on the line. But"—he grimaced—"it's Val I don't understand. For the life of me, I can't figure out what's gotten into her.

She seems to care more about her lifestyle now than her son. Val was an assistant manager at a temp agency when I met her. She was down-to-earth, hardworking. A bit nervous and, I guess, needy, after losing her husband, but she was a devoted mother. I mean, yeah, she always liked nice things, and she was maybe a little too into buying 'stuff,' just for the sake of buying it, but now . . ." He blew out a breath. "Now she acts like having that fancy mansion and lots of rich friends and being married to Mr. Corporate Hotshot are the most important things in her life. I don't even recognize the woman I was married to."

"Grady's lucky to have *you* right now, Travis. And since you're his father legally you have as much of a say as she does about his schooling. About everything."

"That's for damned sure." His tone hardened. "I've already put in a call to a lawyer. And whether he likes it or not, I'm going to have a few choice words for Drew Baylor— even if it means I have to fly out there and crash their fancy party." His eyes glinted the cool blue of mountain frost. "Think it would get his attention if I threw Mr. Big Shot into the swimming pool in front of all their guests?"

"You wouldn't." Mia's dimples popped out as she looked into Travis's determined blue eyes. Suddenly she had to bite back a laugh. "Seriously, Travis, not a good idea."

He pulled her into his arms. "I do have a *few* good ideas, though. Like kissing you. Right now. Long and deep and slow. Sounds damned good to me."

"Um, I don't think so."

Following her glance he saw that Grady, Justin, and Evan had just raced to the front of Ellis's house and were now sharing two skateboards, each of them taking turns riding up and down the street.

Grady waved happily to him and Travis let go of Mia to wave back.

"Bad timing," he muttered as she laughed and slid away, putting a few respectable inches between them.

"Okay, I'll take a rain check on the good stuff." Travis settled his back against the swing, looked at her with a grin. "So how about dinner? You, me, Grady—Lucky Punch Saloon. I hear there's a Monday special on T-bones."

Mia was trying not to stare longingly at his mouth. She knew from past experience—too many past experiences— how those firm lips felt against hers, how they tasted of fire and spice.

She knew what his kisses did to her.

"I have a better idea." With an effort, she willed her attention back to practicalities. The boys were yelling as they skate-boarded, and Samson was barking at them from her front lawn like he'd never seen boys playing before. "I already have chicken ready for frying. And I was going to fix fresh green beans and mashed potatoes, too. There's some leftover chocolate-frosted brownies for dessert." Her head tilted as she studied him. "Why don't you and Grady join me and Britt?"

Britt. He needed to talk to Mia about Britt. But first things first. She was watching him, waiting for an answer.

"Would that be your mom's fried chicken recipe?" Travis's smile was hopeful. He'd been invited to Mia's house for dinner countless times when they were dating. Her mother knew how much he loved her fried chicken and made it more often than not when he was joining them.

"The one and only."

"And your grandmother's chocolate-frosted brownies?"

"None other."

He grinned. "You got yourself a deal. But I get a rain check on the Lucky Punch."

Mia wanted so much to reach out, brush her hand across his dark-stubbled jaw. She wanted to smile at him and lean closer, breathing in his scent, his strength, the easygoing warmth that had drawn her to him since that day when she was fourteen and he lifted up her fallen backpack, making everyone else in the high school hallway fade to a non-descript grayish blur.

Instead she exercised every bit of her willpower and merely nodded and stood up. "Sure," she said casually. "You want a rain check, cowboy, you've got one."

Before he could guess how close she was to doing something impulsive and dangerous, like smiling at him, running her fingers through his dark hair, or kissing him in broad daylight, she walked into the safety of the house and started fixing supper.

⌒

As it turned out, Britt wasn't able to make it home for dinner. She called Mia to say she had a date with Seth and promised to be home by ten thirty.

Grady, on the other hand, devoured his supper. He seemed to love her mother's fried chicken recipe every bit as much as Travis did. After making short work of four chicken legs, a thigh, and three helpings of mashed potatoes, he pronounced it the best supper *ever*. He was halfway through his second brownie when Ellis called Mia's cell, inviting Grady to join her grandsons at a sleepover.

Ellis's daughter and her husband had gone out of town overnight and Ellis said she had the night off from the hospital and would be keeping the boys until tomorrow. "We're going to roast marshmallows in just a few minutes, and then Justin and Evan are planning an Indiana Jones movie marathon. They want to know if Grady can join them. He's very welcome to come."

Grady turned eagerly toward Travis when Mia repeated the invitation, his face flushed with excitement. "Can I? Please, Dad?"

"Sure. It's nice of Mrs. Stone to invite you, so remember to thank her, okay? How about if I go home and pack up your pajamas and toothbrush and bring them back for you?"

He might have offered the boy the moon, the stars, and all of the planets Mia had been teaching him about that afternoon.

Grady leaped out of his chair. "Can I go over there right now? Please?"

Ellis heard him over the phone. "We're about to roast those marshmallows," she reminded Mia with a laugh. "So the sooner he gets here the better."

Mia relayed the message and Travis said, "First you might want to thank Mia for the wonderful supper."

"Thank you for the wonderful supper. It was great!" he added enthusiastically. "Especially the mashed potatoes and the chicken!"

Then he hugged his dad, grabbed his backpack with his books and homework, and raced out the door.

Travis helped her clean up and load the dishes in the dishwasher. He insisted on washing the pots and pans while she wrapped up the leftovers and wiped the table.

"Come back to the ranch with me while I get Grady's gear," he said when the kitchen was tidy. "After we drop his stuff off at Ellis's, we'll go for a ride."

"A ride?" Her brows lifted. "Where?"

"The cabin. It's in pretty good shape now, if I do say so myself. I want to show it to you."

Say no.

She and Travis all alone out there at the old Tanner cabin? Half a mile from Sage Ranch and no one around except the rabbits, deer, and coyotes?

It was a terrible idea.

She opened her mouth to tell him a more tactful version of that. The words *Maybe another time* were on the tip of her tongue. But instead she heard herself say, "I need to take Samson for a walk first."

"Great." He flashed her a quick, easy grin that made her stomach do a few somersaults. "I'll go with you. You never know what kind of lowlifes might be lurking on Larkspur Road."

With that, he picked up the dog's leash from the countertop, and Samson, done with his kibble, came running.

Watching him snap the leash on her little dog, Mia won-dered if she should be running, too. In the opposite direction.

But, she thought as the three of them slipped out the front door into the early evening hush of the neighborhood, maybe it was time she stopped running from her feelings for Travis. Maybe what she needed was to stand her ground and figure out where they went from here.

Chapter Seventeen

During the drive to the cabin, Travis filled Mia in on every-thing that had gone down with Brittany at A Bun in the Oven.

She listened in taut silence, hearing him out completely before speaking.

"And she was frightened? You're sure? Or was she only upset about dropping that pie?"

"She looked frozen." Travis glanced away momentarily from the empty road to note the apprehension in Mia's eyes. "I'm not trying to scare you, but something definitely didn't feel right. I'd never seen the guy before, but from the instant he walked in, Brittany seemed to freak out. Right before he arrived, she was doing fine, and then she dropped that pie and . . ." He shook his head. "She was scared. I'd swear to it. Not that she admitted it when I asked her if anything was wrong."

Tension knotted in the pit of Mia's stomach. Her heart began to race—and not in a good way. "I really don't like the sound of this. At all. Tell me what he looked like."

Travis made a left turn off Squirrel Road onto Hawk's Way. They were nearing the cabin.

"I'd put him at five ten, eleven tops. Husky build, short, sandy-colored hair. Smiled a lot. He wore flashy cowboy boots so I took him for a tourist. I'd put his age around nineteen or twenty. I haven't seen him around before."

A tiny chill quivered down Mia's spine as a memory struck her.

That day she and Britt had gone shopping at Top to Toe. She'd watched Britt head toward the bakery, and Seth hold the door open for her.

A boy was watching from across the street. A boy with a husky build, short fair hair . . .

"I think I may have seen him—or someone who looks like him. There was a boy who stared at Britt one day when she was going back to work. I didn't think anything of it at the time—she's so pretty, and boys always look at pretty girls."

"Where was he exactly? Did he approach her?"

"No, he wasn't anywhere near her. He'd just come out of Ponderosa Earl's. He seemed to be watching her while she was fooling around with Seth. They were just talking and laughing in the doorway of the bakery, like kids do. Then they went inside and . . ." Mia broke off. "He saw me looking over at him. But it didn't seem to bother him at all. He smiled at me and then he walked away. He had a large shopping bag—lots of purchases from Earl's. It looked like one of them was a sleeping bag. I didn't think anything of it. And I haven't seen him around since."

She grabbed her purse and dug for her cell. "Travis, Brittany left Butte for some reason she never explained. She showed up at my house right before Sam left for her honeymoon. She refused to stay with her father as she'd planned, and wouldn't tell me or Sam why." Panic rose in her chest as she finally seized her phone and began punching in Britt's cell number. "What if this boy had been bothering her?

Following her, stalking her or something? And she was trying to get away from him? What if that's why she came to Lonesome Way? I need to talk to her right now and see if she's all right."

Travis was silent as he parked the Explorer in front of the cabin. He hated seeing the tension in her face as she pressed the cell to her ear, her fingers clamped around it. Even the muscles in her slender throat were tight.

"She's not answering. I don't like this." Mia chewed her lip in frustration. "Maybe we should . . . Oh! Britt! Britt, honey, are you okay? Where are you?"

The tension in her face eased as she listened to her niece's voice. "All right, enjoy the movie. But I need to talk to you. As soon as possible. No, honey, your mom's fine and so's your dad. We just need to talk. So come straight home after the movie, okay? Promise me."

Slowly she lowered the phone and dropped it back into her purse. "She's okay, she's with Seth. They met for supper at the drive-through and now they're at a movie." Her shoulders slumped with relief.

"The movie's about to start, but I told her . . . well, you heard. I'll talk to her later and this time I'm going to get some answers."

"If you want I'll hang around and talk to her, too. If you think it would help."

Gratitude welled in her throat. "Thank you. I might take you up on that."

Her heart rate was finally returning to normal. At least, she thought, as normal as it could get with Travis sitting two feet away, looking too handsome for words, and as at ease in this big open clearing as a mountain lion on a bluff.

She pushed the door of the Explorer open and climbed out before she could get lost in those distractingly sexy blue eyes.

But as she closed the SUV's door and glanced around, she got lost in something else—the delicate beauty of the rose and gold sunset—and the sight of the sprawling cabin before her.

Nestled amid tall cottonwoods and pines, the cabin looked big and sturdy against the sunset-painted sky. Her gaze took in the generous-sized porch. There was plenty of space for a garden and a barbecue pit, along with a patio or deck.

The setting couldn't have been lovelier with its backdrop of trees and the sweep of grassland and mountains as far as the eye could see. Tall peaks loomed dark in the distance as the glowing apricot sun dipped behind the pines, and lavender night rolled in like soft thunder.

A sharp wind blew down from the mountains, rustling the summer leaves. Mia had changed into jeans and a tan cotton sweater before leaving her house since even in the summer the temperature could dip into the forties at night, but she realized she could have actually used a jacket tonight. Shivering a little, she turned toward Travis as he came up beside her.

"It's wonderful. I'd forgotten what a beautiful spot this is."

"I'd forgotten, too. I've been away too long." As she shivered again, he took her hand and drew her toward the house.

"Come on, I'll get a fire going, then give you the tour. If we open any of the windows facing west, you can hear the creek. And there's a great view of the Crazies from the master bedroom."

The moment the words were out of his mouth, he wanted to bite them back. Master bedroom. Now she'd think he was trying to steer her into his bed.

But . . . wasn't he?

"I didn't mean that the way it came out," he said, stopping short.

"Uh-huh. Sure you didn't."

Slipping free of his grasp and trying to hide a smile, she moved ahead of him toward the wide porch, leaving Travis to linger a moment behind her, enjoying the delicious sway of her hips. Not to mention the way her snug jeans hugged her curvy little butt.

"This porch looks plenty big enough for a swing," she remarked over her shoulder.

"There'll be one soon. I have some fond memories of porch swings."

He heard her little choke of laughter ahead of him and suddenly wanted her with an intensity that rocked him. No one laughed like Mia. Soft and low and sexy, full of joy. Something about the sound made him hungry to make love to her that very minute. On the swing that he didn't yet have.

He lengthened his stride to catch up to her and caught her hand as they went up the steps.

Inside, he flicked on the lights and waited as she stared around in amazement.

"Travis, it's incredible. I can't believe what you've done. The last time I was here . . ."

Her voice trailed off, but he remembered. The last time he'd brought her here the outside of the cabin had been muddy, the grounds choked with weeds, all the windows smudged and filthy. They'd been in high school then and Travis had wanted to show it to her, since one day, according to his grandfather's will, the cabin would be his.

But it had been dark and musty then, the corners shadowed with spiderwebs, and mouse droppings littering the scarred old floor. It had given Mia the creeps and they hadn't stayed long. She couldn't wait to get out of there.

Now . . .

Now the place shone with light and wood and warmth. She took in the comfortable leather furniture, the gleaming hickory floors and richly colored throw rugs. The big windows and open floor plan. Airiness, warmth, and space.

A big stone fireplace and mantel dominated one wall of the living room.

"I like the new paint," she murmured, sniffing at the faint, fresh scent of the sage green walls.

"It's all new throughout the house. And the new appliances are in, too, except for the fridge. That's being delivered tomorrow."

Travis got busy loading logs into the hearth. "New windows are on the agenda next, as soon as I get around to it. I had everything else renovated about five years ago."

After the fire roared to life, he switched on the handsome brass table lamp beside the fawn-colored sofa. The living room was flooded with more light.

"Denny McDonald and his dad did the work back then. I was still married to Val at the time and I had it in my head that we could come out here with Grady, use the place as a second home on long weekends—and maybe even longer during the summers. But things didn't work out that way," he added as he led her through the wide dining room with its big bay window and view of the mountains. He let Mia precede him into the spacious kitchen with its farmhouse table and chairs, and a curving black granite island flanking the breakfast area.

"Why not? What happened?" She slipped onto one of the caramel-colored leather stools along the island as Travis scraped a hand through his hair and studied her with a rueful expression.

"What I should have guessed would happen. Val balked about coming back after the one time we stayed at Sage Ranch for a few days with Rafe and Ivy."

Mia's slender brows lifted.

"She thought both the ranch and this cabin were too isolated. Said she liked city living." Travis shook his head. "She claimed she could never feel comfortable out here in the middle of nowhere, that she couldn't relax so far from civilization. Lonesome Way being all of ten miles away," he added dryly.

"Ouch." Mia knew living in a small town—or on a ranch outside of a small town—even for a short time wasn't everybody's cup of tea. But for a man like Travis, whose family was firmly rooted in Montana, it must have been a hard pill to swallow.

"The three of us never came back. But then, the three of us didn't last that much longer." He leaned a hip against the island. He was close enough to touch, but Mia didn't dare touch him right now. He looked too good. Way too good in that black polo and jeans. His tall body taut and muscular, his dark hair glinting almost blue-black in the kitchen light.

They were all alone in this house, and if she wasn't careful, she'd be kissing him instead of merely drinking in the nearness of him. And kissing him now . . . *here* . . . could lead to a whole lot more. . . .

Don't even go there, she thought with a hint of panic. She spoke quickly to stop the wanderings of her mind. "I'm sorry. It must have been rough. The whole breakup thing."

"Yeah, it was, but mostly because of how it affected Grady." There was a low note of regret in his tone. And total honesty in his face. "I think Val and I had both begun to realize that we'd rushed into our marriage without knowing all that much about each other. Much as I hate to say it, I suspect part of me was more in love with the idea of being a father to Grady than I was with Val."

He broke off suddenly and looked at her. "Sorry. I didn't bring you all the way out here to talk about Val." He thrust a hand through his hair. "How about a glass of wine?"

"Wine sounds good." She smiled wryly. "It might relax me before I have that little conversation with Britt later."

Plucking a bottle of red wine from a cooler, Travis poured generously into two glasses. He handed one to her and took a seat on the stool beside her.

"To good days ahead." His gaze was steady on hers as they clinked glasses. "And good nights," he added with a grin that made her tingle down to the soles of her feet.

She fought to keep herself from getting lost in those keen eyes, in the warmth of that Travis Tanner grin. Even in the slant of his jaw, where a dark fringe of five o'clock stubble cast a sexy shadow that made her want to reach out and touch him. Everywhere.

"To your new home." Her voice came out sounding a little bit breathless, and she quickly took a sip of wine.

Travis drank, too, then slowly set his wineglass down on the counter.

"How about to getting everything out in the open?"

She froze.

"Everything like . . . what?"

"Like the past. *Us*. More specifically, what I *did* to us."

Her heart began to thud. "Travis, you don't have to—"

"Yes. I do. *We* do. We need to get this out there. Deal with it. Right now," he said quietly. "I've made a hell of a lot of mistakes in my life, Mia. But marrying Val wasn't the biggest one, not by a long shot. And it wasn't the first." He caught her free hand in both of his, and his warm fingers closed around hers. His gaze locked on her face. "Leaving you was the dumbest thing I ever did. Bar none."

"Travis, it was a long time ago. We've both moved on—"

"The hell we have. And we won't. We can't—not until I get this off my chest. I hurt you, Mia. And I don't have any fancy excuses. I was young and dumb as dirt—and that's my only excuse. I was a jerk and an idiot. I loved you and I walked away from you. *You*—the best thing in my life."

It was so long ago. The words shouldn't have mattered. But they did. Her heart trembled. She felt like she wanted to run away from him and toward him all at the same time. Those intense blue eyes were steady on hers. She saw hard determination in his face. And . . . something else. Sorrow. He needed to say this, she realized.

Even though it hurt him, and it would probably hurt her, too.

"Go on." Her voice was soft in the big quiet house. The only other sound was the rustling of the leaves outside as the wind picked up, whistling down from the mountains. In the kitchen, she looked into Travis's eyes and couldn't look

away. "I'm listening. But first I need to say something, too."
She took a breath. "I know now that we were both young.
Too young. We weren't ready—"

"Wrong. *I* wasn't ready. Don't blame yourself." Travis's
fingers gently stroked hers. "None of it was your fault. It
was *me*. I panicked. I . . . lost sight of what we had. What I
felt for you. It started before the prom, a week before. You
remember that I went down to the University of Montana
campus at Missoula that weekend? A week before prom?
To visit Jim Malloy?"

She nodded. Jim Malloy. Two years older than Travis.
He'd been the star quarterback of the Lonesome Way High
School football team when Travis first joined as a linebacker.
Malloy had been a player in every sense of the word.

"We partied that weekend, me and Malloy." Travis shook
his head at the memories. "We partied hard. More than I
told you at the time. I didn't hook up with any other girls,"
he added quickly, scanning her face to make sure she
believed him. "I never cheated on you. But I came damn
close. And a part of me wanted to."

She sat completely still. His words hurt. Like an ice pick
digging in her heart. Even though it was years ago, it hurt
to hear flat-out that he'd wanted other girls. She could *understand* it—he'd been eighteen, as handsome as sin, and on
the brink of a new world: college, freedom, choices . . .

And his girlfriend was only sixteen. If they'd stayed
together she'd have held him back. . . .

She'd guessed at this, but she'd never really known.
Because the night Travis had come to her door and told her
good-bye, he hadn't given her a reason.

"The two of us hit the bars nonstop that weekend," he
continued, his strong fingers laced through hers. "It was a
pretty wild scene. Crazed. I'd never seen anything like it
before. There were tons of college girls there, new girls, who
seemed hot and exciting and who just wanted to have fun.
No strings, no feelings, just . . . freedom. I felt like a mus-

tang turned loose in wide open spaces with nothing to hold me back."

"Except me," she said very quietly.

"Except you." His grip on her hand tightened. He held her fingers carefully, gently, not hurting her, but his grip was firm. As if he didn't ever want to let go.

"I made the decision to break up with you that weekend. Then I almost changed my mind a dozen times the following week before I actually did it. I'd already decided to get a summer job in Missoula and move down there early, so I told myself it would be better that way, better to make a clean, quick break right away. Malloy had an apartment there and he'd said I could bunk with him over the summer until I moved into the dorm and started classes. I wasn't thinking, Mia, at least not with my brain," he added ruefully.

She nodded slowly.

"So I let go of the one thing that mattered to me most. But believe me, I realized the idiocy of that mistake a few months later."

That surprised her and she stared at him. The quiet intensity in his face made it impossible to look away.

"The wild side of college life got old fairly quickly. One day it hit me like a ton of rocks just how much I'd let my studies slide—and my grades reflected that. My parents weren't happy, to put it mildly. But worse than that . . . *I* wasn't happy. I missed you. More than I'd ever realized I would."

Surprise swept through her, but she didn't interrupt.

"By March, I really woke up," Travis continued, his thumb stroking gently across her knuckles. "I started staying up all night studying, not partying. And I managed to pull my grades up by the time finals rolled around. When I came back home that summer, I got a job at Tobe's, but all I could think about was you. I hoped so hard you'd take me back. But you weren't interested. You were dating Curt Hathaway by then." He grimaced. "And every time I came to your house to try to talk to you, you blew me off. That drove me crazy."

"You had it coming," she murmured, unable to contain a smile.

"No argument there. But then . . ." This time when he looked at her, there was a glinting challenge in his eyes. "Flash-forward a whole lot of years. To Rafe and Sophie's wedding. You *still* wouldn't talk to me. You wouldn't even so much as *look* at me."

"I told you." She bit her lip to keep from smiling. She couldn't believe how much her avoiding him at the wedding had bothered him. "I didn't notice you."

Travis was off his barstool so fast Mia barely had time to gasp before he tugged her off hers, plucked the wineglass from her fingers, and set it down with a hard clink on the granite counter. His arms snaked around her waist, pulling her close against his body.

"And I told you," he said, making sure that a dime couldn't have fit between their bodies, "I noticed *you*."

"Are you sure about that? It was more than a year and a half ago and you might not remem—"

Her teasing words were cut off as he kissed her. A kiss that made her forget where she was, who she was. A deep, dark, sensual kiss that had her shivering and hot and wanting more. Her arms tightened around his neck as the kiss went deeper, burning back her laughter and her defenses in one fell swoop. She swayed against him, drinking in the taste of him as Travis's strong hands slid roughly down the length of her body. He caressed her hips, cupped her bottom, lifted her up to her tiptoes, and pressed her close against him as his tongue delved deeper, stirring a whimper of pleasure from far back in her throat. His mouth never left hers, even as he scooped her up into his arms.

"I noticed you," he huskily murmured against her lips. "And I've been wanting to do *this*—and more, a lot more—ever since that damned day at the wedding. You believe me now?"

"I could use some more convincing." Breathless, she traced his lips with the tip of her tongue. Her skin felt hot and there was an ache of need in the deepest place inside her. She knew she should be cautious, but suddenly she didn't want to be. She rubbed her fingers through the thickness of his hair as he laughed and kissed her again, carrying her toward the staircase.

"More convincing, huh? You got it."

"And just where . . . are we going?" she gasped between long, dizzying kisses as he mounted the steps with her tight in his arms.

"I promised to show you the rest of the house. This is Grady's room. . . ."

Mia caught a one-second glimpse of a chest of drawers, and a sleeping bag and pillow on the floor of a good-sized room.

"We camped out last night," Travis told her, striding past it down the hall. "Grady couldn't wait to see what it was like to sleep here. And that's a bathroom, and another bedroom, and this is the master bedroom."

He carried her over the threshold of a huge, high-ceilinged space, cloaked in darkness but for the moonlight streaming in the windows. Perhaps it looked even larger without a king-sized bed to fill it, Mia thought, a little dizzy from the heat of his kisses.

There was no bed. No curtains. No furniture at all other than a low oak bench, a fireplace, and a wide-screen TV hanging on one wall. But a pillow and a much larger sleeping bag than the one in Grady's room lay upon the hickory floor.

"Bed and armoire due tomorrow," Travis said roughly, his gaze hot as he looked into her face. His boots scraped against the floor when he walked to where the sleeping bag was spread out and set her on her feet. "Maybe we should wait another day." His mouth brushed against hers, lingering, tantalizing. "It's a great bed, king-sized, leather headboard, good linens—"

"Oh, no, you don't." Her fingers curled through his hair. "Forget the bed. Forget another day. You and me, we're doing this . . . now. I don't want to leave," she whispered. And smiled into his eyes. "And I don't want to talk either."

He laughed, then kissed her long and hard. He tasted like wine and desire, like strength and sex and *Travis*. His lean, rock-hard body felt like the stone gate to heaven as he swept his arms around her, and pulled her even closer. They kissed like two crazy people, all sparks and spice and lightning, their mouths not parting for even an instant.

Kissing her throat, he lowered her gently down onto the sleeping bag and then gazed at her with an intoxicating mixture of flat-out lust and laughter.

"Last chance. If you want to leave, say the word." He was nibbling at her neck, his teeth scraping gently. "But you'd better say it fast."

"Neither one of us is leaving. Neither one of us is going anywhere," she heard herself say breathlessly as she grabbed ahold of his polo shirt and yanked it over his head. Then drank in the sight of that broad, hard chest, lightly matted with dark hair.

She kissed him again, long and slow, her hands exploring the taut bulge of muscles across his upper body. With just her fingertips gliding down, she traced the hard flat plane of his stomach. Need flowed through her, hotter than coals in a stove. His eyes, midnight blue in the silvered darkness, seemed to pierce straight through to her core.

"Two can play that game," Travis said, his voice so deep and husky she shivered all over. He gripped her tan sweater, pulled it up over her head, and sent it sailing across the bedroom. In the process her hair clip came loose and her pale hair tumbled down past her shoulders.

"Yeah, what else have you got, cowboy?" she challenged him softly, giving her head a shake. As the slow grin she loved spread across his face all the way up to touch his eyes, she pushed him down on the sleeping bag and quickly moved on top of him, both of them laughing as if they were kids again, alone in his bedroom at Sage Ranch, nobody else home, the door locked, and only the two of them, making crazy teenaged love atop his old green-and-blue-striped comforter.

Her mouth was so hungry for him, she could barely breathe. Her whole body was starved for him. She stroked her tongue against his and gasped when he hauled her down, pinning her tightly against him. Their mouths fused in kisses that were long and deep and fevered. Mia's mind whirled with sensation as the last remnants of rational thought spun away into the shadows.

"Hey," she murmured as he unclasped her pale, blush pink bra and flung it aside.

"Your panties go next," he whispered, his mouth burning a path down the column of her throat.

"It's a thong, for your information," she gasped, working at the zipper of his jeans.

"Even better." He licked her ear and smiled at her soft moan, then with a swift, deft move he flipped her over, making her gasp with laughter as he switched places with her, him on top, kissing her all the while.

They tore off each other's clothes, Travis taking his time when she was nearly naked, slowly, so slowly sliding the tiny lavender wisp of her thong down her thighs and tossing it across the room in the opposite direction of her bra.

"I'll have you know that's a very expensive piece of lingerie to be throwing around," she said, her hands fisted in his hair. "I ordered it from Victoria's Secr—"

"I'll buy you ten more. Or maybe you should just stop wearing any." He braced himself above her, his eyes glinting into hers with humor and tenderness before his gaze drifted downward from her flushed face and warm amber eyes to the creamy beauty of her breasts. "You're so beautiful, Mia." His voice thickened. "You're perfect. You always have been. I've missed you. Missed *this*. The way it feels when we're together."

"Show me." Pulling his head down, her mouth clung to

his again. Heat fluttered through her as the kiss grew even hungrier. "Travis," she whispered, "show me how much."

"Baby, I intend to. Don't you worry." Eyes gleaming, he shifted lower, and his mouth found the pebble-hard peak of her left breast.

Mia had been planning to tell him to hurry up and show her, but the words died away in a wordless moan as his clever tongue stroked and circled. Licked and kissed and nipped. Ever so slowly teased.

Her eyes drifted closed. She didn't want him to hurry. Lost, melting, her body pulsed with an aching pleasure.

Travis took his time. She realized with a rush of heat that he *wanted* to drive her wild, and oh, he was succeeding. He nibbled hot kisses and licks down her stomach, then went lower still, past her hips to taste the sweetness at her center.

She could barely breathe as he nuzzled her, flicked his tongue over her, caressing and teasing as if they had all the time in the world. . . .

"Tra . . ."

She forgot his name. She forgot her name. She forgot everything but the feel of him stroking her with his tongue, with his fingers.

He took his time with her, making her writhe, making her moan as a keening pleasure roared inside her until slowly, ruthlessly, he sent her flying over the edge, dizzy and crazy and soaring through space.

She was still gasping when he surged up over her, dark, rugged, handsomer than the devil himself. His eyes burned into hers as she clutched those broad shoulders.

"I . . . want you . . . need you . . . inside me, Travis. All of you, n-now," she gasped, her fingers sliding down those muscled arms, her body straining, aching for more of him. For all of him.

"Ah, Mia, baby." He reached toward his discarded jeans and yanked out a condom, his eyes burning with equal parts lust and laughter. "I can handle that."

"I just bet you can," she gasped raggedly as she wrapped her legs around him, pressed kisses across his broad chest and neck, and opened herself to him, heart, body, and soul.

Travis filled her, his blood roaring in his head, in every part of his body. As her hips began to thrash, he drove steadily, deeper, and harder as they fused together. He breathed her in, watched her damp, flushed face, felt his body ignite at the glazed need in her beautiful eyes. He saw something else, something wild and soft and giving. Her gaze was locked on his, the center of her amber eyes darkening as she cried out and clutched him, nails scraping down his back. *Mia.* He lost himself in her, in her deep hot sweetness. Lost himself again and again and again.

The rest of the world disappeared. In a nearly empty bedroom in a cabin in the woods, filled with two people, a sleeping bag, and the glimmer of the moon, he made love to the woman of his dreams.

And after he finally sank down on the sleeping bag beside her and cradled her in his arms, he stroked her hair and made her laugh with the only words either of them spoke for a long time.

"Now, that gives a whole new meaning to the expression 'coming home.'"

Chapter Eighteen

◈

Larkspur Road was dark and silent by the time they returned. It was almost ten o'clock and no lights shone from Mia's house when Travis turned the Explorer into her driveway. He immediately glanced over at Ellis Stone's home where light still glowed in two of the windows. The boys must still be watching Indiana Jones or playing video games, and Ellis was probably awake, too, waiting for them to go to sleep.

"That's strange. Something's wrong," Mia said beside him, even as he scanned the other houses on her side of the street. He saw several lights gleaming from windows along the block. "I'm sure I left a light on in the hallway and the kitchen."

"You did. I'm thinking it might be a power outage. Only it looks like it's just your house."

"Samson! He's all alone in the dark." Unsnapping her seat belt, she sprang out of the Explorer. Travis was already slamming the driver's-side door and heading toward the porch, two long strides ahead of her.

"Why don't you give me your key and wait in the car? Let me check this out first," he said, easing open the screen door.

"No way. I'm going in with you."

"Mia."

"Here, open the door." She handed him the key and waited, her face tense, determined. "Hurry, Travis—Samson . . ."

He sighed at the set expression in her eyes. And at the worry he saw there. "Stay close, then—right behind me."

Even as he fitted the key in the lock, they could hear Samson barking—sharp, frantic yips from somewhere in the house, and he saw Mia stiffen.

The dog definitely wasn't in the hall or the living room. The barking sounded distant and muffled and much more high-pitched than usual. Agitated.

"Travis, hurry, something's definitely wrong," she whispered as he pushed open the door to pitch-blackness.

"Stay right behind me," he repeated, scanning the darkness ahead of them.

She watched him move toward the light switch in the hall, a big shadow moving with purpose. His entire body seemed to emanate a kind of dangerous power and subtle authority. As he flipped the switch the entry flooded with light.

They both blinked, swiftly scanning the living room, dining room, and what they could see of the kitchen and hallway. Nothing amiss. The only sounds were those harsh, desperate, near-hysterical barks.

"I have to find Samson!" she muttered, but as she started forward, Travis stopped her, his hand closing over her wrist.

"He'll be okay for another minute or two," he said in a low tone. "Follow right behind me now while I check the place out."

As he edged forward, the dog's high-pitched barks intensified to fever pitch.

This was nothing like Samson's normal welcome-home bark—there was panic and alarm in the frenzied yaps. Mia fought back the urge to call out to him or to race ahead and find him. Her throat was so tight she could barely swallow as she forced herself to wait, shadowing Travis from the living room to Gram's sewing studio and then the dining room. Suddenly, in the kitchen, he stopped so abruptly she bumped into him.

She gasped when she realized what had caught his attention.

The back door was wide open. Someone had smashed the window set into it and had no doubt reached in to open the lock. Shards of glass littered the floor she'd left spotless only a few hours ago.

"Travis . . ."

He spun toward her, gripped her arm, and spoke in that same low, calm tone she had to strain to hear. "Hang on. Don't touch anything—the sheriff will have to dust for prints. We need to check the rest of the house, make sure no one's still here. Stay close, okay? You all right?"

"I will be once I see Samson and we catch whoever broke in here," she whispered furiously.

Travis nodded. "And we will. Come on."

Grateful for the calm in his voice and for the cool determination she saw in his eyes, she followed him back down the hallway to her bedroom and adjoining bath.

There was no sign of anything being disturbed either there or in the smaller bedroom in the back of the house she used as an office during the school year. As they hurried toward the guest room—Brittany's room—the sound of Samson's frantic barking grew closer. Louder.

At the last second Mia couldn't stand it anymore and bolted past Travis through the doorway, unable to wait another minute as she heard the dog going crazy on the other side of the closet door.

"It's all right, Samson, I'm here," she cried, yanking the

closet door open even as Travis barreled forward, cursing under his breath, and bracing himself for whatever—or whoever—else might be on the other side of that door.

But only the dog sprang from the small, dark prison, jumping wildly toward Mia. With a cry, she swept him up into her arms.

"You're all right!" Her knees almost sagged with relief. Samson didn't seem hurt in any way and he wasn't whimpering. But he was plenty upset. His eyes shone wild and frantic in the gloom. He was shaking all over, squirming in her arms, licking her hands, her face.

Travis flicked on the bedside lamp, then sucked in his breath. Behind him, he heard Mia's gasp.

"No. Oh, God." Shock knifed through her. She stared at Britt's bed.

The covers were neat, the pillows straight, the comforter only slightly wrinkled. But in the center of the bed sat a cluster of flowers.

Not just any flowers.

Wildflowers. *Dead* wildflowers. Tied together with string. Blood stained their wilted petals and stems, soaking into the pink and yellow-flowered comforter, staining it a sickening shiny red.

"Oh, my God," Mia gasped. Trembling, she met Travis's grim eyes.

Blood. Whose blood is this?

Fear jammed her throat, nearly choking her.

"Travis . . . it's him, isn't it? That boy I saw outside Ponderosa Earl's. It has to be. *He* locked up Samson and left dead flowers in my house. On Britt's bed!"

Travis's mouth was taut. "We'll find out soon enough. It's time to bring in Hodge." He yanked out his cell. "We need to—"

Before he could finish the sentence, they heard a voice in the hall.

"Aunt Mia?"

Brittany.

"We're in here," Mia called shakily and set Samson down. Immediately he raced out into the hallway to greet her. Mia wondered frantically if she should head her niece off—keep her out of here, not let her see the chilling sight of the flowers and the blood.

"She needs to see this." Travis read her thoughts as the sound of Britt's quick footsteps drew nearer.

"Hey, Samsie pie, cutie, what's up—"

She broke off as she reached the doorway. Stared from Mia's white face to Travis's frowning one in surprise.

"What's going on . . . ?" Britt began but her voice trailed off as she spotted the dead flowers on the bed. The blood.

Every drop of color drained from her cheeks.

"Oh, God." Her voice cracked. "He broke in . . . here?" Tears welled, filling her eyes.

"You know who did this." The way Travis said it, it was more of a statement than a question. "Tell us, Brittany."

Mia marveled at how cool he sounded. How in control. He put a light hand on her niece's shoulder. "Was it that boy in the bakery today? The one who made you drop the pie?"

Tears began to stream down her cheeks. She didn't seem to hear Travis's questions. She was staring at Mia, shaking her head back and forth, her mouth trembling. "I'm sorry, Aunt Mia. I'm so s-sorry!"

"Don't be." Mia reached her in three quick strides and threw her arms around the girl. "Just tell us the truth, Britt." She held her for a moment, trying to absorb her trembling sobs, wishing she could take all the fear and pain vibrating off Brittany away. "Everything's going to be all right," Mia told her firmly. "You just have to tell us the truth."

Britt pressed the heels of her hands to her wet eyes. "I . . . kn-know. I w-wanted to tell you! I did! But I didn't want to upset you. Or my mom and dad. I . . . I thought I could handle it."

Mia glanced at Travis. Despite the gravity of his expression, he nodded, encouraging her to take the lead.

Gently, she squeezed Britt's shoulders. "Once you tell us, this can all be over. We'll take care of it, honey. I promise."

"You don't understand—it's not that simple!" Britt's voice rose. Breaking free, she paced to the window and back, her face pale. "You don't kn-know what he's like. He'll *never* give up. And I don't know where he is or where he'll show up without warning. But I never thought he'd break in here, Aunt Mia, I swear!"

"His name, Brittany," Travis said quietly. "Just tell us his name."

Something in his deep, steady tone got through to her. Britt's eyes flew to his face.

"It's Wade. Wade Collins." She drew a deep, shuddering breath. "He's my ex-boyfriend and he won't leave me alone. He'll *never* leave me alone. I'm scared, Aunt Mia, I'm really scared! If I don't go back to him . . . he says I'll be sorry!"

And with a burst of sobs, she threw herself into Mia's arms.

Chapter Nineteen

~~~~

It was midnight by the time Sheriff Teddy Hodge left Mia's house.

He'd questioned Brittany for over an hour and taken photos of the dead wildflowers on the bed. He'd made a detailed report, then put out an APB on Wade Collins. He'd dusted for fingerprints and collected the flowers and blood as evidence to be tested and preserved in the event of a trial.

"A stalker, huh?" Sternness and sympathy mingled in the stare he directed at Brittany as they sat in Mia's living room discussing home invasion, spray-paint vandalism of vehicles, and threats. "This ever happens again, young lady, you'd best tell your parents and the authorities pronto. It's nothing to fool around with."

"Yes, sir," she'd mumbled meekly, her hand squeezing Mia's tight.

In the course of the questioning, she'd shown the sheriff the photo of her on the porch, the one Wade had sent to her phone, and she'd haltingly revealed that the moment she saw spray paint all over Seth's truck at Jackie's party she'd been certain Wade was behind it. The last time she'd seen him Wade Collins had told her in no uncertain terms that he didn't want her dating anyone else. Only him.

"I guess I need to tell Seth the truth, too. Before Sheriff Hodge pays his parents a visit," she whispered to Mia in a small voice as Travis walked Hodge to the door.

"Seth still doesn't know? You haven't told him anything about Wade?"

"I wanted to forget about Wade—as much as I could! I didn't want Seth to have to be involved—or you either. But once Wade spray-painted his truck . . ." She swallowed. "I knew I should have told him right away. But he'd have told his parents and they'd have called you. . . ." Her voice trailed off helplessly. "I was embarrassed that I picked such a crazy boyfriend. I didn't want Mom or Dad to know, and to be disappointed in me—"

"Britt." Mia squeezed her niece's hand. "Parents are here to protect their kids. So are friends—and *aunts*. We can't help if we don't know. Your mom and dad would have helped you with this if you'd told them the truth instead of running away."

"I know." Britt's lower lip trembled. "But Mom was planning her honeymoon. And she was so happy. It was stupid, I know," she rushed on. "I realize that now. I don't blame you for being mad at me. He could've hurt Samson. I'd never forgive myself—" She broke off, staring in dismay at the dog, curled in a fluffy ball on Mia's lap on the sofa. He'd received treats to help him forget his ordeal and now his eyes were drifting closed—no doubt from exhaustion after an evening of being locked up by an intruder and barking until he was nearly hoarse. "I'm so thankful he's okay," Britt said in a choked voice.

You're not the only one, Mia thought. It chilled her to think that while she and Travis were drinking wine, talking about the past, and making love, Wade Collins could have killed her dog, burned down her home . . .

She pushed the awful thoughts away and focused on Brittany.

"We need to get something straight, Britt. Right now. I'm not mad at you—what Wade's doing isn't your fault. None of it. But what *you* did, keeping this to yourself, *that* was wrong. Secrecy doesn't help solve problems. Telling me and Travis—and Sheriff Hodge—*that* will help. In the morning, we'll call your dad. . . ." She trailed off, remembering in dismay that Steve had left for China today. She bit her lip. "You need to email both your mom and your dad, let them know what's going on."

"There's something else you should know." Britt swallowed. "Wade . . . he said he might hurt Tate. That's why I didn't want to stay with Dad and Gwen while Mom was on her honeymoon."

The words came out in a tumble as Mia listened in horror. *Tate? Britt's father's toddler son with his new wife?*

"I had to lead him away from Tate," Britt hurried on miserably. "I thought if I left town and he couldn't find me, he'd be so busy searching for me that he'd leave Tate alone and spend all his time trying to find out where I'd gone. But I . . . I never meant to lead him to you, Aunt Mia. I swear. I didn't think he'd find me here in Lonesome Way. Laura promised she wouldn't tell him or anyone else where I went."

So how *did* Wade find her? Mia wondered. Not that it mattered at this point. He'd tracked her down and now it was his turn to be tracked. Pursued. Mia's responsibility now was to protect Brittany as long as she was here in Lonesome Way—and to call Steve's new wife and alert her to the threat against Tate.

She glanced up as Travis returned from seeing the sheriff out.

"I'll replace that door and lock for you tomorrow," he said without preamble. "And I'll be installing a state-of-the-art security system by tomorrow night."

"You don't have to do that," Mia told him quickly. "I'm sure we'll be fine."

"I'm sure you will be, too, once I get done with this place." Travis's mouth was a set line. "Until Collins is in custody, you're getting the Tanner Security Specialists top-of-the-line protection package. And you . . ." Those dusk blue eyes settled on Britt's drawn face. "You don't walk anywhere alone until this is finished. You understand? When you drive to work, keep your car windows up and the doors locked. If this jerk darts into the middle of the road, go around him or through him, but you don't stop for him, not under any circumstances. Got it?"

"Got it."

She drew a deep breath. And actually managed a watery smile for Travis. His words, his take-charge calm seemed to be reassuring her, Mia realized.

And they're keeping me from jumping out of my skin.

It was hard to believe that less than three hours ago they'd been making hot, crazed love on a sleeping bag. And then had taken a long shower together in that huge glass-enclosed shower stall . . .

His gaze shifted to her at that exact moment and a slow smile touched his lips—even reached his eyes—almost as if he'd read her mind.

It was amazing how her heart lifted. In that instant, she almost forgot about Wade Collins. About the blood on the old comforter, the dead flowers, and her broken kitchen window.

She was beginning to feel like Travis was really back in her life. *But for how long?* Her heart clenched. She didn't know. But for now . . .

For now, she told herself, *it's enough. It has to be. Live for today, isn't that what everyone always says people should do?*

"Aunt Mia, I . . . don't think I can sleep in that room tonight . . . on that bed." Britt's voice was a whisper.

"You don't have to. For tonight, you'll sleep in my room with me." Very gently, Mia set Samson on the floor and straightened. She shot Travis a fleeting smile. It was beginning to feel like everything that had happened in the cabin had occurred days ago, not a mere few hours. Yet she could still feel the heat of his powerful body against hers, could still taste the tenderness of his kisses.

"I'll see you tomorrow?" she asked softly.

"You'll see me a lot sooner than that. I'm not going anywhere."

She stared at him in confusion.

"I'm bunking on your sofa tonight, Mia. Until that window's fixed and the security system's in place, you two are stuck with me."

She swallowed. "You actually think Wade Collins might come back here? *Tonight?*"

"Highly unlikely. But I'm not taking any chances, not with either one of you. Or with this guy." Travis knelt to stroke a hand across the little dog's furry head as Samson's tail wagged furiously.

Meeting his gaze, Mia felt her heart filling with a rush of emotion. She wouldn't have slept for a minute tonight with wondering if Wade Collins would return and find his way into her home again while she and Britt were asleep. Gratitude swept over her. Gratitude that Travis was here, helping her deal with this mess. Gratitude that he was back in her life. . . .

At least for tonight, she reminded herself carefully.

She brought out two fluffy pillows and a freshly washed blanket that smelled of laundry soap and sunshine and laid them across the sofa while he took Samson outside one last time.

Britt had padded off to the bathroom to wash her face. Mia met Travis in the kitchen when he returned and found him giving her dog a treat.

"I don't even know how to thank you. For everything."

She wrapped her arms around him and brushed her lips to his.

"Would that be thanks for earlier tonight—or for right now?" He caught her against him with a grin and drew her close.

The feel of his arms around her made her breath catch in her throat. There was no denying it. Travis Tanner still had the power to rock her world. Just by being here.

"Both. Definitely both," she whispered and rested her head against his chest.

They stood like that for a while, holding each other, and Mia didn't want to think about the future or what tomorrow would bring. She was soothed by the steady rhythm of Travis's heartbeat, by his arms solid and strong around her, and that was enough for now.

Chapter Twenty

❧

"How'd I do?" Grady asked eagerly ten days later. He was sitting cross-legged on Mia's living room floor, tossing Samson's stuffed bear into the hall for the twentieth time and watching the dog chase after it.

"One minute and I'll tell you." Mia was almost finished grading the last section of the English test it had taken him less than forty minutes to complete.

Three pages of identifying verbs, adjectives, and pronouns. And then a paragraph he'd written himself, where she'd asked him to circle his adjectives in red marker, the verbs in blue, and the pronouns in yellow.

"Not bad." Setting the last page aside, a smile broke across her face. "You got every one of them right, Grady. One hundred percent. You didn't miss even one."

"Guess that means I'm not such a dummy after all, huh?" The boy's grin belied his casual words. His face flushed with pride—even the tips of his ears turned red. "Wait'll I tell my dad—and my mom. She won't believe it. She told me not to get my hopes up about getting into sixth grade."

"If I were you, I'd get my hopes way up. Way, *way* up," she said immediately, and then remembered. If Val and Drew Baylor had their way, Grady might not have a chance to get into sixth grade in September. They'd already arranged for him to repeat fifth grade—at Broadcrest Academy.

"Can I call my dad and tell him?" Grady scrambled up from the floor. "He's at work."

"Be my guest." Mia handed him her cell. "This calls for a celebration. How about a slice of peach pie and a glass of milk? Then we'll take a look at your science homework."

"Thanks!"

Mia smiled to herself as she cut a generous wedge of the pie and slid it onto a cornflower blue plate.

All Grady had needed, she thought, was a little guidance, attention, and structure. He was incredibly bright. Very focused when he put his mind to something. And thanks to Travis's encouragement, he'd ventured to believe in himself. He was making great progress and it was crystal clear to Mia that he'd never been a lazy student—just one of those drop-through-the-cracks, unmotivated ones.

Seeing how well he was doing now was a pungent reminder of all the reasons she'd become a teacher. And almost made her forget for the moment her worries about Wade Collins.

Brittany's ex-boyfriend hadn't been seen or heard from in ten days. Everyone in Lonesome Way was on the lookout for him now. But for all anyone knew, he might have vanished into a crack in the earth.

He'd made no attempt to contact Britt since leaving the blood-drenched flowers on her bed. And though forensic testing had revealed that the blood had come from a rabbit, the State Police, Sheriff Hodge, and Deputy Zeke Mueller had nothing more to go on. In all this time, they hadn't spotted any trace of the car registered to him, much less Wade himself.

No one matching his description had been seen anywhere around town, and Travis told Mia privately that either the kid must have taken off for parts unknown or he was hiding out in the wilderness somewhere, biding his time, waiting until the search died down and he could chance sneaking back into town and striking out at Brittany again.

The fact that Mia had seen him outside Ponderosa Earl's with a sack of purchases and a sleeping bag seemed to suggest he was making camp somewhere. Hiding out. Lying low.

And with all of the campgrounds, sprawling forests, mountains, ravines, and isolated bluffs in the vast wilderness spaces of Montana, the odds of finding him before he came back into town again on his own seemed slight.

There appeared little chance that he'd just give up and leave. According to what Britt had told Mia the day after Wade broke in, he had no family to anchor him, no one to return to.

He'd mentioned to her once that his mother had taken off when he was nine and he hadn't seen her since. His dad had kicked him out of the house when he was seventeen. He'd been on his own ever since, tending bar or working as a bouncer. She'd lied to her parents about him from the very beginning—told them he was a college student because she knew they wouldn't approve of her dating someone four years older, someone who worked in a bar.

She'd wanted to help him, Britt had explained tearfully. Mia had listened with a pang of dismay. Her niece had learned some hard lessons—and learned them the hard way. You can't save someone who doesn't want to save himself. And you can't run from trouble. You need to face it head-on.

Seth had been furious when Britt told him she'd guessed who was behind the spray-painting all along and hadn't said a word. And who could blame him? But after a few days of miserable silence between them, the two seemed to have worked it out.

And though Mia at first thought it would be best for Britt to get out of Dodge, Steve was in China and Sam was still in Corfu, though she'd been desperately looking for an earlier flight home. But Britt had cajoled them both in long emails into letting her stay in Lonesome Way a little longer.

"Wade's gone. He must be on the run. I bet he won't dare come back to Lonesome Way—the cops and everyone in town are looking for him. I'm safer here right now than back in Butte—especially with the awesome security system Travis put in. Wade can't possibly break in again, not without the whole world knowing about it the second he touches any of the doors or windows. I swear, the CIA couldn't get into Aunt Mia's house!"

She'd gone on and on about how much she loved working at A Bun in the Oven, though Mia suspected she just didn't want to leave Seth.

Summer love could be a powerful thing.

So after checking with Mia and learning all of the details about the security system, and how Travis was keeping an eye on the entire situation, both her parents had agreed to let her stay. Now it was only a matter of a few more days before Sam and Alec would be home, and Steve was flying back to the States soon after.

After the first few tense days following the break-in, Mia had managed to shake off most of her unease. She *wanted* to believe that Wade Collins was gone for good, but she couldn't help it—she still felt a chill sometimes when she entered her own home. Even with the security system Travis had installed.

It would've been so much easier to forget about how Britt's ex-boyfriend had violated her home and locked up her dog and tried to terrorize Brittany if she knew for a fact he was gone.

Still, as the days passed, life had settled again into a

soothing everyday rhythm that seemed far removed from the fear and chaos of the break-in.

When she wasn't tutoring Grady, or having supper with Travis and him and often Britt, she was checking in with Aunt Winona, bringing her meat loaf and mashed potatoes one day, casseroles and sandwiches or a salad the next—and once, another pie, this time a juicy Dutch apple with streusel topping from A Bun in the Oven.

Bit by bit Mia felt she was making progress. Chipping away at the layers of her aunt's distrust, even though the visits never lasted longer than fifteen or twenty minutes.

Travis had taken Mia on a tour of his office space one day while Grady was having lunch at the drive-through with Evan and Justin and their mom. It was the day before Travis's new office manager—a fifty-two-year-old former judge's secretary from Livingston—was due to start work, and he brought in pizza and Cokes from Pepper Rony's down the street and set up a picnic for them on a red-and-blue-checked tablecloth spread upon the floor.

After lunch they pulled the shades and tore off each other's clothes and made love on the sofa in his private office, ignoring the ringing phones, the high-tech equipment, and the passage of time.

Aside from the Wade scare, Mia couldn't remember any time since high school when she'd had a sweeter summer.

"My dad wants to take us all out to dinner tonight because I got one hundred on the test," Grady announced. "He said you owe him a rain check for the Lucky Punch Saloon."

"I seem to remember something about that." Mia's lips quirked up in a smile as she slid the plate of pie and a fork onto a yellow and white quilted placemat at the dining room table.

"I've never been to the Lucky Punch Saloon." The boy's green eyes were bright and hopeful on hers. "But Justin and Evan said there's a mini mechanical bull that kids can ride. And a saddle on the wall that was supposed to belong to

Billy the Kid. Can we go? Please?" The eagerness in his tone made something tighten in her chest.

Can *we* go. He was asking as if she—and Britt—were family. Part of a tight little unit, each one of them belonging to the whole. A glorious warmth burst through her heart. She had to force herself to take a breath and keep her feet from floating off the ground. Had to remind herself that they *weren't* family. And might never be.

She and Travis cared about each other and had dizzily wonderful, fabulous sex.

That was it.

Except for the fact that her feelings for him were deeper than they'd ever been. That she thought about him a hundred times a day and could barely work on her quilt or plan a lesson for Grady without wondering when they'd see each other again. And when she was kissing Travis or making love to him or even telling him about her day she could barely think at all.

Which scared the crap out of her.

Because beyond all that, nothing was for certain. He'd never once said he loved her. He'd never spoken a word about the future. And neither had she.

She knew Travis had to focus on looking out for his son. Making sure Grady didn't get shoved under the rug by his mother and stepdad. He couldn't let Grady get shipped off to boarding school or left alone to watch a fifty-inch flat-screen TV by himself. The very thought of both of those prospects made Mia burn with anger.

"Can we go?" Grady asked again, yanking her back to her kitchen as he shifted impatiently from one foot to the other, her cell phone still clutched in his small hand. "Please say yes!"

"We-ell," she told him, happy to see the hopeful grin creasing his face as she poured him a glass of milk and brought it to the table, "Britt's coming straight home when her shift ends at five. So, *yes*. It sounds like a plan."

"Yippee!" Grady whooped so loudly Samson dashed over to stare at him expectantly. "Dad wants to talk to you." He handed back the phone.

"Don't pay any attention to what my son just said," Travis told her. "I mean, I *do* want to talk to you. But that doesn't begin to cover it. I want to do a whole lot more to you than that. Things I can't repeat when there's kids around."

"Sounds good to me." She smiled. Grady had slipped into the chair and was whipping through that peach pie as if he hadn't touched a morsel of food in weeks.

"I've got a genius plan for after supper."

"I'll just bet you do."

She almost heard his grin over the phone. "Rafe's taking Ivy and her pals to a movie tonight. Grady and Britt—and even Seth, if he wants to go—are invited along. My brother volunteered to keep an eye on all of them for a couple of hours. Which means you and I can keep an eye on each other."

"Nice." Anticipation curled in her belly.

"Oh, it's going to be a whole lot better than nice." The husky deliberateness of Travis's tone sent giddy shivers through her. "Guaranteed. You. Me. Wine. A real bed. The works."

"I'm so there."

"Me, too." He paused a moment. "I miss you, Mia. We need to do something about that."

"I'd like that, too. Let's."

Careful. He only means we need to spend more time together. Alone, Mia reminded herself after they ended the call. *He's not talking about love. Or marriage. He's not thinking about happily ever after.*

And a wise little voice in her ear warned her that she shouldn't be thinking about it either.

Chapter Twenty-one

~

On the Friday morning that she was taking Aunt Winny to see the doctor, Mia woke up early.

After whipping through a fast shower she pulled on a scoop-necked white tee and dark green shorts, then drove Brittany to her early shift at the bakery, since instead of taking the Jeep to her aunt's appointment, she'd decided to pick Winny up in Britt's convertible instead. It would be easier for her aunt to get into Britt's car than to maneuver herself into the SUV with a cane.

And since Britt's shift ended at noon, Mia had another plan as well—convincing Winny to join them both for lunch after the doctor appointment.

Despite the older woman's earlier objection to setting foot in A Bun in the Oven, Mia suspected that Britt's joining them might just tip the scales in her favor. Winny had a soft spot for Britt.

She's not nearly as tough as she'd like everyone to think, Mia mused on her way back from dropping her niece at work.

Since she had plenty of time before she needed to head
to the cabin, she returned home and took Samson for a walk,
then enjoyed a quick cup of coffee and a blueberry crumb
muffin on the porch with the little dog curled up beside her,
his eyes drifting closed as the sun warmed his fur. Clouds
loomed to the west, though. It looked like rain. Narrowing
her eyes at the sky, Mia had a feeling thunderstorms would
roll in later.

But she still had several hours free, a good chunk of time
to work on her quilt. Settling in at her sewing machine, with
Samson snoozing on the needlepoint rug only a few feet
away, she wrestled the quilt layers under the hopping foot
and set to work, trying not to think about Travis. He was
bringing Grady by for tutoring this afternoon. And she
couldn't wait to see him.

Concentrate on this quilt, she chided herself. *If you let
yourself start daydreaming about Travis, you'll mess something up and won't finish until next summer's quilt exhibition.*

Her work was soon accompanied by the sound of Samson's gentle snores, along with the drone of bees and the
chirps of songbirds drifting in through the open window.

Slowly her Starry Night design was taking shape. The
stars she'd so carefully appliquéd looked perfect against the
dramatic midnight blue background and the swirls of light.
Though the quilt wasn't yet halfway finished, she could
already see it becoming a vibrant reflection of her dreamy
vision, her own version of the brilliant night sky made
famous by Van Gogh.

Mia was so engrossed in her work that she lost track of
time and suddenly was startled to discover that she needed
to leave right that minute if she was going to have a prayer
of getting Aunt Winny to her appointment on time.

She rushed to the door and set the alarm, leaving Samson
safely inside as she took off for Sweetwater Road.

Winny was perched on the ancient rocker on her porch,
a knitted multicolored handbag on her lap, when Mia roared

down the gravel drive and jumped out of the Mustang with the engine still running.

"No need to hang on to me," her aunt complained as she started to help her down the porch steps. "I'm not glass and I sure as shootin' won't break."

"Humor me." Mia held carefully to Winny's arm.

"It's not like I have much of a choice," her aunt grumbled.

Mia noticed the tabby crouched outside, watching them, half hidden in the brush as they started toward the car.

"It looks like rain, Aunt Winny. Don't you want to leave her inside?"

"We'll be back before there's a drop of rain. Those clouds won't get here 'til late afternoon."

"If they roll in faster, she'll get soaked."

Winny frowned. Stopped. Thought about it. "Well, for Pete's sake, if you're going to worry about it . . ." She half stomped, half limped back toward the porch. "Jellybean, you come on up here. Now!"

To Mia's astonishment the cat obeyed, leaping up the steps and sidling against the cabin door with a low meow. Mia helped her aunt up and then down the steps again after the cat was safely shut up inside.

"You underestimate that cat. And me." Winny flicked her a flinty glance as the convertible spat gravel going up the drive. "We've gotten along just fine on our own, both of us, for a good long time. We're survivors. We don't *need* folks fussing over us."

"Everybody needs someone to care about them. Most people just say thank you when someone like that comes along." She smiled as her aunt directed a gaze at her sharp enough to pierce armor. "It doesn't make you a wimp to care about another person or to let them care about you. It just makes you human."

"If I want a sermon, I'll go to church." Winny folded her hands over the knitted handbag in her lap. "You were late coming today."

"I'm sorry. But with this sweet little car, we'll make up the time." She pressed down hard on the accelerator and the convertible shot forward down Sweetwater Road. "I was distracted working on my quilt for the exhibition. I lost track of time."

"So you like to quilt, too, do you? No doubt you're as good at it as Alicia was. You're just the type."

"Type?" Mia's slender brows rose. "What *type* is good at quilting? I don't understand."

"The type who things come easy to. *She* was like that— Alicia. The perfect child." Winny snorted. "The one who always did her chores, followed the rules, minded her manners."

"Is that how you remember her?" Mia asked quietly.

Winny didn't reply for a moment. "Alicia drew people to her," she muttered at last. "It was like she had some kind of invisible charm in her pocket that magically made them love her. My father used to ask me why I couldn't be like her. Every day he asked me." Her mouth twisted. "But I wasn't like her. I wasn't like her at all."

"What *were* you like?" Mia asked. She remembered what Martha had said, comparing Winny to one of those wild horses still running free in Coldwater Canyon.

"I didn't take to being told what to do, for one thing. I liked to climb trees no one else would dare climb—not even any of the boys. I played in the mud, and then I tramped it all in the house because I forgot to wipe my feet before going inside." She chuckled, but it was a dry, mirthless sound. "I made more work for my mother in one day than my sister did in a year, and my father would swat my bottom until I cried and then send me to my room. Alicia never got swatted or sent to our room, not that I can recall."

"So you and Gram . . . you were never close?"

Winny hesitated. "When we were younger. We were close then." Her voice changed. Softened. Mia had never heard that tone from her before. "She was always nice to me when we were younger. Felt sorry for me, I guess, because I was always in trouble. When I cried in bed because my bottom was sore from beating, she used to show me her drawings, try to make me forget about the pain. *Butterflies.* She always drew butterflies. All different colors, sizes. Real pretty, they were. Alicia just loved butterflies. . . ." Winny moistened her lips, remembering. "And when I got sent to our room without any supper, she'd sneak me food from the kitchen. Right after supper she'd duck in with it, and again before she came to bed. As much as she could carry. Those were the only times she ever broke any rules. *She* never got caught."

"I don't understand." Mia couldn't contain the words. "If you and Gram were close . . . if she was good to you . . . what happened? Why did you burn her wedding quilt and run away? If you left because of your father, I can understand that," she added quickly. "But why didn't you and Gram ever speak to each other after you came back to Lonesome Way?"

They were only a few miles from town and the hospital now, she realized as she made the turn onto Squirrel Road. They'd made up the time and she deliberately slowed her speed so they'd have more of a chance to talk. It was the first time Winny had ever opened up about her childhood with Gram, and Mia knew she might never have another opportunity to find out what had gone wrong between them.

As it was, Winny went quiet for so long Mia feared she wasn't planning to answer, but at last, as the road dipped just past a fallen tree, and a hawk swooped overhead, casting a shadow in the sky, Winny let out a sigh.

"I guess you could say as we grew up, we grew apart. By the time we reached our teens, my sister learned to be ashamed of me." She looked straight ahead, into the distance. When she spoke again, the words came steadily, but there was pain beneath them.

"The other girls whispered about me, you see. They

thought I was loose because most of my friends were boys. But I just felt more comfortable with the boys. I had fun with them and I liked the attention I got from them. Abner was one of 'em. And his brother Bill. That was when we became friends—good friends. But the older boys . . ." Winny sighed. "Well, let's just say the older I got, the more attention they paid me. Seemed like they all thought I was pretty, so they used to tease me and flirt with me—and I wasn't one of those girls who shied away from flirting back." Her mouth curved in a faint, reminiscent smile. "And yes, they kissed me on the first date. If I liked 'em, I kissed 'em back. But that's *all* I let 'em do. Not that it mattered," she added, her mouth tightening. "Because I still got a reputation."

Glancing over, Mia saw Winny's eyes brimming with memories. Sour memories, from the look of it.

"Everyone thought I was a certain type of girl—the type who slept with anything in pants. Girls started calling me a slut behind my back. One or two said it to my face. Oh, not Martha or Ava Todd or any of the others Alicia was good friends with. They kept silent, probably out of respect for her. But some—most of 'em, if you want to know—they whispered behind their hands whenever I walked by. But it wasn't true. None of it. I never did all those things they said. I never did *most* of them, except kiss this boy or that one now and then, if I liked him."

Winny peered over at Mia, and in her dark gaze Mia saw a long-ago hurt, a bitterness hard and old, tamped down deep, like tobacco in a pipe.

"The truth was, there was only one boy I cared about. A boy from Billings. Real handsome, he was. We met at a barn dance, and he was the only one I let touch me. Matter of fact," she said softly, "I let him do whatever he wanted— well, *almost* anything he wanted," she added with a wry slant of her mouth that was nothing like a smile. "Because I loved him. And I *thought* he loved me. He told me he did often enough," she rasped in a low tone.

"What happened to him, Aunt Winny? Who was he?" Mia saw the outer fringe of town just ahead. She tried to imagine her crusty aunt as a pretty, vibrant young woman. Brittany's age. Mia's age when she'd fallen for Travis. "Did you . . ." She paused, uncertain how to phrase her question.

"Sleep with him? Have sex with him? Is that what you want to know?" Her aunt was gripping her cane tightly, staring straight ahead, her profile sharp, almost regal. "No, I didn't do that, but fool that I was, I would've if I'd had the chance. I never did."

Mia saw her teeth clench, a timeworn pain tightening her elegant features.

"Why didn't you?" She couldn't stop herself from asking.

Winny's mouth twisted like a gnarled tree root. "Because one day I came home from school and found the boy I loved standing in my very own house. Shaking my father's hand. Paying my mother some flowery compliment. You want to know why? Because he'd just become engaged to marry my sister."

Chapter Twenty-two

❦

The instant Travis glanced at his cell phone and saw it was Val calling he had a bad feeling.

Up until that moment, his day had been rolling along great. His office phones were ringing constantly. Potential clients were emailing all day long, his security teams were shaping up, and inquiries for his company's services were pouring in from D.C. to Sacramento, from Frankfurt to Damascus.

He'd hired five top-notch former Navy SEALs in the past week and he had a video interview with a major potential client in Madrid scheduled at five.

Grady was out in the reception area with his new office manager, and while she fielded phone calls and set up appointments, his son was curled up in a gray-and-black-checked wingback chair, his mouth pursed in concentration as he finished up a take-home quiz Mia had assigned him for homework—comparing how earthquakes, volcanoes, and plate movements affected the earth's surface features.

In an hour the two of them were going to grab some burgers from the drive-through and then later on shoot over to Mia's for Grady's tutoring session.

I'll see her in a little more than two hours, Travis had thought, grinning because he was as eager as a teenager. Not only would he see Mia when he dropped Grady off, but she and Britt were joining him and Grady for a barbecue tonight at the cabin.

Every day he saw Mia was a good day. He looked forward to her sexy little smile, to getting close enough to smell the grapefruit and sunshine fragrance of her shampoo. Hearing her laugh was a bonus. And making love to her was the closest thing to heaven Travis had ever known.

The sight of her triggered a million lustful thoughts and kept him busy trying to figure out ways for them to be alone so they could act on them.

The only fly in the ointment was that Wade Collins hadn't been caught yet. Travis knew that just because the kid hadn't been spotted didn't mean he wasn't around. Snakes liked hiding under rocks. And just because you couldn't see them, that didn't mean they weren't there. Hidden. Coiled. Ready to strike.

He wasn't about to let down his guard until Britt's ex-boyfriend was locked up where he belonged.

He'd been trying to shove his concerns about Collins out of his mind, to focus on Tanner Security and the evening ahead.

And then Val called and it all went to hell.

"You're *what*?"

He listened to her in disbelief, his stomach clenching.

She and Drew. Moving to London in the fall.

Travis heard her out, fighting to control his growing anger. Apparently this had been in the works for a while now. And suddenly it dawned on him. This was probably the real reason for all that talk about boarding school. Drew had been angling toward this all along. Baylor wanted to personally be in London during the launch phase of the UK branch of his hotel line. He'd known for a while now that he and Val would need to relocate overseas for a minimum of six months. Possibly a year. Val didn't admit that to Travis, though.

His jaw tightened as he listened to her breathless, rapid-fire words. The woman didn't give him a second to jump in, just kept on talking. No doubt not wanting to hear him say what she had to know deep down. How disgusting it was to toss a struggling kid off on a bunch of strangers at a boarding school while chasing your own—or your husband's— career aspirations around the globe.

They were renting out their L.A. house, she told him. And planned to settle Grady in at Broadcrest Academy before they left for London on the twenty-third of August.

"Broadcrest Academy is the last thing our son needs right now," he told Val bluntly when she finally paused for breath.

"I disagree." Her tone was defensive. A little shrill. "Drew thinks it's *exactly* what he needs. Structure and discipline. A chance to grow up—and shape up. Drew says if his grades improve after a year, we can rethink everything. Maybe, if we're still based in London then, Grady could transfer to a school there. . . ."

Her voice trailed off, and he heard the doubtfulness she couldn't quite hide.

"I know you think this is a mistake, Travis, but Grady's interview with the headmaster is scheduled for next Thursday. It's only a formality, since Drew has already pulled enough strings to get him in—but if you don't want to take him then I'll just have to fly into Billings on Wednesday and pick him up myself." She hurried on as if expecting him to interrupt. "It's all settled, Travis. Believe me, Drew and I have gone over and over this. There's no other choice."

She was trying her best to sound firm and unshakable, but Travis knew Val, knew that note of hesitation in her voice. Deep down, she knew as well as he did how wrong this was.

"There's always another choice, Val." He spoke evenly, but there was steel in the words. "Drew Baylor doesn't get to call the shots when it comes to our son. So we're going to talk about this. Hear me out."

Unfortunately, at that moment, the door opened and Grady poked his head in.

"I need some help with my homework, Dad. Can I ask you something?" he whispered.

Travis's first instinct was to say *Not right now*, and finish his conversation. Get this settled. His gut was trussed up in knots, and he needed to get everything straightened out, pull out the big guns and make sure Broadcrest Academy and its stuffy halls and messed-up rich kids and manicured lawns was taken off the table. But Grady had already waited too long for him to reenter his life, to be a real, full-time, hands-on father. His son was watching him with urgent need in his eyes.

Dealing with Val would have to wait a little longer.

"I'm going to have to call you back," he said into the phone even as he forced a smile for the boy's sake and waved him in.

"When?" Val's voice rose to a near-screech as it always did when she was stressed. "I have a *thousand* things to do here, Travis. And I'm supposed to meet Drew and the rental property agent in *fifteen* minutes—"

"Soon," he interrupted her tersely. "As soon as I can. I'll get back to you in an hour."

Ending the call, he studied his son. "What's up, buddy?"

"I don't understand what causes magma to rise in a subjection zone. And I have to *explain* it. They talk about it in my science book, and Mia told me about it the other day, but it's kinda confusing. Can you help me?"

"Subjection zones, huh? They're a little out of my area of expertise." His brow wrinkled as he pulled a spare chair up to his desk for the boy and moved his coffee mug out of the way. "Let's take a look at that book and I'll give it my best shot."

As Grady grinned, regarding him with absolute trust and the hopefulness only a child can feel toward his parent's steadfast ability to make everything better, Travis felt his determination multiply fiftyfold.

No way was he letting his son get shunted off to boarding school like extra baggage shoved into a storage facility.

Not while he still had blood left in his body.

Chapter Twenty-three

～

"What happened when you walked into your house, Aunt Winny? What did you say to him?"

They were only a half mile from town now. But Winny Pruitt wasn't responding to Mia's question.

Mia braked at a red light at the intersection of Grace and Pine. Glancing at her aunt, she saw the frown lines etched deeply around her mouth. For several long seconds Winny clung to that silence, and Mia had almost given up on learning anything more when her aunt suddenly began to speak as if the words had been corked up inside her too long, and there were too many of them to contain any longer.

"Henry Clayton behaved as if he'd never seen me before, that's what happened. Smooth as a worm in mud he was. He shook my hand and told me he was honored to meet me and happy I was going to be his sister."

Henry Clayton? Grandfather?

Mia's heart lurched. She couldn't seem to form any words, but fortunately, she didn't need to because Winny suddenly appeared to want to spill all those bottled-up memories out into the open.

"Smooth he was. Lied as if he did it every day of his life, which he no doubt did. It didn't sink in on me until later, how ambitious Henry was in those younger days. He saw himself as a man on the rise. A man with a future. My parents owned a prosperous farm, even had two hired men to help with the chores, and he no doubt saw the benefits of marrying the cherished eldest daughter. Alicia's reputation was spotless, while mine . . ." She gave a short, bitter bark of laughter. "A week or two in town and he knew as well as anyone what my reputation was. He knew I might be good enough to fool around with in the dark shed near the railroad tracks, but not good enough to be seen on his arm in public. Or to walk down the aisle of a church and say 'I do.' "

"But he left Gram—after only a few years—when my mother was still a little girl!" Mia burst out. "He abandoned them both for some barmaid and was never heard from again. What did he get from the marriage?"

"Well, I was long gone by then, but Abner wrote me later what *he* heard. Henry stole nine hundred and seventy-five dollars from my father's safe before he ran away. A fortune in those days. So I guess his true nature won out in the end. Henry wasn't cut out for staying in one place any more than he was cut out for marriage. He was an opportunist who grabbed his chances as they came and lit out whenever the urge took him. I'd bet my horse, if I had one, that he dumped the barmaid for a banker's daughter as soon as the opportunity came along."

The streetlight changed to green and Mia stepped on the gas and accelerated, cruising past the park and the Toss and Tumble Laundromat, her aunt's words whirling through her head. As she neared the hospital entrance, it suddenly occurred to her that her grandfather hadn't been all that different from Peter. Peter Clancy had left her in similar fashion, taking every dime of the savings from their joint account.

"Chalk it up to the wedding quilt." She didn't realize she'd spoken aloud until the words tumbled from her mouth.

Beside her she heard Winny's indrawn breath.

"I'm sorry, Aunt Winny," she said quickly. "It's just that Gram always used to say none of the women in our family had any kind of marriage luck except the bad kind after the wedding quilt burned up. It's seemed to hold true."

"I never should have burned that damned quilt," Winny muttered. It sounded like she was talking to herself. Suddenly she glanced over at Mia. "I did it out of spite the night I left. Hurt feelings and rage got the better of me. I was sorry for it later, but I couldn't bring myself to go back. Not for a long time. And by then . . . it didn't matter anymore."

"You said you left home because your family threw you out." Mia hesitated. "Was that because you burned the quilt?"

"*That's* what you think?" Winny stared at her incredulously. "So it's true. No one ever told you what happened. Any of it. All these years, I figured they passed down the stories about the family tramp. The wild, no-good daughter. Winona." She drew a breath and stared out the window at the hospital, at the half-empty parking lot.

Mia had the feeling she was seeing something else.

Not a tidy hospital shaded by willow trees near a park where children played. Not a town where people called out to friends and shop owners knew all of their customers' names. She was seeing something dark, something ugly. And far away.

"The night my father ordered me to leave his house, I tried to tell him the truth. What really happened. I tried to tell all of them. But they wouldn't believe me," she said heavily. "Not my parents, not my sister—they believed Henry. Guess I shouldn't have been surprised."

Mia pulled up at the curb in front of the hospital, her throat tight at the bitterness in her aunt's voice. It was 11:32. But if she didn't find out right here and now why Winny had been forced from her home, her aunt might never choose to talk about it again.

"I'll believe you, Aunt Winny, I promise. Whatever it is." Reaching out, she placed her hand over her aunt's thin, veined one with the defiantly bright fingernails. "Tell me what happened."

Winny closed her eyes for so long, Mia thought she wasn't going to reply, but finally she opened them and stared—not at Mia—but into the distance, at something, or someone, Mia couldn't see.

"It was two weeks before the wedding," she whispered. "I was in the kitchen, alone, making a dish to bring to my aunt's home. She was hosting a small dinner party in honor of Alicia's engagement. My mother had one of her headaches—she was resting in her room before dressing for the party. My father and Alicia were on an errand. And Henry showed up at the front door early to see my sister."

Mia watched as a young woman was wheeled out of the hospital, a newborn baby nestled in a pink blanket in her arms, her husband at her side, carrying a small suitcase and a clutch of release papers and instructions.

"What happened then?" she pressed quietly.

"I told Henry Alicia was out, and I tried to close the door." Winny spoke in a monotone. "But he grabbed it and held it in place. Then he pushed right past me, into the hall, bold as you please, and declared he'd wait for her."

From the park a few streets away, the sound of children's laughter floated like faint music to Mia's ears, but Winny didn't seem to hear it. Just as she hadn't seen the woman and the baby. She seemed to have forgotten that they were parked in front of the hospital, that Doc Grantham was waiting to check her foot. She was back on her family's farm, trapped in the past, facing a man who'd hurt her.

"Instead of waiting in the parlor, like I told him, Henry followed me into the kitchen. I ordered him to get out, but he . . . he wouldn't go." Anger shimmered in her eyes. "He pushed me against the wall. *Hard.* Covered my mouth with his hand. I was scared, fighting him. Struggling to get free, but he just laughed. He told me he still wanted me, that he kept thinking about me. He told me we could still have fun times together, that no one need know. I kicked him—I was trying to get away. But I couldn't," she whispered. "I couldn't get away."

Mia felt sick as her aunt drew a deep breath.

"Suddenly Henry pulled his hand from my mouth. He pinned my hands to my sides and held me against the wall beside the pantry and he kissed me. I tried to twist away but he only held me tighter . . . and he . . . he wouldn't stop. . . ."

Disgust shook Mia to her core. Even though it had all happened long ago, pain still trembled through her aunt's voice and glazed her eyes.

"I tried to push him away, but he wouldn't budge, wouldn't let me go. He just laughed at me and started groping me—" Winny broke off with a shudder. "And then Alicia and our father walked through the kitchen door and found us like that. It must've looked like we were embracing . . . kissing."

"No. Oh, no." Mia didn't even realize she whispered the words aloud. But her aunt seemed not to have heard.

"Soon as Henry saw them he shoved me away and pretended he was shocked. He told them he'd been waiting for Alicia to return, passing the time with me to be polite. He told them I suddenly threw myself at him, kissed him, and he was caught off guard—" As Mia's breath froze in her throat, Winny's mouth twisted. "They believed him. My own family. My own sister. They wouldn't listen to a word I said. They thought I'd actually *do* something like that. That I'd hurt my sister."

Her voice was dull now. Dulled with an old, rusty pain and the resignation that came with time. "No matter how I tried to deny it, all of it, they wouldn't listen. My mother came downstairs in her shift and they told her. All of them stared at me with contempt in their eyes. None of them believed me. They took his word over mine."

Finally, she lifted her head, met Mia's stricken gaze. "My father told me I'd been nothing but trouble from the day I was born. Told me I was to get out of his house and never return. My mother looked heartbroken, but she was angry, too. She asked me how I could do this to my sister. And Alicia, she stared at me. I'll never forget the sadness in her eyes. She said to me in the coldest tone I'd ever heard her use—'I know him. He's a good man. And you're so jealous of my good fortune you're trying to ruin it. I'll never forgive you.'"

A clutch of pain ripped through Mia's heart. *Gram . . . sweet, kind Gram.* She must have felt so betrayed. But it wasn't her sister who'd betrayed her. And those words had ripped the two of them apart.

"My father gave me until morning to leave, but I lit out that same night after they all went to my aunt's." Winny leaned back against the seat and closed her eyes. "Before I left, I set fire to that quilt out back in the yard. When nothing was left but some fabric threads and a pile of ash, I doused the fire with a bucket of water and walked away. Never looked back."

Winny's sigh seemed to hang in the air between them. "I wanted to hurt them. All of them. Especially Alicia. I wanted her to think her marriage would be cursed. Joyless. I didn't learn until much later that it was just that. Not to mention short-lived."

"But . . . where did you go? How did you disappear so completely and quickly?" Mia had to know.

Winny told her how she'd hitched a ride to the train station and used the little money she'd saved up to buy a ticket, heading east. In each town she came to, she found work as a maid or in a diner, staying on until she earned enough money to travel farther. She rode the train all the way to Bismarck, North Dakota, where she met her husband, Harley Pruitt. They'd moved around a lot, never had any children, and Abner was the only person from her past she ever kept in touch with. She didn't return to Lonesome Way until well after her parents were gone and Harley was killed, struck by lightning in Abilene.

"After Abner wrote me that his brother Bill was moving to be closer to his daughter in Boise, selling his cabin, and did I want it, I decided why not? It was far enough away from town that I figured there'd be no need to see anyone I didn't want to see. There was nothing for me in Abilene anymore with Harley gone, so I picked up and moved back."

Opening the door of the convertible, Winny eased carefully out onto the pavement. She leaned on her cane. "It's true, part of me wanted to see my sister again. I don't know why. But when she came to see me out at the cabin . . ." She shook her head. "I couldn't bring myself to open the door. I got angry all over again, and even when she begged me to let her in for just a minute, I wouldn't. Like when you came out that first time."

Shock washed over Mia like a splash of icy water. *Gram reached out to Winny?* As she tried to absorb this, her aunt said something that made her go still.

"Alicia said she was sorry."

"She . . . *what?*"

"She said I was right about Henry and she was sorry she didn't listen, didn't believe me. She'd written me a letter she wanted me to read. But I wouldn't take it. Wouldn't even open the door. Didn't think I could ever forgive her and I told her so. She never came back."

Mia stepped out of the Mustang and hurried around the hood. Her mind was racing. "Did she leave the letter, Aunt Winny?"

"On the porch. But I never opened it."

"Why not?" The words burst from her. "Gram *apologized.* Weren't you curious to know what was in that letter? Didn't you want to give her another chance?"

A heavy sadness seemed to weigh down Winny's shoulders. "In my mind it was too late. I thought it would only bring back the hurt—and for what? Nothing could be changed at that point. Or fixed. Too many years had gone by."

Her dark sable eyes were shiny with tears. "I should've opened that door. Should've talked to her and read that letter. I wish . . . I wish I'd forgiven her when I had the chance." Her shoulders slumped. "I'll live with that the rest of my days."

Suddenly she looked utterly spent. She managed to reach out her free hand and lightly touched Mia's arm. "Guess I shouldn't have bent your ear with all that. But I figured close to sixty years is enough time to hold a secret. I haven't said so many words all at once since I was a child who didn't know any better. If you want to leave before I come out, I'll understand."

Mia gazed into that proud, stubborn face. Winny was fighting it with everything she had, but two tears leaked from her eyes. Sympathy, sadness, pain, and regret all seemed to thicken in Mia's throat.

She reached out without thinking and wrapped her arms around the old woman's shoulders. For a moment she just hugged her tight.

"I'll be here, Aunt Winny," she whispered. "You don't have to worry that I'll be gone when you come out. I'm not going anywhere."

⌒

Mia sat for a while, the engine running, trying to absorb it all. It hurt to know that Gram had tried to make peace and Winny hadn't accepted her overtures. She ached for her grandmother. Yes, Gram had made a terrible mistake, but she'd lost her sister forever because of it. She'd died without reconciling with the one person she should have been closest to.

Mia couldn't imagine what it would be like to never speak to Sam again.

So many years wasted, she thought. *Sisters who grew up together spending their lives as strangers.*

But at least Gram had *us,* she reflected. *Mom and me, Samantha and Britt. She had Martha and Ava, all of her quilter friends, and everyone in town who loved her.*

Winny had only her husband and the folks she met while moving from place to place. And Abner. Everyone else, everyone in Lonesome Way, still thinks of her as an outsider. Someone who's never belonged and never will.

She drew a breath as she remembered she hadn't told Winny yet that they were meeting Britt for lunch at A Bun in the Oven.

Could be a problem.

Her aunt would probably just as soon ride a six-hundred-pound bull out of a rodeo chute than face the citizens of Lonesome Way in broad daylight.

But the past is gone. And Winny's not that wild and scorned young girl anymore. If things are ever going to change, why shouldn't it start now? Today.

Mia pulled away from the curb, into a parking spot, thinking that sharing sandwiches and cupcakes and lemonade at the most popular spot in town might be as good a way as any to begin.

Chapter Twenty-four

Forty-five minutes later, Mia, Winny, and Britt were seated in one of the comfortable middle booths at A Bun in the Oven, enjoying spicy turkey wraps and creamy cole slaw accompanied by cups of icy lemonade. Pink frosted cupcakes sat beside each plate. All three women were trying to act as if Aunt Winona came into town for lunch every day.

For a while there, Mia had thought Winny would never agree to set foot inside the bakery. Her aunt had sat in the car and refused to budge, insisting they pick up burgers or fried chicken from the drive-through and take it all back to the cabin.

"You can't avoid people in this town forever," Mia had reasoned. "It's been almost sixty years since you left, Aunt Winny. You don't have any reason to hide from anyone."

"No one ever liked me in this town."

"They're going to like you just fine now."

"The last time I came here to buy something at Benson's

Drugstore two years ago everyone stared at me. Dorothy Winston, Ava Todd . . . all of Alicia's friends."

"Nobody's going to stare. And if they do, you and I will stare right back. We'll get Brittany to help and all three of us will stare them down."

A guffaw broke from her aunt's lips. Then she'd grown quiet. Finally she said, "You're not going to give up on this, are you? Then we may as well get it over with before we starve to death."

As they walked toward the bakery, Gram's friend Martha Davies hustled out of the Cuttin' Loose. She stood outside her pink-painted door and watched Winny hobble alongside Mia.

"Told you they'd stare," Winny muttered under her breath.

For the first time Mia was uneasy, worried now that Martha might say something that would hurt her aunt. Today the salon owner's hair was tinted such a deep wine color it looked almost purple, and on her long, thin frame she wore belted tan slacks and a striped green and tan silk blouse. At least five bright rings sparkled on her fingers.

"Winona," she said suddenly, "Tell me the name of that nail polish you're wearing."

Winny blinked at her. "Nail polish?"

She stared down at her nails, which shone vivid pink in the sun.

"I have a metallic pink in my shop, and a coral pink and a blush pink, of course, but yours is prettier. Zestier, you know, not so demure. After you reach a certain age, nobody wants to be plain old demure. I know I don't!" Martha grabbed her hand, beamed down at her fingernails. "So what's it called? What's the brand? Don't you know?"

"I didn't pay attention." Winny shrugged. "I bought it over at that drugstore in Livingston."

"We can check the bottle for you when I drive Aunt Winny home," Mia offered.

Martha's eyes lit up. "Well, now, would you? That would be real nice. I'm always looking for new hair products and new nail polish for my customers. Georgia Timmons is partial to pink and told me I need a bigger selection. You tell me and I'll order it."

Martha started to turn back toward her shop and then stopped, eyeing Winny's hair. "You ever want to go more silver on top, you come on in. I've got a real pretty shade that will brighten you right up. I give a ten percent discount for new customers."

Winny stared at her. "Now why would I want to . . ." She caught Mia's chagrined look and clamped her mouth closed. "That's right nice of you, Martha," she said after a brief pause. "I've never touched hair dye in all my years, but . . . if I can put polish on my fingernails and toenails, then why not a little color on top? I might just take you up on that."

Martha grinned as she headed back into the Cuttin' Loose. Over her shoulder, she called, "Don't you be a stranger now, Winny."

Winny stood stock-still for a full minute, trying to digest what had just happened.

But now, inside A Bun in the Oven, she seemed less self-conscious as she bit into her wrap. She was clearly relishing it, and she listened closely as Brittany told them with a sigh that her mom had sent an email to Britt's phone—she was coming home from her honeymoon early. She and Alec would be back in Butte tomorrow.

"She's too freaked out about Wade to stay any longer, so she and Alec changed their plans. And they're coming to Lonesome Way the day after tomorrow because Mom doesn't want me driving home alone, even though I told her I'd be fine." Her face was a study in dejection. "I just wish I could stay, like . . . another week."

Even as the words left her lips, her gaze strayed to Seth at the bakery counter. He was filling a cupcake order for

Joanie Hodge, the sheriff's wife, his good-natured laugh drifting through the shop.

"You need to leave this town, Britt. The sooner the better." Mia caught her niece's hurt look and added quickly, "It's not that I don't want you to stay, honey. I do. But what if Wade's still hanging around? He *could* be," she pointed out despite the alarm that flickered in Britt's blue eyes. "Once he realizes you're gone he might panic. Travis said it could lead him to make a mistake. One that could get him caught."

"But I don't want to go. I feel safe here now that Travis put in that security system. And you and Mom both promised I could stay the entire summer."

"That was before they knew that boy was stalking you." Winny waggled a finger at her. "It's best you go home now and lie low. Give that boy the slip. Not that anyone's asking my opinion—"

Winny broke off as Ava Louise Todd suddenly emerged from the kitchen bearing a magnificent three-layer cake with caramel frosting atop a cut-glass platter.

She stopped short on her way to the front counter and stared at Winny.

"Well, now, I guess there really is a first time for everything."

Winny stiffened, but Sophie's petite white-haired grandmother broke into a gentle smile. "Welcome to A Bun in the Oven, Winona. It's been too long since we've seen you in town. What do you think of my granddaughter's shop?"

"I think I'll be back for a taste of more before you notice I'm gone."

That won her an even wider smile from Ava.

"What kind of cake is that?" Mia wanted to know. "It looks scrumptious."

"Praline carrot cake. Two dollars and seventy-five cents a slice. We make two a day, every other Friday." She winked at Mia. "And when they're gone, they're gone."

"Do you have any of your red velvet cake this afternoon?" Winny asked out of the blue.

"Matter of fact, we do. How do you know about our red velvet cake, for goodness' sake?"

"Abner." Winny shrugged. "It's his favorite. He stops by for a slice now and then and is always going on about it. I was thinking . . ." She trailed off with a glance at Mia. "Abner and his brother should get back from their fishing trip by suppertime and I thought . . . well, he's been so good to me, taking me to my doctor appointments and checking on me every day or so. Think I'd like to bring one of those red velvet cakes over and leave it for the two of 'em when they get back. I have a key to his cabin," she added. "And he'd sure be surprised. I do bake him my oatmeal cookies now and again, but this would be special."

"You're in luck," Ava said. "Tuesdays and Fridays are red velvet cake days. Deanna Mueller is another one who can't get enough of 'em. You want a whole, a half, or a couple of slices?"

"Whole," Winny said. "I've never been one for half measures."

"That's the truth." Ava nodded, then grinned at Mia and Britt. "Way back in the day, all of us girls so wanted to wear our hair just like Jane Russell, but your aunt Winny was the only one who pulled it off every single day. I'll never forget your beautiful waves and curls," she told Winny. "It must have taken you hours. You had those long legs and a figure like she had, too. Everyone said you looked just like her. We were all so envious."

She seemed not to notice the shock on Winny's face at the idea that anyone had been envious of her.

Ava moved forward with the cake platter. "Seth will ring up that red velvet cake soon as you're ready," she called over her shoulder.

Glancing at her watch, Mia realized they'd lingered too long at lunch. Now they'd have to hurry. Especially if they were making an extra stop. Travis and Grady were coming at two and she didn't want to keep them waiting. "Time to make tracks," she announced, pushing back her chair.

Winny was quiet, lost in thought, as they drove toward Sweetwater Road, the roof on the convertible now up since clouds had begun tumbling in from the west. The sky had faded to a cool steel gray, and the first sprinkles of rain splashed against the windshield.

It wasn't until they were almost past the nearly invisible turnoff to Abner's cabin that Winny shook herself out of her reverie and pointed urgently.

"It's right there, Mia, quick. On your left—the turnoff. There's no sign, never has been. Abner's always liked the idea of living on a road with no name."

Mia managed to twist the wheel just in the nick of time. The bumpy, twisting little side road leading to Abner's cabin wasn't in much better condition than Winny's, she realized as the Mustang jolted down the narrow track. Apparently Abner Floyd and her aunt shared a love of isolated, hard-to-reach spots.

But instead of perching on the shoulder of the mountain like Winny's cabin did, Abner's place boasted an old weathered barn and a thick wood and ravine winding behind it.

Peering at the time again, Mia had to swallow a sigh. It was nearly two and there was no help for it. She was going to be late.

She pulled out her cell phone to call Travis and let him know.

"Wait here, Aunt Winny—I'll run the cake in," she ordered as she slid out of the car a few dozen feet from the cabin. Casting one more glance at the threatening sky, she tossed the cell down on the seat.

Better to get the cake inside first, before the heavens opened up.

But even as she raced around to the passenger side and grabbed the white bakery box from her aunt a damp wind gusted furiously down from the mountains, blowing her hair into her face.

Winny had hobbled out of the car and after handing off the cake began fishing around in her knitted bag for the key.

"Where *is* that damned thing?" she muttered as Britt hopped out of the backseat.

"Why can't a person ever find what they're looking for? Ah, here it is. I *knew* I had it."

"Let me open the door for Aunt Mia. You get back in the car, Aunt Winny, before you get drenched." Britt snagged the key and spun toward the cabin as rain began to pelt down.

"Thank you, girls, both of you," Winny called after them, ducking back into the Mustang as adroitly as she could with her cane.

Mia and Britt sprinted toward the cabin as wind and rain shook the trees. Reaching the porch, they gasped with laughter as rain ran down their faces. Britt shoved the key in the door, then caught her breath as it suddenly swung wide open from the inside.

Abner's home early, Mia thought instantly with a jolt of surprise.

Then she saw the man inside the cabin.

Not Abner.

It was a husky young man in a black tee and jeans, and he moved like lightning. Before Mia had time to blink, Wade Collins grabbed Britt by the hair and yanked her toward him.

As Mia screamed he raised his other arm and pointed a gun straight at her face.

⌒

Winny had shut the Mustang's door and dragged her gaze off the sky long enough to watch Brittany push the key in Abner's lock.

When the door swung open and the man seized Britt by the hair, her heart nearly lurched out of her chest with fear.

"Inside! Now!" she heard him shout, his voice bellowing

shakily through the rain. Her blood froze as he stared toward the convertible.

"You, too, Granny!" he yelled. "Outta that car! Get in here *now*. Or . . . or . . . I'll shoot them both!"

Horror ripped through her. Britt was sobbing, terrified, as he clamped her up tight against his chest. Mia stood in frozen shock, still holding the cake as the rain slashed down on her and she stared down the gun inches from her face.

Winny couldn't breathe. She clutched the dash of the car.

Then he yelled at her again. Her hands shook as she groped for the handle to open the Mustang's door.

At the same time, Mia's cell phone trilled on the seat beside her.

Chapter Twenty-five

⌒

"Mia? Are you there?"

Travis distinctly heard someone pick up Mia's phone. But instead of her voice, all he could make out was labored breathing. And then a muffled shout.

It sounded like: *Get your ass over here now!*

A male voice.

"Mia. What's happening?" This time his words were as sharp as blades. Every one of his senses was on edge. He'd been waiting on Mia's front porch for her to get home. It wasn't like her to be late.

Inside her house, Samson was peering out the window, eager to come out and play. Across the street, Grady had joined Evan and Justin as they tossed a football beneath darkening clouds and spatters of rain that hinted at a downpour to come. A moment ago Ellis had appeared on her porch, inviting the boys to come in for hot chocolate.

"Help . . . we need help." A woman's scratchy whisper reached his ears, hammering cold fear into his heart.

"Who is this? Where are you?" His voice was taut, cool, steady. But his insides were churning.

"Winny Pruitt," she whispered. "We're at Abner's cabin. Call the sheriff. . . . He has them, that boy has them—Britt and Mia. And he's got a gun. . . ."

She said something else, but the words were drowned out by another shout, more like a roar.

"All right, give these old bones a minute," Travis heard her call out. Her voice was shaky, more shaky even than it had sounded talking to him and he suddenly wondered if she was playing old and frail, stalling for time. "No need to yell," Travis heard her say, a quaver in her voice—and then abruptly the connection went dead.

He heard silence. Dead silence.

Thunder boomed overhead even as he shot across the street like a linebacker headed for the goal line.

"Grady, you stay here with Ellis! Ellis, keep the boys inside!"

He pounded back to his Explorer without hearing the torrent of questions that followed him and vaulted in, gunning the vehicle down Larkspur Road, swearing under his breath even as he punched in Hodge's number.

"Teddy Hodge here; who's this?"

"Travis Tanner. Wade Collins is at Abner Floyd's cabin. He's armed and he has Mia and Brittany. Tell me where that fucking cabin is, Hodge! *Now*."

Chapter Twenty-six

"Let Brittany go." Mia's nails dug into her palms. "Please. You're hurting her, Wade. I'm sure you don't want to. Just let her go."

Collins stared at her, blinking rapidly. Panic and rage burned in his ocean blue eyes as if he weren't sure how he'd gotten to this point, or what came next. One thickly muscled arm was wound like a noose around Britt's throat, and he was holding her pinned against him as if he'd like to keep her that way forever. But Mia saw him swallow hard, and he looked pale beneath his tan.

Perched on Abner's old sofa beside Winny as rain drove against the cabin windows and thunder cracked across the sky, it was all Mia could do not to leap up and rush toward him. She needed to tear Brittany out of his grasp. The only thing stopping her was the gun. Collins had it pointed in the general direction of her and Aunt Winny. Anguished, she watched the terror mounting in her niece's face.

"*I'm* hurting *her*? You're kidding me, right?" Collins's

voice rose a notch and almost cracked on the words. Nervous tension seemed to ooze from every pore of his beefy frame. "Let's get this straight. She's the one who hurt *me*, okay? Over and over again, she hurt me. I've done everything I can to show her how much I love her, but does she care? *She refuses to listen.* So I guess I have to prove it to her."

"Wade . . . I . . . I know you love me. I know you didn't want to break up. I'm . . . sorry, really sorry. If you let me go, I won't run. I p-promise. I'll stay right here with you, and we can t-talk. If you let them go . . . just let my aunts go!"

Britt had given up trying to wrench his arm from around her throat. At first she'd struggled—until he threatened to shoot Mia and Winny if she didn't stop fighting him. She was trembling now uncontrollably, tears she couldn't stop streaming down her cheeks as she pleaded with him.

"I'll stay here and we can talk. But . . . we need privacy, Wade. It needs to be just you and me—"

"You and me? What about that other guy?" His face tightened. "The jerk I always see you with. At that party . . . at the movies. At the bakery. You think I don't see you? Kissing him, letting him touch you—*what's his name?*"

"His name doesn't matter—"

"I want his name!" Collins shouted, and he fired a shot across the room that missed Winny by only a couple of feet. She ducked sideways instinctively and Mia's body jerked in shock as the bullet slammed into the wall behind them.

"Seth!" Brittany gasped. "His name is Seth!"

"I knew that." Collins's furious expression gave way to bitterness. An agonized despair glimmered in his eyes. "I just wanted to see if you'd tell me the truth. And you should know, the next time I fire this gun, I won't try to miss." He spoke into Brittany's ear with what sounded to Mia like forced bravado, but Britt seemed to shrink a little bit smaller with each word. "You believe me, don't you?"

"Y-yes. D-don't shoot anyone. I'll do whatever you say." Fresh tears dampened her cheeks as she gasped out the words.

Mia struggled to contain the fear rising in her chest. *Stay calm,* she told herself, taking deep breaths to keep panic at bay. *When you make a move, it has to be the right one.*

She couldn't focus on Britt's terror. Or on that frighteningly erratic glint in Wade Collins's eyes. He was nervous, on edge, and therefore dangerous. He looked as wretched now as if he were the one being held against his will. She knew as surely as she knew her own name that he'd shoot her or Winny or Britt without compunction if he lost it and acted on his amped-up emotions.

Her gaze swept the cabin, looking past the cake box she'd set on Abner's three-legged side table, past the old, faded furniture and the ancient television, trying to spot something—anything—she might be able to use as a weapon.

From the condition of the cabin it was obvious that Wade had been squatting here, probably ever since Abner and his brother left on their trip. The sleeping bag rolled up on the floor, the open backpack stuffed with clothes, a flashlight, camping supplies, and the assortment of opened beer cans scattered on tables and across the old wood floor all told her he'd been here several days at least.

But the only weapon in sight seemed to be the one in his hand.

Then her gaze returned to the beer can lying squashed and empty on the round table beside her. It wasn't much. But if she had a chance, any kind of chance, it would be better than nothing.

How long had they been here now, listening to Collins yell at them how much he loved Brittany, how much she'd hurt him? Telling her how he'd been sleeping on the hard ground in the middle of nowhere for weeks, just to be close enough to stay near her, to keep an eye on her? How he'd probably lost his job for taking off after her, spending every waking moment trying to prove to her how much she meant to him?

It felt like hours since she and Britt had run up to Abner's door, but in all this time, she hadn't found an opening yet to do something. Anything.

She had to stop him.

All she needed was an opportunity. . . .

"How did . . . you find me?" Britt gasped as he dragged her to the rocking chair a few feet from the sofa, sank down, and forced her to sit on his lap. Glancing uneasily back and forth between the two women on the sofa, he kept the gun trained on Mia.

"Didn't I tell you I'd follow you wherever you went? You're my girl, I'd do anything for you." He pressed a kiss to her cheek, then scowled as she tried to pull away.

"Finding you was easy peasy. All I did was pay my cousin Ralph fifty bucks. He's a computer programmer, remember? He can hack into anything under the sun. Once I offered him the dough—and the added bonus that I wouldn't tell his mom he smokes weed on the weekends and does a little dealing on the side—he got right to work. Didn't take him long to track the location of the computer you used once you got to this dump of a town. Led me straight to your aunt's pretty little house. Nothing's too much trouble when it comes to you, baby." He sounded defiant and more than a little desperate. "I thought you knew that."

Winny was holding tightly to her cane, her fingers rigid as she, too, watched Collins. Mia could almost sense the heat of her aunt's fury.

So she was surprised when Winny spoke in a voice that sounded unsteady.

"Young man, I . . . have to use the bathroom."

His head jerked toward her. "No way. Stay where you are."

"Please. I . . . I'm scared and I . . . need to go. I'm an old woman and you've frightened me."

"Let her," Britt begged softly, tilting her face toward him. "Please, Wade. She's not in good health. Let her for me."

His skin darkened with an angry flush, but uncertainty

hovered in his eyes. "Haven't I already done enough for you? I gave up my job, I've been hanging around this dump of a town . . . I've done nothing but try to show you . . ." He stopped, swallowing down the tremble in his voice. Then he scowled at the pleading look on Winny's face.

"Hell, Granny, why not? Go ahead, use the can." He stood up, clamping Britt to him again and training the gun on Mia once more. He was struggling now to keep his voice steady. "But you just remember—you do one thing I don't like, make one little move, and I'll have to shoot her. You got it?"

"Y-yes. Th-thank you." Winny's voice sounded more frail than Mia had ever heard it. She didn't sound like Winny at all. Mia's heart began to thud. She braced herself for whatever was coming next as her aunt leaned heavily on her cane and began to hobble across the room.

She limped past Collins and Brittany, moving more slowly than Mia had ever seen her move, and Wade turned slightly to keep her in his line of vision. For an instant, the gun no longer pointed straight at Mia.

Suddenly everything happened at once. Winny slammed her cane with astonishing force at Collins's knee. Even as he screamed in pain, Mia snatched the beer can and launched herself at him, ramming the can into his jaw, and at the same time, Britt drove her elbow backward into his rib cage. She lurched free of his grasp at the same moment Mia grabbed for the gun.

Desperation fueled Mia as she used every ounce of her strength and will. Her fingers latched onto the cold metal with strength she never knew she possessed as pain suffused Wade's face. Then Winny hit him again with her cane, and as he howled with the impact, Mia gritted her teeth and wrenched the gun from his fingers.

Suddenly the front door flew open. Travis sprang into the cabin, soaked from the rain, water streaming down his taut face, his shirt clinging to his chest. Yet the Glock in his hand was trained with cold, impervious efficiency on Wade Collins.

"Freeze, Collins. Don't move."

But Wade, his face bloodied, wheeled and took his chances, dodging for the back door like a wounded jackrabbit confronted by a mountain lion. Travis swore, his eyes narrowing as in that split second he chose not to shoot. An instant later, Collins was gone, fleeing into the rain.

Travis reached Mia in two strides just as she set the gun down on the floor. His free arm caught her to him, holding her close as she clung to him. He searched her face, his throat so tight he couldn't even swallow.

"Are you all right?" he asked hoarsely. Finally the terror that had clamped hard and heavy on his chest during the endless drive to the cabin began to ebb. She was deathly pale and she looked shaken, but otherwise she was unharmed. Relief sagged through him. "He hurt you? Any of you?" he demanded.

"N-not me. Travis, he hurt Britt." Mia gulped back tears. "Britt, honey . . ." She whirled toward her niece, wanting to enfold the sobbing girl in her arms, then saw that Winny was already holding her, murmuring words of comfort. Aunt Winny was stroking the girl's hair with a gentleness Mia had never seen in her before.

"Stay here, all of you. Lock that door after me." Travis fought against his own overwhelming sense of relief. The knowledge that he could have lost Mia today shook him to his core. He could have been too late. . . .

His voice was husky as he told them, "Hodge will be here any minute."

"Go, Travis, we're fine. Go get him," Mia urged as she joined Winny in hugging her arms around Britt.

"No fears, baby." He shot her a grim, gentle smile that belied the deadly look in his eyes when he'd entered the cabin. "That bastard's as good as got."

Then he was gone, pounding into the storm after Wade.

Mia cradled Brittany in her arms, rocking her as the girl began to hiccup with her sobs. Gently, Winny stroked Britt's hand.

"It's okay, honey," Mia said firmly. "You're safe now. We all are. Travis will get him. You won't ever have to worry about Wade Collins hurting you again."

Over the wind and the thunder nearly shaking the cabin Brittany clung to her as the shriek of police sirens suddenly filled the air, screaming down the road with no name.

⌒

Travis tore through the trees, ignoring the rain slamming like bullets into his face, soaking his clothes. Collins was zigzagging wildly through the woods, moving fast with adrenaline and fear despite the injury to his knee. But Travis was gaining on him. Gaining fast.

No slipping away this time, asshole, he thought as he leaped across fallen branches and plowed toward his quarry. Collins was less than twenty yards ahead—fifteen. Travis could practically hear the kid's chest heaving.

He couldn't let himself think about what Collins had done to Mia and Brittany and their aunt. He forced himself to focus solely on pursuit as he single-mindedly bore down on him. He was drawing closer . . . and closer. His own breath was coming fast but he wasn't winded. Collins stumbled and Travis gained another yard. *Two.* The wind tore at his face and he blinked the rain from his eyes, jumped over a tree stump in his path, and saw Collins start down an embankment.

No, you don't, pal. Travis pumped up his speed, calculated, and leaped at the kid in a flying tackle that had brought down far tougher men. He hit him with a sickening thwack and then they were both rolling down the grassy embankment, over rocks and twigs, twisting and grunting. He managed to get in one good punch before they reached the bottom. Collins tried to fight, to land a blow, but Travis pinned him easily to the ground and slugged him again.

Blood streamed from the punk's nose as he screamed, "Britt! I love you, Britt!"

"Shut up," Travis said. Turning his head quickly, he saw Teddy Hodge and Zeke Mueller behind him, tearing down the embankment. "The only time you're ever going to set eyes on Brittany again is in the courthouse—right before they send you away."

And then as Collins tried once more to kick and twist, Travis hit him again and this time the punk slumped, his head rolling to the side, the fight going out of him like a whoosh of air from a deflated balloon.

"Good . . . job . . . Travis!" Hodge called, huffing as he reached the bottom and stalked toward them, grim faced.

Mueller got there before the sheriff. As Travis stood, the deputy flipped the dazed kid over and snapped on the cuffs.

"You have the right to remain silent," Mueller began, but Travis didn't hear the rest. He was already running back up the embankment. Back to the cabin.

Back to Mia.

Chapter Twenty-seven

⌒

"Sure you're all right?" Travis asked that night when the police had finished with their questions, when Collins was locked behind bars, when Brittany had let everything out in a two-hour crying jag and then gone out with Seth for ice cream—and he and Mia were finally alone.

Travis had left Grady at the ranch with Rafe and Sophie so he could come back to Larkspur Road to check on her.

Mia lay nestled in his arms on her living room sofa wearing clean jeans and a pink tank top, her feet bare. Her freshly showered skin glowed in the lamplight.

"I'm good," she assured him. "A little shaky still, but . . . thank God you got there when you did!"

"If anything had happened to you—" His voice was so thick he suddenly found he couldn't even finish the sentence. He'd never forget that godawful drive out to Abner's place. Knowing all the while that Mia, her niece, and her aunt were trapped there with Collins and that the kid had a gun and was plenty unstable enough to use it.

Raw terror the likes of which he'd never known had gripped him during that drive. Terror of losing Mia. Of her being hurt in any way . . .

He wouldn't have been able to bear it.

Every muscle in his body tight, he pressed a kiss to her cheek and she turned in his arms so she was lying in his embrace, her beautiful face uplifted to his.

"You reached us just in time."

"If it hadn't been for your aunt answering your cell phone I wouldn't have known. No one would have—"

"Shh." Mia touched her finger to his mouth. "We're all okay, Travis. You got him. Now all of us—me, Aunt Winny, and most of all Britt—we're safe."

"You're the one who got the gun away from him," he reminded her, pressing a kiss to her temple. "I'll have nightmares for years thinking about how *that* could have gone wrong."

"Hey, there were three of us fighting back. We had it in the bag. Unless, of course, he'd gotten the gun away from *me*. . . ."

Her voice trailed off and Travis felt her shiver.

His arms tightened around her.

"It's over," he said quietly. "You're safe. He'll never get near any of you again."

With a smile she reached up, pulled his head down toward her, and kissed him. A long, soul-stirring kiss that soon had them both lying on the sofa, as close as two people could be, thinking how grateful they were to be alive and together, alone in this house except for Samson, who was snoring gently on the hall rug.

"Um . . . Brittany and Seth . . . they could be back soon. They only went for ice cream. . . ."

"Then I guess we'd better hurry." Travis grinned. He was off the sofa in one swift, smooth lunge, reaching down and scooping her into his arms. He loved the sound of her laughter as he carried her into the bedroom and kicked the door shut with his foot.

"Lock it," she ordered with a grin as he lowered her to the bed. "Hurry."

"Hey, always happy to oblige a lady." His lips quirked and his eyes were warm as he obeyed, then moved back toward her, watching her peel that pink tank top over her head in one smooth movement and toss it to the floor. Suddenly they couldn't get each other out of their clothes fast enough.

But for all their hurry, once they were free of their clothing they made slow, gentle love. They kissed and nibbled and stroked. Took their time. Celebrated being alive and being together, and knowing they had tomorrow and the next day and the day after that.

It was only when they were both dressed again, and had shared coffee and scones in the kitchen, and she was walking him out onto the porch so he could pick up Grady and take him home to the cabin, that he remembered the conversation he'd had earlier in the day with Val.

Mia listened in shock as he clasped her hand in his and told her about it.

"His interview's next *week*? They can't do that to him, Travis. You can't let them."

Her eyes blazed into his, and Travis pulled her to him, kissed the top of her head. "Don't worry, I won't. I never had a chance to return Val's call today—but tomorrow . . ." He sighed, and his eyes narrowed with purpose. "Tomorrow I'm calling my lawyer, and I'm telling Val that we're revisiting our custody arrangements. If she can't—or at this point won't—care for Grady full-time, I sure as hell can. And I want to. Let her go to Europe or wherever she wants, or should I say, wherever *Drew* wants, but they're not dumping our son at Broadcrest Academy, not for a single day."

"Will she listen?" Mia's face was tight with worry.

"I'll make her listen. Val knows deep down this is wrong. She's trying to please Drew."

"Going a little overboard, don't you think?" Mia muttered. "Throwing her son away."

He touched his forehead to hers. "Believe me, I don't understand this any more than you do. All I can think is that she's become so caught up in this supersized lifestyle she and Baylor have going that she'll sacrifice anything, even her own son, to hang on to it. To hang on to Drew. And somehow, she's justifying it in her own mind. Who knows, maybe she's convinced herself it will be good for him in the long run. But deep down, I think Val knows it's wrong. Wrong on her part and wrong for Grady. I hear it in her voice. She feels guilty as hell but she's trying to drown it in denial."

Mia could only pray that was true. "Travis, if he could stay with you, stay in Lonesome Way . . ." Her eyes searched his. "He's been making such good progress. He's worlds happier than he was when you first brought him here—that first day he looked like he didn't have a friend in the world. Now he's blooming. He's so incredibly bright—with the right guidance and structure, he'll not only pass that proficiency test, he'll probably get straight A's in sixth grade. And he has friends here already and he could have so many more—"

Travis stroked a gentle hand across her cheek. "You don't have to convince me, baby. Maybe I should let *you* talk to Val," he added with a laugh in his voice.

"I'd be glad to," she shot back, chin up, a martial light in her eyes.

There on the porch, with misty moonlight streaming down and only the faint howl of a faraway coyote and the hum of a thousand insects breaking the deep silence of the Montana night, he stared at her. At her lovely upturned face, at the care and willingness to fight for his son that shimmered in her eyes.

He was overwhelmed by the generosity of her heart. By

the light and kindness that seemed to flow effortlessly from her, like the purest water cascading from a falls in the wild.

Something hard and almost painful swelled and tightened in his chest, in his throat. Every muscle in his body clenched. He tugged her closer, into the circle of his arms, breathing in the clean, flower-light scent of her, feeling that gorgeous, sexy body pressed to his, hardly able to believe his good fortune—that he'd somehow been granted a second chance with her.

"Do you have any idea—any idea at all—how much I love you?" His voice was low, almost fierce. The words seemed to come of their own accord from someplace deep within his soul. He saw the smile curve her lips even as a glaze of shock softened her eyes.

"No . . . but I'm listening." Her arms slid around his neck. Her voice was slightly unsteady. "Feel free to tell me in great detail."

"I can do that." His mouth brushed hers and his eyes glinted in the moonlight. "How much time you got, Ms. Quinn?"

"Enough to tell you that I love you, too."

Pulling his head down toward her, she kissed him. He gripped her waist and their mouths made silent promises their bodies yearned to answer. But just as he tugged her back toward the door, their lips and hearts locked together, the sound of a car's engine turning into the drive drove them apart.

Travis groaned. Was this some kind of a joke? He wanted to kiss her all night long. It almost physically hurt to let her go.

"Damn." The growl came from his throat but it seemed pitifully unequal to the situation as Britt and Seth got out of the car.

"Hi, Aunt Mia, hi, Travis." Mia's niece sounded quiet but calm. Her face was pale, Travis noted, watching the teens' approach, but after the explosion of tears earlier, she seemed to have remarkably pulled herself together.

"To be continued," he vowed in Mia's ear as Samson barked, demanding to be let outside to join the group.

"You know where to find me," Mia whispered, longing filling her as his words—*Do you have any idea how much I love you?*—circled through her head.

And the heat of his kisses singed her heart.

Chapter Twenty-eight

❧

"Dad, is Mom *really* coming here to see me before she goes to London?"

Travis stood at the kitchen counter in the cabin, pouring himself a second cup of coffee. He and Grady were finishing their breakfast before heading to Sage Ranch for a ride.

Outside the window, an early morning rain had stopped, and the sun peeked out above the mountains in a clean-washed sky the color of a denim shirt fresh out of the dryer.

"Absolutely. Your mom promised she won't go overseas without seeing you first." He returned to the table with his steaming mug and saw that Grady had polished off his fried eggs and hash browns and wore a trace of a milk mustache. His son was oblivious of this, though—oblivious even of the buttered biscuit still on his plate as he studied Travis, his eyes big and worried.

"She misses you, buddy. She'll come. And if for any reason she *can't* make it out here," he added carefully—because who knew if Val might for some crazy reason decide ultimately she didn't have time for a trip to Montana?—"then I'll take you to L.A. to see her before she leaves. That's a promise."

"I don't have to stay in that house, though, do I, Dad? I hate that house."

I know you do, Travis reflected, a pang twisting through him at the thought of how much time Grady had already spent in Drew Baylor's home. *Way too much time.* "If we end up going to L.A., we'll stay in a hotel. One with a swimming pool," he added, eyes twinkling.

"Awesome!" With a satisfied grin, Grady suddenly noticed his uneaten biscuit. He popped it into his mouth. "And if we don't have to see Drew, even better," he said, chewing. "That guy's a jerk."

I know that, too, Travis thought, but he didn't say it aloud. "You'll have to see him and stay at that house sometimes, remember, but not this time," he warned the boy, who already knew the score.

Travis and Val had talked extensively in the past weeks— almost as extensively as their lawyers had.

After Travis had made it clear he wanted full-time custody of Grady and that he'd fight full-out in court if Val refused to let the boy stay in Lonesome Way, it hadn't taken anywhere near as long as he'd expected for her to throw in the towel.

He'd guessed she wouldn't have the time or the will for a protracted legal battle and all its entanglements. And that Baylor didn't have the patience for it—or the willingness to spend an exorbitant sum of money trying to retain custody of a boy he had no interest in and who didn't measure up to his standards.

So with a quickness that filled Travis not only with relief but also with disgust, she'd agreed to drop the whole Broadcrest Academy notion *and* to let Travis take over custody. All in return for generous visiting privileges.

Obviously Val and her new husband had decided she had

better things to do than to be saddled full-time with the raising of an adolescent son.

She could see Grady on prearranged weekends and on spring and winter breaks, and she had the right to visit him in Montana once a month if she chose after she returned to the States.

"I know what you must think of me, but I'm not abandoning my son," she'd insisted to Travis the last time they talked. Defensiveness had bristled in her tone. "I'll see him a lot—as often as I can. It's just that all of these opportunities have opened up for me. Things I could never dream of before. And after everything I've gone through, being a widow so young, a single mother . . ." Her voice wavered. "Travis, that was all so hard. My therapist says I deserve this. And I do. It doesn't mean I don't love Grady with all my heart. I've always been a good mother, you know that, don't you?"

"I know you love him, Val." *As much as you're capable of loving anyone besides yourself—and Baylor—right now.* But Travis hadn't said that aloud. He'd chosen his words carefully and left it at that.

She didn't need to know that Grady had been overjoyed when he learned he didn't have to go back to school in L.A. Or that he'd been thrilled at the idea of living full-time with his father in Lonesome Way, only a stone's throw from his aunt and uncle and cousins.

He hadn't been able to stop talking about being able to ride Pepper Jack whenever he wanted and learning from Rafe and Will Brady how to start horses.

Not to mention his excitement about going to school with Evan and Justin—a school where Mia taught, where he already had a teacher who was an ally and a friend.

He was a little torn about not seeing his mother regularly, but for the most part he'd taken it so much in stride it made Travis wonder just how little time Val had been spending with him once she married Drew. During all the weeks he'd been living with Travis, the boy had talked more about Drew and the housekeeper than he did about Val.

"Can we take Evan and Justin camping with us when we go?" Grady took a last swig of his milk. "They want to see the planets, too. And Evan said he checked out a library book about the stars. We need to go on a really clear night so we can see as much as possible."

"I'll speak to their parents, and if they give the go-ahead, it's a plan."

Grinning, the boy snagged another biscuit. As he broke it in half, a serious look came over his face. "There's something bothering me, Dad."

That hint of worry still hovered in his eyes.

"What is it?" Travis asked, bracing himself.

His son leaned forward, his face earnest. "I can't make up my mind. About what I want to be when I grow up," he explained.

A grin broke across Travis's face. He tried to hide it by taking a quick swig of coffee.

"Some days I want to have a horse ranch like Uncle Rafe's. I want to start horses and raise them and ride them all the time. But other times I think I want to be an astronomer or maybe even an astronaut." The worry left his eyes. They began to gleam. "I want to learn everything there is to know about the stars and the sky and the planets. I want to go to Mars. Wouldn't that be cool? Or maybe Mercury. What would it be like? I could be an explorer and find out all kinds of new stuff. But on the other hand, I love horses and riding. So what should I do? I can't pick."

"Well." Travis studied him calmly. "Seems to me you don't have to pick anything yet. You can learn about both. See where it leads. There's no rush."

"But Justin wants to be a football player. His mind's made up. And Evan knows he wants to own a hardware store because he loves being around tools and making things and stuff. I'm the only one who can't decide. I think there must be something wrong with me."

Travis fought back a smile. "There's nothing wrong with you. You're bright and you're curious. You have all kinds of options—and some of them you don't even know about yet. For now, go to school and do your best. And be a kid. When you're older, like another seven, eight years, then you'll have a better idea."

"But what if I still don't know?" Grady fretted.

Travis looked into that young face and saw a boy so full of ideas and dreams and worries that a thick, almost over-powering rush of love swept over him like a tidal wave.

"If you still don't know, then you'll try one thing. And if something inside you tells you it's not right, you'll try another." He set down his coffee. "Always listen to what's inside of you, Grady. Your instincts will lead you to the right thing."

"Instincts," Grady repeated, trying out the word. "Okay." He took a breath. "Thanks."

Scrambling to his feet with a thoughtful expression, he carried his plate and empty milk glass to the sink. "I have one more question," he announced.

"Good, because I probably have one more answer." Travis leaned back with a grin.

"This is serious, Dad. Are you going to marry Mia? You're always holding hands and stuff, and I know you kiss when you think I'm not looking. I heard Evan and Justin's grandma talking on the phone. She told some lady in her book club she'd bet every book on her shelf you two are getting married."

"Did she?" Travis pushed back his chair, a slight glint in his eyes. "And how do you feel about that?"

"I think it would be cool. Then we could have that fried chicken she makes and those chocolate-frosted brownies all the time. *And* she could help me with my homework if I ever have trouble."

"Hey, I can help you with your homework, too."

"But she's a teacher. Plus I like her. And"—Grady's eyes lit—"then Samson would be my dog, right? I've always wanted a dog. And he's the best. I mean, I like Starbucks and Tidbit a lot, too," he added quickly. "But they're Ivy and Aiden's dogs. So . . . are you? Going to marry her, I mean. Can she and Samson move in with us?"

Travis's eyes gleamed in the sunlight pouring through the kitchen window. "What do your instincts tell you?"

The widest grin he'd ever seen broke across Grady's face. "My instincts say *yes*!"

Travis nodded, unable to keep his lips from twitching. "Well, what did I just tell you? Always trust your instincts."

Chapter Twenty-nine

While Travis and Grady were eating breakfast together, discussing camping trips, planets, dogs, and marriage, Winona Sullivan Pruitt was sitting in her old Ford pickup at the edge of the cemetery, where graceful aspens and carefully tended rosebushes guarded old and fresh graves alike.

She was staring down at the letter she'd left unopened for years. Turning the sealed envelope over and over again in her hands. Setting it down on the passenger seat. Picking it up.

Finally she took a deep breath, grabbed the envelope, and headed toward her sister's grave. She could manage without the cane now and from the moment she was able to be out and about on her own this idea had been taking over her brain.

She could think of little else.

"Just get it over with," she told herself.

Her heart was pounding uncomfortably.

The deep, lush grass she walked across was still damp

from the morning rain, soaking her purple canvas sneakers. The morning air still held a hint of a chill.

Or maybe the chill's inside me, Winona thought as she searched for her sister's grave.

Finding it in a quiet, shady spot beneath a weeping willow tree, she stared down at the simple pale gray headstone.

Her big sister was down there. Deep in the cold, damp ground. The sister she'd shut out of her life. The sister who'd tried to make amends.

"You wanted me to read this, Alicia, so I guess I will. Maybe it's coming too late, but it's all I can do now. I should've let you in that day you came to see me—I guess we both know that. But I didn't—and I can't change that now. So I'll read your letter. Maybe that will be enough."

It wouldn't be, though. How could it?

Still, she told herself, it was something.

She had to try to make some measure of peace. With herself.

And with Alicia.

Her fingers shook as she unfolded the plain ivory paper and began to read her sister's neat, tiny, airy script.

When she reached the last word, she returned to the top and read the letter through again.

Pain arced through her like a carving knife slicing through bread. First one tear, then a flood of them streamed down her cheeks.

"I never knew," she whispered into the silence hovering over the graves. "I never imagined."

The words on the page blurred as she stared at them, read them yet again.

I admired you so, Winny. And I never told you. I was jealous of your daring, your freedom. All those chances you took. The way you defied our father, and held your head up no matter what he said to you or how he tried to shame your spirit out of you, took my breath away. Everything about you filled me with jealousy. You did things I never had the courage to do. All those times you climbed out the window in the night and went off dancing, or running wild in the woods with the boys and didn't come home until the sun was up—oh, how I envied you your courage. I used to dream about going with you just once—to see what it felt like to do something adventurous. Something our father wouldn't approve of. To be different from all the other girls.

But I liked being the good daughter too much ever to do anything that would make Papa frown. I never had an ounce of your courage. And here's what's the hardest thing of all to admit. I always tried to make myself look good, sometimes at your expense. In those days, I loved being praised and petted. Something inside me needed to make sure I was the one Papa was always proud of.

But I'll tell you what shames me the most. Not believing you about Henry.

Winny thrust the letter down, her heart clenching. Closing her eyes, she tried to fight the sea of emotions sweeping over her.

It wasn't until a full minute later that she managed to pick up the letter with trembling fingers and start reading again.

You'd never done anything to hurt me before that day. Never. I should have known you didn't kiss him, that he was to blame. I should have believed you. My own sister. If I had, things might have been so very different.

Maybe you'll forgive me after you read this letter. I can only hope and pray. No matter what, there's something else you need to know.

I forgive you. I forgive you for burning the good luck wedding quilt. There wasn't any way I could have had good luck with Henry, not with the sort of man he was. So it hardly would have mattered even if that quilt had been draped across our marriage bed every day and every night. Henry would have left me, cheated on me, no matter what. That was the nature of the man. I need you to know this, so that if you ever find your way to forgiving me back, we can be sisters again. I would like that more than almost anything in this world.

Winona, please come tell me if you find it in your heart to forgive me. I will hope and wait. With love, Alicia.

Winny's knees trembled. A gust of wind fluttered the leaves of the willow and she swayed, too, as the impact of her sister's words struck, and shook her deep into her bones.

"It's too late, isn't it?" she whispered. She thudded painfully to her knees in the grass beside the grave as tears began to drip from her eyes. "I wasted . . . all that time."

Her throat closed up. Reaching out an unsteady hand, she brushed a clump of dirt from the gravestone.

"In case you can hear me—I forgive you, Alicia," she whispered. Images of her sister sneaking supper to her, hidden in her red and white print apron, rolled through Winny's mind. "Do you hear me, Alicia? *I forgive you, too.*"

As the words left her lips, she felt something. Something light as air. Brushing against her cheek. A splash of color flitted suddenly across her line of vision. Winny blinked.

Stared.

It was a butterfly.

Tiny and quick, its wings alive with light, it fluttered in a circle, then came back to settle on her hand. The hand that rested on the grave. The tiny wings stilled. Quivered against her skin. Winny held her breath.

A butterfly.

An instant later, wings glowing like stained glass in the sunlight, it flew upward again, whisked along her cheek softer than a feather—or a kiss—and was gone. A fairy whirl of light and color, vanishing in the glare of day.

Gone.

A butterfly.

"Alicia," Winny whispered hoarsely, staring at the air around her. It was impossible to hold back her tears. "I miss you . . . Alicia. I always missed you."

It was a breath, a whisper, and a prayer all at once.

She didn't know how long she knelt there. But finally, painfully, she pushed herself to her feet.

A sense of peace came over her. A kind of peace she hadn't known in years. Perhaps she'd never known it.

But she suddenly realized one final thing she had to do.

She had to tell the truth about the only lie she'd ever told.

She had to tell Mia.

⌒

"Aunt Winny, I wasn't expecting you." Swinging the screen door open, Mia smiled at her aunt. Winny had a large wicker basket with a matching lid hooked over her arm. Her expression could only be described as purposeful. "Are we having a picnic? Did I forget?"

"You didn't forget a thing."

Samson dashed around the older woman in happy circles, trying to be noticed and petted as she stepped inside.

"There's something I need to show you, that's all. It's past time we cleared this up once and for all."

Mia searched her face, mystified, but led the way into Gram's little sewing studio. She offered Winny some iced tea, but her aunt shook her head.

"Sit," Winny instructed, pointing at the small sofa, though she herself stood a moment longer, gazing at Gram's butterfly quilt on the wall.

"What's going on?" Mia asked as Winny settled at last on the sofa, placing the basket between them. Samson leaped up, his paws on Winny's knee, his little face begging to be acknowledged.

"I see you, you little mutt," Winny murmured. "Don't be such a pest." But she reached out and gently scratched the dog behind his ears. "Go lie down now," she told him and, to Mia's amusement, he obeyed, curling up at her great-aunt's feet, his chin resting on his paws.

Winny didn't waste any time getting to the point. "You know the good luck wedding quilt I burned?"

"Yes, of course. You told me. You burned it the night you ran away."

Meeting Mia's gaze, Winny swallowed hard. "This isn't easy to say. I've kept this secret all these years. Along with all the others," she added ruefully. "But you have a right to know. And so do Samantha and Brittany."

"I already know why you burned the quilt. You were angry when you ran off because no one believed you that night about what happened. It's all right, Aunt Winny," Mia said quietly. "I understand. None of us blame you and we're not angry—"

"I didn't burn it."

Mia stared at her. *"What?"*

"It's here. Right here. I've had it all along."

Pushing back the lid of the basket, Winny drew out a quilt and spread it across her lap with careful fingers. Mia couldn't stop staring at her in shock, but Winny wasn't ready yet to meet her eyes.

"I burned a different quilt," she confessed. "One I'd been working on in secret. I wasn't anywhere near as good a quilter as your grandmother in those days, and I couldn't bear to be compared to her." She sighed. "So I kept the quilt I was working on well hidden under my bed, and I didn't show it to a soul. But that night, I was so angry with Alicia, with everyone, that I wanted to burn the good luck wedding quilt. I actually brought it outside—I was ready to set it on fire. I itched to do it. But . . ." She looked away. "Something stopped me. I guess because it was part of our family history, I just couldn't bring myself to do it. But I wanted so badly to punish Alicia for doubting me. And to show my parents how angry I was. So . . ."

As her voice trailed off, Mia at last found hers. "You burned the *other* quilt," she whispered, stunned. "You took the good luck quilt with you!"

Winny's nod of assent made her heart squeeze tight in her chest. Mia gazed at the faded old quilt spread across her great-aunt's lap. There was no doubt. It was the most unique, lovely quilt she'd ever seen. That rich, rose-colored background. Those beautiful scalloped edges. The graceful arcs of vintage calico in the double wedding ring pattern.

A sense of wonder filled her as she ran her hand gently over the yellow and blue and lavender patches. "So you've had it all these years," she breathed.

Winny nodded. "I was married to my Harley for forty of those years, so I suppose it did bring me some good luck after all." She touched a finger gently to the quilt, then her gaze lifted.

"If I'd left it for Alicia, she might've had better luck in her marriage. Maybe they'd have stayed together, been happy. . . ."

"It's only a quilt, Aunt Winny. An extremely beautiful one," Mia added, "but still a quilt. It's not magical and nothing could have changed my grandfather's nature. *He* was responsible for deserting Gram, not your taking this quilt away."

"I know that. I do. But I never should've . . ." Winny stopped herself, straightened her shoulders. "What's done is done," she said half to herself.

Then she stared Mia in the eye. "I want you to have it and I don't want any arguments. Take care of it. Maybe you'll marry that handsome Travis Tanner and keep it safe and pretty on your bed for the next sixty years or so."

"Aunt Winny—"

"That's all I'm saying." Her aunt held up a strong, imperious hand, whimsically painted in a bright lime hue. "You just keep it safe. You won't be seeing another one like it anytime soon. And don't thank me, whatever you do."

A rush of emotion swamped Mia. This quilt had passed through the hands of countless women in her family. It was an heirloom, a one-of-a-kind treasure she'd never thought to see. She could hardly wait to show it to Brittany and Sam.

"I'm so grateful it's here. That's all *I'll* say," she added with a laugh as Winny shot her a warning glance. "You know, I'd love to display it at the fund-raiser. Everyone in Lonesome Way would enjoy seeing it. And it would definitely be one of the oldest quilts there. An oldie but goodie," she said softly. "Would that be all right with you, Aunt Winny?"

"I can't believe I'm saying this," Winny muttered gruffly, "but I like the idea. And I think Alicia would like it, too."

Mia reached over, clasped her hand. "I'm sure Gram has forgiven you, Aunt Winny. Now it's time for you to forgive yourself."

"Working on it."

"Good. You'll stay for supper?"

"Depends." A faint smile touched her eyes, then spread down to the corners of her lips. "What's on the menu?"

"Meat loaf and mashed potatoes. Green beans and salad. Apple pie for dessert. Travis is coming with Grady. Britt will be joining us, too."

Now that the threat of Wade Collins was gone, Samantha had dropped her insistence that Britt come home to Butte as soon as possible. She and Alec had driven to Lonesome Way, and she'd hugged and kissed her daughter, shown Britt and Mia photos of her honeymoon, stayed over two nights, and then relented—allowing Britt to remain at Mia's until at least after the fund-raiser.

"We'll have a party," Mia continued, smiling at Winny. "A good luck wedding quilt party."

"I don't like parties. Never did," her aunt responded bluntly. "But I'll stay. Only because of that apple pie." But Mia saw the glimmer of humor in her eyes and, for no reason at all, she put her arms around her aunt and hugged her tightly, the wedding quilt smushed between them.

"We're having a real family dinner, Aunt Winny," Mia whispered. "I bet Gram would like that. Very much."

Chapter Thirty

❧

"Well, imagine that. Less than an hour to go and the sun's still out. That rain's holding off, thank goodness." Martha Davies bustled toward Mia in the small, brightly lit side room of the Lonesome Way Public Library, where Mia was stationed to supervise the special exhibition of fragile older quilts.

The good luck wedding quilt was among nine others considered vintage quilts, displayed with special care and attention inside the library.

The weather forecast for the quilt fund-raiser had been foreboding all week, but by some miracle, the day had dawned sunny and the clouds in the west had shown no inclination to drift closer.

So far so good, Mia thought, watching several older women pause to admire Gram's butterfly quilt and then the good luck wedding quilt, both carefully presented on hanging racks.

The small sign beside the butterfly quilt showed a grainy

black-and-white photo of Gram with the quilt draped across her arms at age seventeen, the year she'd made it. The sign also noted Gram's name, the date the quilt had been sewn, and the fact that Alicia Rae Sullivan had won first place at the tri-county Fourth of July fair.

"I'm your replacement—you've been shut up in here long enough," Martha announced, sweeping toward Mia at the small rectangular table. "Go on out and have some ice cream while you have the chance. Before you know it, you'll be up on that podium announcing the grand total."

"Is there still a nice-sized crowd?" Mia asked as a very pregnant Deanna Mueller wandered past the doorway, browsing the quilts displayed in the main room of the library.

"You'd better believe it. In the last hour and a half just about everyone in town has shown up. And most everyone's sticking around to see how much money we've raised. Should be a tidy sum, especially now that the community quilt's been raffled off." Martha's big silver hoop earrings swung wildly as she nodded in satisfaction. "A caravan of folks from Livingston and some more from Billings came by a few hours ago. A few of the women chatted with Karla—real excited to see our quilts. Said they might want to do an ice cream social with their exhibition next year, too. But," Martha added, "it's time you got back out there to see for yourself. Spend a little more time with your sister and niece—Samantha *did* come all the way from Butte, didn't she?"

It was true. Sam and Alec had driven in for the day to attend the exhibition. They would spend the night at Mia's house and then take Britt home with them in the morning. At Britt's pleading, Sam had agreed that her daughter could still drive in to work at A Bun in the Oven, but only weekends for the rest of the summer, giving her a chance to see Seth and to spend the night at either Mia's house or Jackie Kenton's.

It had been wonderful having lunch outside with Britt, Sam, and Alec, drinking strawberry lemonade from paper cups while the sun poured down and the Lonesome Way High School marching band serenaded the crowd.

Travis had invited Samantha, Britt, Alec, and Aunt Winny, as well as Sophie and Rafe, Lissie and Tommy, and all the kids, back to his cabin for a big barbecue tonight under the stars. Though if the weather acted up, as expected, he'd be forced to move everything indoors.

Winny had been particularly surprised—and pleased— to be included. But nowhere near as surprised as Mia had been when she learned that her crusty aunt had volunteered to help sell tickets to the quilt exhibition outside the library entrance today.

If she isn't careful, Winona Pruitt might become a real honest-to-goodness force to be reckoned with in this town, Mia thought in amusement as she made her way through the main room of the library, past the vivid array of beautiful quilts draped across tables and chairs. She was thrilled to see how many people were roaming through the main room, knowing every one of them had made a donation before coming inside to view the quilts. More than a dozen quilts had been raffled off, among them Mia's Starry Night quilt.

With any luck the total proceeds this year would top those from last year. The Loving Arms shelter needed every penny Bits and Pieces could raise.

Stepping outside, she peered at the crush of people. It looked like almost half the town was gathered near or around the library, in the parking lot, and across the grassy picnic area, or lined up for the ice cream cones and sundaes all donated by Lickety Split.

The high school marching band still played, drums and trumpets blaring, adding color and noise to the celebratory atmosphere.

And the sun was still out. But she noticed with a thrum

of unease that some dark clouds were moving in. The sky was subtly changing, darkening to a hue more gray than blue.

Damn.

Automatically she glanced around to see if Travis and Grady were anywhere in sight. A little wave of disappointment pinged inside her as she failed to spot them even though she knew exactly where they were and why they weren't here.

Travis had stopped by this morning while she was helping set up the quilts and told her he and Grady would need to spend a good portion of the afternoon back at the cabin preparing for the barbecue.

We'll have the whole evening to be together, she reminded herself as she spotted Lissie strolling toward her. Molly, adorable in a ruffly yellow top and matching shorts, toddled at her side, clutching a small plastic spoon and a cup of melting ice cream.

"You need to try the Crazy Mountain Caramel Hot Fudge Sundae," Lissie informed her without preamble as Mia knelt down to give Molly a kiss on the cheek. "Best. Sundae. Ever."

"Bestiss!" Molly added, nodding vehemently.

"You've talked me into it, both of you." But the words were scarcely out of her mouth before Karla McDonald's voice flowed out from the loudspeaker.

"Can I have your attention, please? Due to the quickly changing weather, and the latest forecast, we've decided to move up the final ceremony and to begin taking down the quilts displayed outdoors. At precisely five o'clock we'll make the announcement of our grand total. So if anyone wishes to make a further donation or purchase a quilt, this is the time to do it," she told the crowd. "I need Becky Hall and Mia Quinn to join me at the podium in ten minutes."

A ripple of anticipation ran through everyone on the library grounds. People began to glance at the sky and to gravitate toward the raised platform twenty feet from the entrance, where the final tally would be revealed.

"Too bad those clouds didn't hold off for another hour," Mia muttered, scanning the increasingly darkening sky with trepidation. "You haven't seen Travis and Grady back yet, have you?" she asked as Molly held out a spoonful of melted ice cream to her. She took a lick. "Yum. Thanks, sweetie. That's delicious."

"Car-mel. Da-wicious." The little girl grinned.

Lissie shook her head. "Travis and Grady? Haven't seen 'em. Guess they're still setting up for tonight. Or more likely, starting to move everything indoors as fast as they can."

A speculative sparkle gleamed suddenly from her eyes as Mia turned toward the podium. "Wait a sec. Since you brought up the subject of my brother . . . and if you don't mind my asking . . . care to share where things between you two are headed these days?"

"Oh, no, don't you start, too." Mia brushed off the question with a laugh.

But she had to admit that she sometimes found herself wondering the same thing. The truth was, she had no idea where things were headed with Travis.

She only knew one thing. That she loved him more than she'd ever thought possible. And that when they were together, everything somehow seemed to fall into place. Her heart felt whole. Her world happier than she ever remembered.

Did she want a home with Travis and Grady? A baby or two—or maybe three? Cribs and bunk beds, squabbles and homework, birthday candles to blow out and holidays to be celebrated around that big table in the cabin's kitchen? A table built to be laden with food, flanked by family, the heart and center of a home . . .

Yes. She dreamed of all that. And more. With her whole heart she dreamed of it.

But she knew Grady was making a lot of adjustments right now. In the course of little over a month he'd gone from visiting his father for the summer to living with him full-time. He and Travis deserved some father-son time now—alone time. A chance to deepen their bond, to make this transition to living together full-time as smooth and comfortable as possible.

There's no rush, Mia had told herself. No need to plan, or spell everything out, put a name to it. She and Travis knew how they felt and they would wait . . . and see. . . .

"There you are! Mia, Karla needs you. She and Becky are about to have a meltdown." Sophie hurried breathlessly toward them, Rafe striding alongside, a chubby-cheeked Aiden snug in his muscular arms. Mia marveled that Sophie looked almost as fresh as she had at the start of the day, her toffee-colored hair swept up in a loose tail, her green eyes bright and glowing.

"Someone heard it's already raining in Big Timber," Sophie said. "Panic is setting in onstage."

"I'm going up there right now." As if to punctuate the words, a low rumble of thunder sounded in the distance. The sky was changing before their eyes to an ominous shade of charcoal. "Can you two pitch in and help take down some of the outdoor quilts? Rafe, maybe you can watch the kids?"

"You've got it," Rafe told her.

"See you guys at the cabin later," Mia called over her shoulder, sprinting toward the platform.

A slight, ominous wind began to rustle along the library grounds.

Mia ran faster. She passed Ivy Tanner and her best friends, Shannon and Val, laughing with some boys near the scattering marching band. Spotted Aunt Winny in a bright violet top and khaki pants working desperately alongside Evelyn Lewis, the Bits and Pieces recording secretary, to gather up quilts.

Rain could move in quicker than a gunshot in Montana. She only prayed they could finish the ceremony before everyone watching got soaked.

As she rushed up the steps of the platform she saw Martha hurrying in the same direction from the library. Becky Hall was already up there, staring nervously as members of the group and other volunteers snatched quilts from their displays and ran inside with them as the crowd pressed forward, everyone looking eager and expectant in between uneasy glances at the sky.

The moment she reached Becky's side she felt the first drop of rain. *Just hold off a few more minutes,* Mia thought desperately, biting back a groan. In the crowd now she saw Aunt Winny joining Brittany, Sam, and Alec. They were pressed close among the throng near the podium.

"Good luck, Aunt Mia," Britt called out.

"Woo-hoo! Go, Bits and Pieces!" Samantha whooped.

Winny smiled up at her.

Aunt Winny? Smiling? Now, that was something you didn't see every day.

"May I have your attention, everyone?" Becky spoke into the microphone as another rumble of thunder shook the sky.

"We want to rather quickly thank you all for coming today. I think we've had the best turnout ever and I know all the money we've raised here, thanks to your generosity, will be of great help to all the women at the Loving Arms shelter. We'd especially like to thank all of our wonderful Lonesome Way businesses that have contributed so generously to this effort—"

"Just announce the total!" a man yelled from the back of the crowd. Someone else hushed him, and Becky continued, speaking even more rapidly. "As you know, the community quilt raffle was won by Benson's Drugstore. . . ."

Mia didn't hear the rest. She'd suddenly spotted Travis and Grady at the edge of the crowd and her heart lifted. They must have just arrived and she was touched that they'd come all the way back to town just to watch the closing ceremony.

The sight of Travis made her smile despite the stress of the impending rain. He looked effortlessly sexy in a crisp black shirt open at the neck, the sleeves rolled up, pressed jeans and boots, his Stetson on his head. He looked all cowboy and all man and her throat went dry just looking at him.

As his gaze zeroed in on her, a grin broke across his face and he tipped back his hat. A rush of warmth and love swept over her.

Faintly she heard Becky tell the crowd that Mia would now reveal the total amount raised today. Stepping quickly to the podium, she noticed Grady waving at her and she waved back before adjusting the microphone.

Then Karla was beside her, her face flushed with excitement as she handed Mia her grandmother's delicate silver box. It felt warm and familiar in her hands, and as her fingers closed around its corners, she couldn't help but imagine Gram gazing down at her, proud that her butterfly quilt had been displayed today. Delighted that the good luck wedding quilt was back among the women of her family.

The crowd held its collective breath, waiting for the rain, the thunder, and the total as she lifted the lid of the box.

How much money did we raise? Hopefully enough to make a difference for all the women and children in need at the shelter.

She reached for the slip of paper nestled inside and felt another drop of rain splash against her cheek.

"The grand total for this year is . . ." She unfolded the paper with rushing, trembling fingers.

And then stared at what she saw printed there. A bold, black scrawl of words. Not numbers. *Words.*

Will you marry me?

What? She stared down at the letters, dazed.

"Tell us the total!" someone in the crowd yelled.

Mia glanced down at the paper again, her heart beating so fast she couldn't think. She could only stare at those words. It couldn't be . . .

"I think there's been a mistake," she began, trying to keep her tone even.

"There's no mistake. You read it right."

Travis's voice.

But he wasn't speaking from the front of the crowd. He was right beside her on the platform.

Karla was gone. So was Becky. Travis was here, looking at her with gleaming eyes. A few feet behind him, she spotted a smiling Grady.

"I'm afraid everyone's going to have to wait another minute for that total, folks," Travis said into the microphone. "There's something I need to do first and I want you all to be a part of it. I'm either going to embarrass the hell out of myself right now or I'm going to be the happiest man on earth."

"What are you *doing*?" The words burst from Mia in a gasp. She felt her face burning red. "Are you crazy?"

"Yep. Crazy in love with you." The microphone carried his voice throughout the crowd and suddenly laughter and applause broke out. Cheers, too.

"Go for it, bro!" Rafe called.

"It's about time!" Lissie's voice rang out happily.

"Hurry up and ask her already," Aunt Winny warbled through the warm air. "Any minute now we're all going to be wet as fish in a pond."

"You heard the lady." Travis spoke softly. His gaze held hers as he took the slip of paper from her numb fingers and set it inside the silver box, which he rested on the podium. Then he caught her hand, cradling her fingers in his as he drew her over to the center of the platform and the crowd whistled and cheered.

"You really are crazy," Mia whispered on a breathless laugh. Her throat was tight, and her heart felt ready to burst wide open and spill out all the love she could barely contain.

"How did you . . . do this?"

"I haven't done anything yet." Still holding her hand, he dropped down onto one knee. His eyes never left hers as he pulled a small gold box from his pocket and popped it open.

On a bed of palest cream velvet glistened a brilliant round diamond ring set in platinum.

"Mia Quinn, I left you once and it was the dumbest damned thing I ever did. But I was an idiot kid then, and I've learned a lot since that day. I've learned that you're the only woman for me, I've learned that you own my heart. And if you say yes now, I'll do everything in my power to make you happy for the rest of our lives. I love you, Mia."

His deep voice thickened. "I want to spend every precious moment of our lives together. I want to hold you every night and kiss you good morning every day. I want us to be a family. I want us to raise a family. And I want us to be together forever and ever."

Mia felt hot tears squeezing from her eyes as he turned her palm up and brushed a gentle kiss against her skin.

"Will you marry me, Mia? Will you be my wife, for now, for always?"

The words were said aloud for everyone to hear, but the love and hope in Travis's steady gaze were meant only for her.

"Yes." Mia watched the grin spread across his face even as she began to smile. She held her breath as he slid that gorgeous ring on her finger and stood.

Happiness mingled with shock as she stared at the brilliantly shining diamond, then at the tall man who tugged her close against his chest and wrapped his arms around her.

"Yes, yes, yes," she whispered, caressing his jaw, smoothing her hands through his hair as he lowered his head and kissed her long and deep. There was tenderness in the kiss, but also wanting.

A flash-fire heat rippled between them, quickening her blood as his mouth took all he wanted from hers.

The crowd erupted into cheers and then the rain fell. Lightning slashed across the Crazies, people yelped, a woman shrieked as rain pelted down like stones, but still Travis kissed her, and still everyone stood their ground, clapping.

Finally Travis plopped his Stetson onto Mia's head as the rain tumbled harder and a soaked Grady scampered toward them. Laughing, they knelt to include him in a hug, and then Rafe yelled, "Okay, everyone, we'll save the rest for the wedding. Run for the hills!"

Laughing, soaked, and thoroughly satisfied, the crowd scattered and everyone raced toward their trucks and cars.

"The grand total!" Becky Hall pushed forward to scream into the microphone. "Two thousand and four hundred—" The rest was drowned out by a long crack of thunder.

Mia found herself bundled into Travis's Explorer, with Grady perched in the backseat.

"Samson's going to be my dog now, too, isn't he?" the boy asked her, leaning forward.

She met Travis's grin with a smile and then turned to press a quick kiss to the boy's cheek. "You bet he is. We all belong to each other now," she told him. "And we always will."

Chapter Thirty-one

The wedding took place in August at Sage Ranch. Nearly a quarter of the town attended, and the day was sunny, without a single cloud drifting in the blue Montana sky.

A huge luncheon buffet was served outdoors. Platters of prime rib, lemon chicken, roasted asparagus, Parmesan potato wedges, and sweet corn and peppers were arranged upon long tables bedecked with lacy white cloths. There were five kinds of pie served for dessert, along with an assortment of cupcakes and cookies and an elaborate three-tiered wedding cake baked by Sophie with chocolate ganache and buttercream frosting.

Travis was dazzled when he saw Mia in a simple gown of palest ivory silk, her shiny blond hair flowing loose and sexy, exactly the way he liked it. She carried a bouquet of peach and white roses and Sophie, Lissie, Samantha, and Brittany were all bridesmaids in flutter-sleeve gowns of delicate peach silk. Aunt Winny, in blue taffeta and fuschia-colored nail polish, gave the bride away.

There was champagne and wine, beer and whiskey. Rafe handed out cigars. Grady made a speech. So did Jake, Travis's younger brother, the rodeo champion who was the only one of the Tanner boys who'd never been married, and who proclaimed himself immune to love.

"You're next," Rafe had told Jake after the ceremony. "Mark my words."

"Your number's coming up," Travis had warned him.

"Not in the cards for me," Jake had retorted cheerfully. "Never met any woman who'd make me want to give up all the other ladies I haven't even met yet."

"You'll fall, little brother," Travis assured him. "And when you do, it's gonna be hard. You'll never see it coming."

"Don't hold your breath." Jake had laughed before sauntering over to his little niece, Molly, pretty in a raspberry lace dress, and swinging her up into his arms.

While people chatted and danced on the patio, accompanied by a local country band that covered everyone from Garth to Reba, Travis tugged Mia up the steps and down the hall into his old bedroom. He closed the door, leaning his back against it.

Dusk blue eyes gleamed at her.

"What are you up to? This is our wedding. We can't—"

"Sure we can. Five minutes alone, then we'll go back down. I need to tell you how beautiful you are. How happy I am today."

She nestled in close, pressed against him, lifting her mouth to his kiss. "I'm happy, too. So happy."

It was a long kiss, even deeper than the one that had sealed their marriage vows. Joy shimmered in the air between them.

"You know, I've already got that good luck wedding quilt at the cabin, folded right across the foot of our bed," Travis told her when they came up for air. "Not taking any chances."

"Smart man." Mia laughed as he pulled her toward his old double bed and sat down, yanking her onto his lap. "I'm thrilled to have it back. But . . ." Her amber eyes were soft on his as she stroked his jaw with the tips of her fingers, as his arms encircled her tightly and happiness soared in her heart.

So much happiness filled her that she thought she might burst.

"But what?" He nibbled at her throat. Hot shivers raced through her.

"But I don't believe in the good luck wedding quilt."

That got his attention. He looked into her eyes. "No?"

"I believe in *us*. You, me. Grady. And however many other little members of *us* come our way."

His slow grin made her heart turn over. "Expect lots of us. Think you can handle that?"

Mia was lost in his eyes, in the love she saw there. She forgot about the guests downstairs, the cake, the gifts and champagne. She saw only Travis, and the years of love and laughter awaiting them. Together.

Her voice came out in a whisper choked with happiness.

"I think I can hardly wait."

Read on for a preview of the first
Lonesome Way novel
from *New York Times* bestselling author
Jill Gregory

Sage Creek

Available now from Berkley Sensation!

LONESOME WAY, MONTANA

A charcoal and rose dusk streaked above the Crazy Mountains as Sophie McPhee turned her Blazer onto the private gravel drive that would lead her home.

The drive was called Daisy Lane, and the rambling two-story timber house looming a half mile in the distance was the Good Luck ranch house built by her mother's grandfather more than ninety years ago.

Three generations of her mother's family had called it home, and it had been *her* home the first eighteen years of her life. Sophie wondered with quiet desperation as darkness stole over Lonesome Way if it truly could be her home again.

Would this house or this town *feel* like home, after all this time, after everything that had happened? Would any place ever again feel like home?

She swallowed, hoping it would. But the emptiness inside her seemed as if it would never go away, never allow her to feel anything but loss and anger ever again.

Back in San Francisco, friends had told her she wouldn't

always feel this way, that things would get better. The platitudes sounded nice and Sophie knew they were well-meaning, but they bounced off her like drops of cold water hitting a sizzling skillet.

Her throat tightened as she neared the head of Daisy Lane and the Blazer's headlights caught the gleam of the big white house and the familiar landmarks of the now empty Good Luck barns and sheds and paddocks. The same-old, same-old words of encouragement weren't doing a thing right now to help her fight the fist of pain squeezing her heart.

She didn't have any idea what—if anything—ever would.

All she'd been able to think to do was to leave her old life with all its tears and mistakes behind, and to start over.

And here in her hometown of Lonesome Way was the only place where she'd imagined having the strength to try.

As the flaming rose sun slipped behind the mountains, and darkness swallowed the foothills, a tiny flicker of hope made Sophie catch her breath. The sage-scented air, the vast miles of rugged rolling land, were familiar. Comforting.

Home.

On that thought, the kitchen window suddenly glowed with a bright, cheerful light. Her mother was expecting her. Sophie had called from the road. Next on was the living room lamp, gleaming with welcome. And then the porch light sprang to life, illuminating the old white wooden swing and her mother's carefully planted rosebushes.

A crystal wind chime tinkled sweetly, swinging in the night breeze, and there were the wide porch steps where she'd perched on countless summer afternoons as a girl, playing jacks with Lissie and Mia.

A rush of emotion filled her as she switched off the ignition and climbed down from the Blazer on tired feet. Even as she grabbed her purse, the front door of the house swung open and her mother appeared in the doorway. Not quite as tall as Sophie, she was thin and angular, wearing a loose blue cotton top and jeans, her feet bare in the summer night.

Diana McPhee hurried out onto the porch. Her chin-length fair hair was peppered with gray, her eyes reflected a mixture of eagerness and concern. Sophie was struck by the fact that nearing sixty, her mother was still a strikingly pretty woman.

"Sophie! Thank heavens. I was starting to get worried."

As Sophie moved toward her, her throat ached with unshed tears.

"I've been holding dinner. Guess you must've hit some major traffic on—"

Then her mother saw her face and broke off. Sophie knew how she must look—pale, sad, tired, with the tears that were always close shimmering in her green eyes. She was so sick of the tears. She blinked them back and forced a smile.

"Sorry to keep you waiting, Mom. There was construction, and at one point, believe it or not, I was so distracted that I took the wrong turn and had to backtrack."

"Well, now, that happens. You have a lot on your mind." Her mother's arms went around her, hugging very gently as if she were afraid Sophie would crack in pieces. But her voice was brisk and bracing as she touched her daughter's toffee-colored hair, tumbling in soft curls around a beautiful face with wide cheekbones a model would covet, a generous mouth, and dimples when she smiled. But Sophie was definitely not smiling now.

"You're here, Sophie, that's all that matters." Her voice was overly cheerful. "Leave your bags, we'll get them later. Let's go inside. I've fixed your favorite—meat loaf and biscuits, garlic mashed potatoes, and a big salad—oh, Sophie . . . honey, what's the matter?"

Sophie's feet had frozen on the threshold of the ranch house. Behind her flowed the night, full of stars and a crescent of moon, the buzz of insects, the lone cry of a hawk.

The cool night wind rustled delicately through the ponderosa pines. And ahead of her loomed her past, the house of her childhood and teen years, warm and faded yet so familiar it was startling.

She felt herself teetering between two worlds.

She couldn't move, could only stare past the entry into the rectangular living room, with its big chintz-covered sofa and matching love seat, warm maple end tables, and the black walnut TV stand centered along the far blue wall. She took in the massive stone fireplace, the bookshelves, and her father's favorite tan leather chair in the corner beside the reading lamp.

How many times had she torn through this door, or downstairs from her room, to see his long legs stretched across that chair, his feet propped on the footrest, his hooded eyes intent as he watched a football game or devoured the newest Tom Clancy novel—or slanted a stern glance at her as she hovered uncertainly in the doorway, just as she was doing now?

Her father's granite voice seemed to scratch the air around her, blasting his opinion of all the ways she fell short of his expectations.

You forgot your spelling list at school. How do you expect to pass the test? That's just plain irresponsible, Sophie. You're eight years old. I expect more from you than that.

How much time have you wasted talking to Lissie Tanner on that phone? You weren't raised to spend half your day jabbering about nonsense.

All your daydreaming is nothing but foolishness. Stop living in the clouds, Sophie. There's plenty of work around here that needs to be done.

Worst of all, that F in Geometry during her junior year.

Damned laziness. You wouldn't know hard work if it kicked you in the butt. Why don't you use your God-given brain, girl?

She'd never been able to please Hoot McPhee. But then, no one had. Not even her mother, though, somehow, for most

of the years they'd been married, she'd put up with him—
Sophie didn't know how. And finally, when he stepped way
over the line, even her mother couldn't look the other way
anymore.

Hoot had perhaps been hardest on her brother, Wes,
who'd responded to the never-ending reprimands by leaving
for Missoula and the University of Montana at the age of
eighteen, and never looking back.

Wes had gone on to law school at the University of Texas,
taking out student loans and working two jobs all the while
so that he never had to ask his father for a dime above basic
tuition. And he hadn't called home or come home more than
three or four times in the years after his high school gradu-
ation. He hadn't returned to Lonesome Way for Hoot's
funeral either.

Hoot McPhee had been gone five years. But for a dizzying instant as Sophie stared into the living room, she could
have sworn she sensed her tall, formidable father in that
chair.

"It's the first time I've been back . . . since the funeral,"
she murmured as her mother came up behind her. "For an
instant, I could almost see him sitting there—"

Sophie drew a breath and told herself to stop acting crazy.
She walked into the living room, her flats clicking across
the hardwood floor, and touched her hand to the back of the
tan chair.

"Sorry, Mom. I know if he were here, you wouldn't be."
After her mother had divorced him, Sophie's father had
spent the last few years of his life living alone—or with one
or another of a succession of women—in a cabin on Bear
Claw Road. "I probably wouldn't be here either," she added
with a rueful smile. "I'm just being stupid. Emotional, as he
would say."

"No, you're not, not in the least. I don't wonder it seems
strange to you to come in here and not see him. But a lot of
things are different on the ranch now, Sophie. I've sold all

the livestock and leased most of the grazing land. It's not the same as when your father was here, running cattle, running everything." Her mother's gaze held hers. "All the years you lived at home, he was here—we both were, together. So you've barely been in this house without him here—of course it feels odd to walk in and not see him."

Sophie studied her mother. She didn't look the least bit upset. Which was a wonder. Sophie couldn't imagine how her mother could talk about Hoot so calmly, almost dispassionately, as if he hadn't been discovered having an affair with the mayor's wife, Lorelei Hardin, during Sophie's junior year of college—and who knew how many other women he'd cheated with before that?

Sophie was still reeling from finding out about her own husband's infidelity. When would it stop, that ice-pick-to-the-heart pain? After a year—or two—a decade?

It's only been a few months, she told herself. *You won't always feel this rage, this pain. This blinding sense of betrayal. Mom survived. She's a normal, rational human being. You'll become one again, too.*

But she knew she'd never trust any man again. Sophie couldn't ever see that happening. No way.

And she would be careful not to share her heart again, much less give it away. To anyone. The pain was too intense. The risk too great. She understood that now.

"You know, Mom," she said quietly. "It's because of Hoot that I tried so hard to make things work with Ned. I always dreaded the possibility of a second generation of divorce in the family. I needed someone different from Hoot, someone who'd hold to his vows. Who'd encourage me and laugh with me and not tear down the people he was supposed to love. I thought I found him. So I kept trying for so long even after . . ."

Even after Ned became so distant, burying himself in his work. Putting Sophie and their life together on the back burner.

Somewhere along the line, Ned had let go of her and their marriage, and committed himself instead to his drug of choice—his own ambition.

In the end he'd had much more in common with Hoot McPhee than Sophie could have dreamed the day she walked down the aisle in swirls of white silk, seed pearls, and taffeta, making promises to love, honor, and cherish.

But she didn't know that—not until the day she found out about Cassandra Reynard.

"I really thought we'd last. Forever." She turned away from her father's chair. "Which just goes to show how much *I* know."

"There's no sense in blaming yourself. None at all." Taking her hand, her mother determinedly led her into the kitchen, lips pursed and concern sharpening her gaze. "Not one bit of this is your fault. I know Ned told you it is, but he's full of it. Don't let him screw with you any more than he already has. Divorce isn't a family curse, passed on from one generation to another. It just happens. And *he* cheated, not you. You gave him countless chances to keep your marriage together. A damn sight too many, if you ask me."

Sophie had to grin as she carried the wooden salad bowl brimming with greens and tomatoes and peppers to the square table. Her even-keeled mom rarely got so worked up. Obviously, Ned was high up on her shit list.

"Good to know you have my back, Mom."

"Family sticks together." Diana brought over the platter of sauce-laden meat loaf surrounded by garlic mashed potatoes and set it down. "That man better never show his face around here or he'll *really* get a piece of my mind."

The table was set with a robin's egg blue tablecloth and her mother's prettiest blue and yellow dishes. Matching napkins were folded atop each plate. Sophie's gaze was drawn to the bouquet of wildflowers filling an oval white vase in the center.

It all looked so festive and inviting.

Mom's trying so hard to make this easier for me.

But nothing was easy these days.

Sophie needed to lift her own mood, or else fake it, for her mother's sake. Which meant not thinking about Ned or about how she had to find a job, or wondering how she was going to restart her life.

"Everything looks great. You made too much food, though, Mom." *Especially since these days I have the appetite of a flea.* She slid into a chair, reached for the salad bowl. "How's Gran?"

"Same as always." Diana gave a tiny smile at the mention of her mother. "She still has more energy than a windstorm and still thinks good always wins out in the end. Not such a bad philosophy, I guess. She's coming to dinner tomorrow night. Be prepared, she's planning to tell you how to fix your love life."

"What love life? I'm done with a love life."

"Not if your grandmother has anything to say about it. I give her a week at most before she seriously gets on your case."

"Maybe coming home wasn't such a great idea." Seeing her mother's alarmed expression, Sophie regretted her flip words. She felt a rush of warmth for her mother, for this house, for the Montana night that seemed to enfold them, at least at this moment, in a cocoon of safety.

"I'm just joking." She hugged her mom. "I'd rather be here than anywhere else in the world right now."

And she meant it.

⌒

After putting away her clothes and storing her suitcase in the back of her walk-in closet, Sophie gazed around her small, high-ceilinged room brimming with knickknacks and memories. The familiar lemon scent of Pledge, freshly washed cotton sheets, and fresh air wafting through the open window stirred her senses.

With the soft white lace curtains rustling in the breeze, she realized how little these four walls had changed since she'd left the ranch for college. She was twenty-nine now, single again, and staring at the remnants of innocence and childhood.

From the photographs and posters hung on the walls to the peach and yellow quilt folded neatly over her double bed, the room whisked her back through time, to days when she and her best friends Lissie Tanner and Mia Quinn spent almost every minute together, and if not together, gabbing on the phone.

All of her old stuffed animals from kindergarten through senior year in high school, including the huge stuffed lizard Wes had won her at the state fair, still slouched on the top shelf of her oak bookcase, which took up half a wall, and her creaky old six-drawer dresser occupied the other half.

Her mother had told her at dinner that Lissie—now Lissie Norris—was pregnant. And that Mia was throwing her a baby shower a week from Saturday.

I'll look for a gift in town tomorrow.

She was thrilled for Lissie and Tommy—they'd been together since high school and had been trying to have a baby for over a year.

But suddenly, the hollowness inside Sophie became a hard, tangible ache in her chest. So many of her friends were pregnant or had babies now. She'd gone to all of their baby showers. Watched them hug and feed and bathe their infants, bundling them into tiny coats and hats, strapping them into strollers and car seats, caring for them with a joy and total intensity that Sophie could only yearn for.

Soon, Ned had told her, over and over. Be patient. We'll start trying soon. In six months. Then it was another six.

Then a year.

The timing needed to be perfect, according to him. And that meant after his career was firmly on track, rolling along in the ideal groove. After he landed a cable or network job

and could cut his ties with the local affiliate crap Ned felt
was so beneath him.

Her ex-husband had been a local news producer on
WBBK in San Francisco, and he was good at his job. Damned
good. Under his direction, the nightly news ratings had
climbed from third place to number one in just under a year.
But Ned had wanted more, a whole lot more. He wanted to
become executive producer of a cable or network news show,
one that was big and important and would get national
attention—and that would thrust him into the big time.

With the big budgets, he'd told Sophie, pacing across the
bamboo floor of their Potrero Hill condo, wound up the way
he used to get before a final exam in college. *Not to mention
big players, big media attention—and big money.*

Sophie wasn't sure exactly when the cute, brown-haired
guy with the serious eyes and a cleft in his chin, with the
perfect manners and a double major in journalism and business, the guy she'd studied with in the library, gobbled pizza
with at Dewey's, lived with in a tiny studio apartment off
campus their senior year, and married ten months later, had
morphed into a man with tunnel vision—burrowing straight
ahead toward his career goals and forgetting the life and
family and home he'd promised to build together with her.

Maybe it was sometime after her own small bakery business, Sweet Sensations, had taken off, becoming as popular
as her cinnamon buns, which flew off the shelves every
morning and were gone by noon.

Sophie had gradually expanded the offerings in her shop
beyond baked goods and coffees. She'd added a couple of
soups and a handful of sandwiches and several unique gourmet salads to the menu, and eventually, at the suggestion of
her friend Rosa, she'd begun taking on some catering jobs.

Somehow, over the next few years, the orders ratcheted
up until she had to add staff and take out a loan for more
equipment and supplies.

Sophie Sinclair's Sweet Sensations soon earned a designation as one of San Francisco's top three go-to caterers for upscale corporate events. Her business had grown beyond her most optimistic daydreams. Written up in local gourmet magazines, in newspaper food columns and online reviews, Sweet Sensations had flourished, and the clients had poured in.

But all along, Sophie had been prepared to hire managers and as much staff as were needed to take over, just as soon as she and Ned got pregnant.

She'd been craving a baby ever since she turned twenty-five. Day after day, she'd found herself smiling at every infant and toddler she encountered at the grocery store or the movies, or being swung by the hands by his or her parents down the street, and the ache of wanting a child of her own filled her with a pang that was almost physical.

But things hadn't gone the way she'd hoped. They'd originally planned to start trying for a family early in their marriage, but Ned had changed his mind, persuading her that they should get more established in their careers first. So they'd put it off.

By Sophie's twenty-eighth birthday, her biological clock was in full racing mode, turning her yearning for a child into a longing that reached into the deepest parts of her heart.

But by then, Ned's head—and a lot more of him than that, Sophie reflected bitterly—was fixated elsewhere.

Cassandra Reynard, to be exact.

The vice-president of the cable network that was tops on his list, and that had been considering hiring him for months, was carrying Ned's child. The baby Sophie had longed for.

And to top it off, Ned was enough of a bastard to blame her for the destruction of their marriage.

"You caused this, Sophie," he'd had the nerve to tell her on the phone two weeks after she accompanied a pregnant friend to the obstetrician, only to find her own husband seated in the waiting room, holding hands with another woman.

Cassandra Reynard, a red-haired, Julia Roberts look-alike, had still been nauseous at the beginning of her second trimester.

"All you could think about was what *you* needed—a baby. You couldn't let up on the pressure, Sophie. You didn't give a damn about my needs, my goals. Just because your stupid bakery took off like a firecracker, you thought it should be easy for me, too. You have no idea what I've been going through to give us a shot at the life we wanted—"

"I definitely know what you've been going through, Ned."

"Don't—"

"Sleeping your way to the top must be terribly hard work. Pure torture."

"I was doing this for *us*, Sophie. Things just got out of control. It doesn't mean I don't love you."

"Is that what you call it?"

"Sophie, look, I gotta go. Cassandra's beeping in, I'll get back to you."

Her hands were shaking so much as she punched off her cell that she dropped the phone on the floor.

For a moment, she'd struggled to fight back her sobs, then had given in to them and let the tears burst from her. She'd snatched up her leather notebook and a pen as tears streamed down her cheeks, and had sat down to scribble an addition to her list.

Imagine Ned as a football. In the center of the stadium. And it's kickoff time at the Super Bowl.

A sound somewhere between a laugh and a sob escaped her throat. A counselor at a group divorce session she'd attended at the library a few days before had suggested the participants keep a list of thoughts that made them feel good—or bad—so they could get in touch with their inner selves as a way to relieve stress and deal with anger toward their former spouses.

"How's that for being in touch?" Sophie had wiped the tears with the back of her hand and shakily stuffed the notebook into her tote bag.

She wasn't sure how, but somehow she'd held it together through the next few months. Packing up the condo, listing it with a Realtor, meeting with lawyers.

Yesterday, she'd signed her name to a contract officially selling Sweet Sensations to the Cramer Restaurant Group, and faxed it, and her divorce agreement, back to her attorneys.

Then she'd rolled her luggage into the hall and closed the door forever on the chic San Francisco condo where her marriage had begun—and where it had ended.

Catching Ned with Cassandra had shaken her out of the dream that they could somehow save their marriage and have the life she'd thought they'd been building. She'd been fooling herself for much too long, ignoring the truth.

That was over now.

Grabbing an old comfortable hoodie, Sophie hurried into the hall and down the old stairs. Softly, so as not to wake her mother, she eased open the front door and stepped out into the Montana night.

"Compelling and beautifully written."

—Debbie Macomber, *New York Times* bestselling author

FROM *NEW YORK TIMES* BESTSELLING AUTHOR

JODI THOMAS

THE COMFORTS OF HOME

A HARMONY NOVEL

Twenty-year-old Reagan Truman has found her place and family in Harmony, Texas. But with her uncle taken ill and her friend Noah lost and disheartened with his life, Reagan is afraid of ending up alone again—and she's not the only one. When a terrible storm threatens the town, the residents of Harmony are forced to think about what they truly want. Because making the connections they so desperately desire means putting their hearts at risk...

KAKI WARNER

Heartbreak Creek

A RUNAWAY BRIDES NOVEL

*From Kaki Warner comes an exciting new series
about four unlikely brides who make their way west—
and find love where they least expect it . . .*

Edwina Ladoux hoped becoming a mail-order bride would be her way out of the war-torn South and into a better life, but as soon as she arrives in Heartbreak Creek, Colorado, and meets her hulking, taciturn groom, she realizes she's made a terrible mistake.

Declan Brodie already had one flighty wife who ran off with a gambler before being killed by Indians. He's hoping this new one will be a practical, sturdy farm woman who can help with chores and corral his four rambunctious children. Instead, he gets a skinny Southern princess who doesn't even know how to cook.

Luckily, Edwina and Declan agreed on a three-month courtship period, which should give them time to get the proxy marriage annulled. Except that as the weeks pass, thoughts of annulment turn into hopes for a real marriage—until Declan's first wife returns after being held captive for the last four years. Now an honorable man must choose between duty and desire, and a woman who's never had to fight for anything must do battle for the family she's grown to love . . .

Praise for the novels of Kaki Warner

"Emotionally compelling." —*Chicago Tribune*

"Thoroughly enjoyable." —*Night Owl Reviews* (Top Pick)